A Family's Second Chance

Gary Herland

This is a work of fiction. Names, characters, businesses, places, events and incidents are either the products of the author's imagination or used in a fictitious manner. Any resemblance to actual persons, living or dead, or actual events is purely coincidental.

Text copyright © 2017 Gary Herland

Library of Congress #4725465551

All Rights Reserved

No part of this book may be reproduced or used in any form without the express written permission of the author.

Front and back cover by Gary Herland

A Family's Second Chance

CHAPTER 1

"I thought I knew what I was doing. I had all the answers. I was wrong, and for that I'm sorry." The middle-aged man with a scraggly salt and pepper beard sat on the ground in front of two black granite tombstones. The stones have roses carved into them as they rest side by side in the cemetery. The man stands up and walks away, never looking back.

Eight Years Earlier

Joe Walker sits in his car watching a man get into a SUV parked in front of the auto parts store with large letters on it. Joe and his partner Bill Simmons are private investigators following a man suspected of cheating on his wife.

"You got your eyes on him Bill?" Joe says into his two-way radio.

"I got him, Joe," a voice responds. Joe pulls out behind his partner's black SUV as the target and Bill drive past him. The engine revs loudly as Joe punches the gas to catch up to the vehicles. Joe and Bill talk back and forth over the radio about the man they are following.

"Hey Joe, are we working Friday night?"

"I can't. I have plans on Friday night."

"What are you doing?"

"Something very special buddy. I will tell you all about it on Friday. Do you know how far away the girlfriend lives and where?"

"She lives about five minutes down the road on Algers Drive."

"OK, I will cut over from here and intercept the car. When the subject gets to the street, break off and I will follow the car to the girlfriend's house. Once he pulls in, I will take pictures then meet you at the office."

"OK see you at the office," Bill replies.

Joe comes home from work at dinner time. He and his family live just outside of Jacksonville, Florida in a quiet community. He opens the front door and immediately hangs a garment bag in the closet. He takes a moment to breathe in the aromas of dinner cooking, and hears the excited chatter of his two daughters and his wife. As soon as he walks into the kitchen two little girls, with long blonde hair and huge hazel eyes run to their father, arms stretched wide.

"Daddy, Daddy!" Calie and Talia, ages seven and five, scream as they run into their father's arms. This is Joe's favorite daily ritual. He can always count on his girls to welcome him home, flashing their beautiful smiles and throwing their little arms tightly around his neck. Joe scoops them up as they giggle and ask him a million questions as he walks over to his wife. Kim is a strikingly beautiful, tall and slender blonde with the most dazzling blue eyes Joe has ever seen. She smiles appreciatively as he comes up from behind and gives her a kiss on her cheek. He is still amazed at how lucky he is to have somehow won over the heart of this amazing woman.

Kim had been the new girl at school in the middle of his senior year of high school and had every boy in the school falling all over her. Joe had certainly taken notice, but he was too involved in his sports and studies to be competing for her attention. Joe was the quiet type in school. He studied and played hard staying clear of the drama of high school. There were a few good friends from his football team who always razzed and teased him about not going to the parties. Joe was seemingly unfazed by the flirtatious attempts from all the hot teenage girls who were attracted to his good looks and strong, muscular physique. He didn't care about any of that. He had goals and he didn't want anything getting in his way. It was exactly that aloofness that caught the eye of Kim. From the first time they talked in the library at school he knew she was different and that they shared a similar vision for their future.

"How was your day, babe?" Joe asks.

"I had a good day," Kim replies as she looks at Joe with a smile. "Go on upstairs and get ready for dinner. It should be done in a few minutes." Joe walks over to the closet, pulls out the garment bag and goes upstairs with it to wash up and change. He comes down a few minutes later looking relaxed and comfortable in his favorite old tattered football sweatshirt and jeans.

"Let's eat," Joe says as he walks into the kitchen and picks up the salad bowl from the counter. Calie and Talia, who share the same beautiful long blonde hair as their mother, jump into their seats. Joe slaps some mashed potatoes on the girl's plates. "How was school today girls?" Joe asks.

Calie and Talia both say at the same time, "good."

"Daddy?" Calie says.

"Yes sweetie," Joe replies smiling at Calie's sudden look of seriousness.

"I think there is a boy in my class that likes me," she explains. Joe stops eating and sits silent for a few seconds staring at Calie as she smiles at him.

"What's this boy's name?" Joe demands in a stern but low voice. Calie knows that her father isn't really mad, but this is how he plays it off.

"William," Calie says.

"Hmmm, does William have a good job?" Joe asks.

"Daaad," Calie says. "He's only in second grade."

"Ohhh, well I'll have to meet him before I can allow you to go on a date with him," Joe replies as he gives Talia a wink from across the table.

"Dad, you're silly," Calie giggles.

"Hey girls, do you know what tomorrow is?"

"Friday?" Calie asks while looking curiously at Talia.

"Well yes, but it's also the Father-Daughter Dance." Calie and Talia's eyes light up with excitement. "I was thinking of asking two special little girls if they wanted to go. Do you know anyone who might want to go?" Joe teases with a smile.

"We do, we do!" Calie and Talia scream while jumping out of their chairs and smothering Joe with hugs.

"Why don't you two go look on your beds and see if there is something there for you," Kim said. The girls run upstairs to their bedrooms and find beautiful white dresses arranged neatly on their beds. Both dresses are white with a lace overlay and tiny pearl buttons that go down the back. Calie's has a pink bow that ties around her waist and Talia's has a red bow. It's their favorite colors. Joe and Kim sit at the dinner table looking at each other with a knowing smile as they listen to their girls shrieking with joy.

"You're such a good Daddy," Kim whispers with a smile. Joe's taking the girls to the Annual Father-Daughter Dance that's held every Valentine's Day.

"They make it easy, don't they?" Joe replies. "To be a good parent? How did I ever get so lucky?" Joe gets up to refill his glass and gives Kim a quick kiss on her head before heading into the kitchen.

⊲▥⊳⊲▥⊳⊲▥⊳

Later, Joe and Kim put the kids to bed. As Joe reads Calie a story while lying on her bed, Kim reads to Talia in her room. He finishes the book and kisses Calie goodnight on her forehead.

"Who's the love of my life?" Joe asks.

"I am," Calie responds in a quiet sleepy voice as they gaze into each other's eyes.

"That's right, and don't forget it. Goodnight Princess, I love you," Joe says softly.

"Goodnight Daddy, I love you." Joe and Kim then switch rooms in order to say goodnight to both girls. This is their nightly routine. Joe lies down on Talia's bed, cuddles right up to her and gives her a soft kiss on her forehead.

"Goodnight Daddy," Talia whispers.

"Goodnight Princess, I love you," Joe whispers back.

"I love you too," Talia says softly as her eyes start to get heavy.

"Who's the love of my life," Joe whispers to Talia as her eyes slowly close.

"I am," Talia responds with a whisper before falling asleep with a smile.

Joe sits up in bed under the covers watching a news story on human cloning while Kim reads next to him.

"This is amazing," Joe says in disbelief. The story is about a scientist in San Francisco who claims to have perfected the process of human cloning.

"Oh my God," Kim replies in a disgusted voice. "This is the worst thing we as humans could start doing."

"Why do you think that?" Joe asks. "This has the potential to rid the world of cancer or other diseases that genetics hand down through the generations."

"The human race wasn't made in a few years unlike the amount of time research for cloning has been around. Something bad is bound to come from this. You shouldn't mess around with human DNA and human nature. That should be left to God," she says.

"Well I think it's a great idea," Joe explains. "Just think about this. What if I died in a plane crash and you couldn't go on without me. You could make a clone of me and have me back," he says jokingly.

"That's just sick," Kim remarks. "I would never do that. You wouldn't be the same person I fell in love with. Besides, who says I would want you back?" Kim teases.

"I bet if your precious dog died, you would clone her."

"That's different. She is cute and cuddly and doesn't fart," she laughs as she reaches for her light on the side table and pulls the switch. "Goodnight, I love you."

"Goodnight, love you too." Joe gives her a kiss and turns off the TV and light.

CHAPTER 2

It is 5:30 a.m. and Joe is getting ready for work earlier than usual. Before leaving, he walks into Talia's room and peaks at her sleeping peacefully with her favorite stuffed bunny tucked under her arm. Joe smiles, walks over to the side of her bed and leans over. He kisses her softly on the forehead and whispers into her ear.

"I love you princess." Joe can't help but stare at her for a moment longer as his heart swells with love for this amazing little being who he somehow managed to play a part in bringing into this world. Next Joe walks into Calie's room, kisses her forehead and whispers, "I love you too my second princess." Calie stirs just enough to reach her arm around his neck and with her eyes still closed she wraps him in an embrace that nearly brings Joe to tears. He treasures these moments knowing the day will come too soon when they will want nothing to do with him.

Later that afternoon, Joe sits in his office looking at Calie and Talia's school pictures on his desk. He can't wait for the day to be over so he can take his princesses to the dance. Joe and Bill Simmons own a security consulting firm called Target Security. Not only are they business partners but they have been best friends since high school. Their storefront office is located in downtown Jacksonville. Joe calls his partner on the speaker phone.

"Bill, what's going on man?" Joe asks.

"I just left the Pizza House on South Street. We have a new client, partner. They want a new alarm system at all 10 of their locations, with multiple cameras and monthly monitoring," Bill says with enthusiasm. "This is going to be a good client for us that will make us a lot of money."

"That's great Billy. Good job," Joe replies with equal enthusiasm. "Hey, I'm leaving a little early today."

"What's going on, you got a hot date or something?" Bill asks curiously.

"Actually, I do," Joe replies as he glances at the tuxedo hanging on the door in front of him. "I'm taking Calie and Talia to the Father-Daughter Dance tonight," Joe says with a big smile.

"Oh man, I'm so jealous. Have a good time, and I want to hear all about it," Bill says envious of the family Joe has. Bill is a single man who enjoys the bachelor life but loves to spend the holidays with Joe and his family.

Kim picks the girls up at Jacksonville Elementary School at 3 p.m. She's secretly looking forward to the dance and getting the girls ready. The prospect of having a whole evening to herself is also appealing to her. She has a bottle of her favorite wine, a movie picked out, and her favorite blanket already on the couch just waiting for her to curl up in.

"How was school, girls?" Kim inquires as they jump into the SUV.

"Good, but Mom, I can't stop thinking about the dance," Calie said.

"Me too, when are we going?" Talia asks.

"Patience girls, first we have to get ready for the big dance." As Kim pulls into the driveway and stops the car, Talia jumps out.

"I want you to do my hair first!" Talia shouts as she runs into the house. Calie and Kim follow behind giggling.

Kim brushes Talia's long curly blonde hair and Calie sits next to them on the bed. "When I was your age, I would get so excited about the dance too. My mom would drive us to the dance and my dad would walk up to the car and open the door for me and my sister like we were princesses going to the ball. I loved to dance with my father. He would let me stand on his toes and dance us around the room." Kim stops for a moment lost in the memories and smiles. "The father-daughter dances are some of my best memories with your Grandpa."

"Mommy, do you miss your dad?" Calie asks softly. Kim turns and smiles as she looks at Calie. She puts her arm around her and pulls her close.

"I do, baby. I miss him very much." Kim kisses the back of Calie's head then continues to brush Talia's hair. "He would have loved you girls so much!"

Once the girl's hair is done, pinned up in the back with elegant curls along their face, she helps Calie into her white dress and buttons up the back. Talia stands in front of the mirror. Happy with her reflection, she smiles at what she sees then spins around making her dress flow around her. "I look like a princess Mommy, and Daddy is my prince." Calie walks over next to Talia. "He's my prince too Talia," Calie protests.

"Daddy is the prince for both of you princesses," Kim replies, taking pleasure in her daughter's quarreling for their father's affection.

Joe's in a flower shop picking out wrist corsages for the girls. He picks out a red rose and a pink rose corsage from the case.

"Looks like someone has a very special night planned for himself," the gray haired middle-aged woman behind the counter says.

"I'm trying to make it as memorable as I can for my daughters," Joe says proudly as he hands her his credit card.

"You're a good dad, have fun."

"Thanks," Joe replies as he signs the receipt and takes the bag. He pulls his cell phone from his coat pocket, looks at the time, and calls home as he walks out the door. Kim answers the phone on the first ring as the caller ID displays Joe's cell phone number.

"Hi babe, Kim says. Are you getting excited about the dance?"

"I am. Are the girls almost ready?"

"We are just about done. We're doing some last minute touch ups with their hair."

"So it's 5:35 and I'm on my way home. I changed at work already so I'll just pick them up and bring them to the dance. I should be there in about 10 minutes. I am hoping we can get there a few minutes early to beat the lines."

"Joe, I wanted to bring the girls and meet you at the dance."

"That's OK honey. I'll pick them up."

"Please Joe. I really want to bring them, like my parents used to do with me and my sister when we were young." Joe is silent for a moment.

"OK. I will meet you at the school. Try and be there by 5:50 and meet me at the front entrance."

"Thanks babe. See you in a few minutes."

It's 5:45 p.m. "Girls, let's go, you're going to be late for the dance. Your Prince awaits you!" Kim stands at the bottom of the stairs looking up as the girls come running down the stairs. "Get your coats on, its chilly outside."

"Is Daddy meeting us at the dance?" Talia asks with anticipation.

"Yes, he will meet us at the front entrance," Kim explains as she ushers the girls out the door. The sun is starting to set, but it's still light out. The girls climb into the car. "Buckle up," Kim says as she sends Joe a quick text. Kim backs out of the driveway and begins driving down the street. Kim turns onto the main road heading into the city. The school is about a mile or so away from their house on a rural road.

Joe is standing on the sidewalk in front of the school, waiting for Kim to pull up so he can open the doors. He anxiously waits to see them with a smile he cannot contain on his face. He starts rehearsing in his mind how he will open the door and take his girls hands as if they are the arriving at the ball and he's helping them out of the carriage. Joe's thoughts are interrupted by his phone beeping. He pulls his phone out of his pocket and looks at the screen.

"We are pulling out of the driveway now. Sorry running a little late," the text reads. Joe takes a deep breath as he continues to wait patiently for his girls to arrive.

Kim looks in the rear view mirror at the girls sitting quietly in the backseat. She turns her attention back to the road again just as a large box truck drives into Kim's lane and hits the car from the side. BANG! Kim and the girls scream in horror. The truck smashes into the rear end driver's side of the car sending it skidding out of control and off the road to the right. It rolls over and over again until finally coming to rest on its roof. The car is mangled, smoke billows from the hood and all is silent. Cars start pulling to the side of the road and people run to assist.

Joe looks up and his face becomes momentarily serious as he heard the unmistakable sound of a car accident in the distance.

"Oh God, I hope those people are OK," Joe says to himself as he looks down the driveway for Kim's car and checks his watch again.

He starts to hear sirens in the distance coming towards him, getting closer and closer. He looks down at his watch again which reads 6:05 p.m. He looks up to see police cars, ambulances and fire trucks race by on the main road as a sudden sense of fear and anxiety fills him.

A fireman is yelling into the smashed out driver's side window, but there is only silence. Kim's eyes open slightly and she looks at the fireman and can see him yelling but hears nothing. The fireman looks in the back seat then stands up and yells to the other firemen.

"There's kids in the back seat." Firemen come running to assist. Kim's in shock and can't hear as she struggles to find her voice to call out for help. There are firemen and police officers everywhere running around the vehicle and back and forth to the fire trucks. Colored lights are flashing and there's an overwhelming smell of burning rubber surrounding her, making it hard to breathe. Kim starts to cry out in pain. Her legs are pinned under the steering wheel and she is bleeding from her forehead. "Can you hear me?" the fireman yells to Kim.

"Yes!" she screams. Blood covers Kim's head as a gash on her forehead streams blood. Kim looks in the rear view mirror and sees firemen working to free both Talia and Calie. The girls are unconscious; their bodies limp in their seats as their arms hang down. Kim screams in horror as she tries to reach for the girls. "Talia! Calie!" Her screams become more frantic and desperate as her understanding of what's happening becomes clearer. There's no response from the girls.

The girls are pulled from the car while Kim watches, helpless and crying. Talia and Calie's limp bodies are carried to the road and placed on waiting stretchers. As the stretchers are being pulled to the waiting ambulances, EMS workers are frantically performing CPR on the girls. As Kim watches in horror, one of the EMS workers shakes his head back and forth as if to say that he's getting no response from one of the girls. Kim's eyes close as her world goes black.

Joe looks at his watch and sees that it is 6:15 p.m. He takes his cell phone out of his pocket and dials Kim. Joe looks up toward the main road and watches as ambulances and police cars are traveling with their lights on, now heading back towards the city. The phone rings six times then goes to voice mail. Joe slowly lowers the phone to his side while holding it tight. He looks down at the phone again as Kim's name is flashing on the screen, then looks toward the main road again. Panic has engulfed Joe's body and his breathing begins to accelerate. Joe's eyes start welling up and fill as tears trickle down both cheeks. "No, no, no," Joe says softly to himself. Fear and the realization of what may be happening takes over as he runs toward the parking lot and jumps into his car. The few remaining fathers and daughters walking into the dance stop and watch the man run in terror to his car. They silently hope that the accident has nothing to do with the stranger who just ran to his car. They watch as Joe speeds out of the parking lot.

Joe drives towards the scene of the accident praying out loud in desperation, "Please God, no," he begs. "Please, please, please!" He wipes the tears streaming down his face as the red lights of the fire trucks get closer. As Joe's car approaches the scene, the interior of the car fills with red from the emergency lights. Joe's bloodshot eyes focus on an object in the grass, off the road and he can see that it's Kim's car. He parks the car behind a fire truck, exits his car and runs as fast as he can towards the wrecked SUV. A fireman and police officer standing on the side of the road try to stop the man.

"Hey, come back here!" the police officer yells. "You can't go over there!" Joe slides into the grass on his knees without a second thought about the rented tuxedo. He peers into the driver's side window to find Kim not there. There is blood all over the interior of the car. He looks in the back seat and also finds that the girls are gone. Joe reaches in and touches a patch of wet blood on one of the seats. He pulls his hand close to his face and stares at the blood. Joe wipes his bloody hand on his white shirt then looks towards the road. His despair turns positive for a moment as he thinks that his family may be OK. After all, if anyone died in the accident, they would surely still be trapped in the vehicle or lying next to the car under a sheet.

"Hey, you need to get away from the car!" A police officer grabs Joe by the arm. He looks at Joe's face and realizes who the man is he was yelling at a few seconds ago. "Joe?"

"Rick, where's Kim and the girls? Are they OK?" Joe has known Rick for years from when Joe was a detective on the force. Joe resigned from the PD to pursue the private investigation job.

"Oh God, that was Ki..," Rick stops short.

"Rick!" Joe yells.

"You better get to the hospital fast, Joe!" Joe runs back to his car and starts driving to the hospital. He searches for his cell phone and finds it in his pocket. While he attempts to watch the road, he dials a number.

"Hi, you have reached Bill Simmons," his voicemail answers.

"Bill, its Joe. Kim and the girls were in an accident! I'm on the way to the hospital." Joe cries while attempting to stay in as much control as possible. "I hope you get this soon! I need you!" His car screams into the parking lot. He barely puts the car in park before jumping out and running into the ER.

"Kim Walker, where is she?" he begs, grabbing the first nurse he sees.

"Sir!" the shocked nurse replies.

"My wife and daughters were in an accident, where are they?" A doctor comes over and puts his hand on Joe's shoulder.

"Mr. Walker, I'm Doctor Russo. Your wife and kids are in the operating room being attended to."

"Are they OK?"

"Sir, your family came into the hospital with very serious injuries and the doctors are doing everything within their power to save your family." Joe stands motionless in the middle of the ER, unsure what to do.

"Please, sir. Come over here and have a seat." A nurse gently assists Joe over to a seat in the waiting room. Joe sits down, bends forward and puts his face in his hands. "Can I get you some water or something?"

"No, just please tell me if there's any news," Joe says to the nurse pleadingly as he looks up at her.

"I will, sir."

Two hours later, a doctor comes into the waiting room. Joe is sitting in the corner with his back to the doctor. He looks at Joe and then looks down to the floor. "Mr. Walker," the doctor says softly as he approaches from behind. Joe jumps up from his chair and meets the doctor.

"Doc! Are they OK? Can I see them now?" Joe asks with anticipation.

"I'm sorry Mr. Walker, we did everything we could, but we couldn't save your daughters."

Joe stands motionless. Unable to believe what he just heard.

"What?" Joe says, shaking his head as if he was trying to clear his mind.

"I'm sorry Mr. Walker. Your daughters both suffered serious internal injuries that were too severe to repair. Your wife has serious injuries and she's still in surgery. We will be moving her to the critical care unit when she's out of surgery. I'm very sorry." Bill appears from behind the doctor and runs over to Joe and hugs him. Joe breaks down and screams uncontrollably yelling for his girls.

"CALIE! TALIA!" Joe yells as he falls to the ground on his knees in the middle of the waiting room.

"If there is anything we can do for you, please let us know," the doctor says to Bill then turns to walk away.

"I need to see them. I need to see my girls," Joe cries out as the doctor starts to walk away. Bill backs Joe up to a chair and helps him into it then runs over to the doctor.

"Doc, can you give him some time with his daughters, please?" Bill asks. "Let him say goodbye. Those girls are everything to him," Bill pleads.

"Let me clean them up a little first. He can't see them like they are."

"Thanks Doc." As he slowly walks back towards Joe who has now buried his face in his hands and is hunched over in the chair crying, Bill breaks down and cries too. He sits down next to his friend and puts his arm around him. "I'm so sorry Joe!" Bill says as they cry together.

"Why is this happening? This can't be happening!" Bill grabs Joe and pulls his head towards his shoulder and holds him tight.

"I don't know buddy. I don't know."

Joe and Bill are escorted into a recovery room by the doctor. As they walk into the room Joe sees his daughter's lying on the bed side by side, motionless. The girls have hospital gowns on with bandages on their heads and cuts on their faces. Joe's posture droops slightly then his whole body weakens before he starts slowly crying.

"Oh God!" Joe says softly. Bill tries to hold himself together.

"Take as much time as you need sir," the doctor tells Joe softly. Joe doesn't respond as he stares at the girls.

"I will wait for you in the hallway," Bill says as he pats Joe's shoulder and exits the room. Joe slowly walks over to the bed and bends over so his face is close to the girls. Delicately he caresses their heads as tears are running down his face. His head comes to rest on Calie's chest as his crying intensifies.

"No!" Joe screams then cries loudly as Bill cringes in the hallway. Bill leans against the wall with tears running down his face and with every scream and bellow, he winces and cries more as he feels his friend's pain.

Joe attempts to soften his cries as he lifts his head up off Calie. He wipes his nose and the tears from his face and again caresses Calie's head, then Talia's.

"Daddy is sorry girls," Joe says. "I promised you that I would never let anything happen to you and that I would always keep you safe," Joe says as tears pour from his eyes. "I guess that's a promise I couldn't keep," he says softly. "Daddy loves both of you very much. You're the best daughters anyone could have ever hoped for." Tears continue to stream down his face, dripping onto Talia's hospital gown. "I am so proud of both of you. You're the most beautiful daughters in the world and I will always love you," he whispers to them as he sobs uncontrollably.

Joe picks up Calie and Talia and holds them in his arms, as he has done hundreds of times, as if they were sleeping. Calie's head is resting on his right shoulder and Talia's on his left. He sits down slowly in a chair in the room and sings to them over and over again. A half an hour goes by before Bill and the doctor come into the room. Bill walks over to Joe and touches him on his left shoulder.

"Joe, we have to go buddy," he says softly.

"Joe, I have to take the girls now, I'm sorry," the doctor says compassionately. Joe doesn't move.

"Come on Joe, it's time to let them go," Bill says. Joe looks at his friend then looks at the doctor. The doctor is nodding his head slightly as if to say, "it's OK."

"I will never get to hold my girls again," he cries. "I love you," Joe whispers softly in Calie's ear as he allows the doctor to take Calie from him after giving her a kiss on her cold bandaged forehead. The doctor lays her back down on the bed delicately. Joe stands up, holding Talia's head close to his. He gives her a kiss on her forehead as he begins to cry out loud. He whispers in Talia's ear softly, "I love you sweetie! You will always be my little girl." Joe sets Talia down gently on the bed next to her sister. He gives both girls one more kiss on their foreheads then stands up straight. As he steps back, Bill puts his arm around his shoulder and guides him towards the door. They watch as the doctor covers the girls with a sheet.

Joe walks into a room in the critical care unit in a daze escorted by the doctor that saved Kim's life. He looks at his unconscious wife lying in the bed with a bandage wrapped around her head. Her left eye is black and blue and swollen shut. She has a tube for oxygen under her nose and needles in her arm attached to an IV line. She doesn't look anything like the woman he left this morning. The woman, who exudes strength and grabs life by the horns, is now broken and fighting for her life. Joe is emotionally drained and looks feeble as he shuffles towards Kim.

"Joe, Kim is stable but in a medically induced coma," the doctor tells him. "She has some very serious internal injuries that were bleeding, but we stopped it and repaired the damage. She has a concussion, a broken left leg and lots of cuts and bruises but like I said, the most important thing is that she's stable for now." Joe can't take his eyes off of his wife. He is afraid if he stops looking that she might be gone too. Dark red engulfs Joe's bloodshot eyes, his skin is pale and he isn't able to listen to anything the doctor is saying. He's fixated on Kim. Bill stands next to Joe looking at Kim but listening to everything the doctor says.

"Thanks Doc," Bill says for Joe. He knows that Joe may be hearing the doctor but isn't really listening to what he's telling him.

"Joe, your wife will be in a coma for at least two weeks, maybe longer so we can make sure her body is healing from the internal trauma she has endured," the doctor says.

"Can she hear me?" Joe asks. "I have to tell her about Calie and Talia."

"No, she can't hear or feel anything right now. Joe, I can't stress enough that Kim is not out of the woods yet. The next 24 hours are the most critical after the body suffers severe trauma like this." Joe looks at the doctor. "You should prepare yourself for the worst and hope for the best. I will leave you two alone for a while." Joe looks back at Kim.

"I'll be in the hallway waiting for you, buddy." Joe looks at Bill and nods slightly. As he walks out of the room, Bill closes the door softly while looking back at Joe. The beeping noise from the heart monitor is deafening in the room. Emotionally and physically exhausted, Joe slowly lowers his face to Kim's forehead and gives her a soft kiss. He stares at Kim for a few moments and touches her cheek with the back of his fingers. After sitting down in a chair next to the bed, he bends over and cups his hands into his face. Joe begins to cry as he has done so many times the past few hours.

The car comes to a stop at the end of the driveway as Bill shifts into park. They both stare out the window at the dark house. The black tuxedo Joe was so looking forward to wearing to the big dance is stained with dirt and blood.

"I'm scared. I don't think I have ever been alone in this house."

"Do you want me to stay with you tonight? You know I will. All you have to do is say the word," Bill says softly. Joe's eyes are barely open as he looks straight ahead, fatigued and dejected.

"Thanks Bill, you're a good friend."

"I probably won't get much sleep tonight, so if you need some company give me a call," Bill tells Joe.

"I'll need your help to get to the hospital tomorrow since my car is still there."

"Don't worry about that, I'll be here tomorrow as early as you want." Joe looks at Bill and nods then exits the car and walks to the front door. He's in no hurry to get into the house. Joe gives him a thumbs up to say he's OK as Bill starts backing out of the driveway. He opens the door with the key from his pocket, enters the foyer and closes the door behind him.

"Daddy!" Calie screams. "Daddy, help us!" Joe runs down the street towards the crash site. He just can't seem to run fast enough to get to the car. "Help us Daddy, please!" As Joe continues running towards the car, firemen are pulling the girls out of the car and running towards the ambulance. Joe sees the girls, he's almost there but doesn't get there quick enough. It feels like they keep getting farther and farther away from him. The ambulance drives off as Joe reaches the car. He can hear the girls screaming for him. The white double door opens into the operating room. The doctors are working on the girls as Joe stands motionless next to the doctor. Calie turns her head and reaches out for her father. Joe reaches out for her hand but he can't reach far enough.

"You said you wouldn't let anything happen to us," Calie cries to her father. Talia is lying next to Calie on the bed and looks at Joe.

"Daddy, I'm scared. Don't leave us here," Talia cries as Joe slowly moves backwards. He continues to reach out for the girls but can't reach them.

"DADDY!" both girls scream.

Joe sits up in bed, covered in sweat and breathing rapidly. His heart is beating out of his chest as he lies back down slowly, then takes a deep breath and stares up at the ceiling. Joe begins to cry violently. The pain in his cry is like salt on an open wound.

CHAPTER 3

It's a cloudy day at the Springfield Cemetery. The air is heavy with the promise of impending rain. Joe sits in front of two small white caskets covered in pink, white and yellow flowers. Joe's sister, Sarah Landry, sits beside him while she wipes the tears from her eyes with a tissue. Her arm is around her brother, as she struggles to provide even a small means of comfort during this horrific and tragic time. Bill is on the other side of his friend looking around at all the people who have shown up for the service. There's an overwhelming turnout for the funeral service with friends, family, community leaders and people he has never met. They all stand around the caskets mourning the unfortunate and sudden loss of children from the community.

Joe sits motionless, staring at the caskets with his unshaven face and bloodshot eyes. The bags under his eyes get bigger as the days go by from not sleeping. He hasn't showered in days and his clothes are wrinkled. One week has passed since the girls were killed tragically. Joe has become angry and depressed during these emotional days, just going through the motions of daily living. Kim continues to be in a medically induced coma at the local hospital. A long-time family friend and retired pastor,

Anthony Levardi, is standing in front of the caskets with an open Bible. Anthony, wearing an all-black suit, is a large round man with a bald head.

"My friends, we are gathered here today to say goodbye to Calie and Talia Walker who were called by God to join him in heaven. Although Calie and Talia leave this world, their light will never leave our hearts and will live on in our memories." Joe isn't hearing anything the pastor is saying but is tuning the words out with the girl's voices in his head. Ten minutes later, Anthony finishes his eulogy. "On behalf of the Walker family, we thank you all for coming out today. Your thoughts and prayers are appreciated for the family and especially for Kim who is still fighting for her life."

As the last mourners walk to their cars, Joe walks over to Anthony. "Thanks Tony, I appreciate you coming out here today." Joe extends his hand to shake Anthony's but he pulls him in for a hug. There are no words to provide the comfort and understanding Joe is aching for.

"If you need anything at all Joe, please give me a call. I'm here for you and the family. I will stop in and see Kim in the next few days," Anthony says while still holding Joe in his embrace. "Keep in touch. OK?"

Joe releases Anthony and looks at him with his eyes looking empty and lost. "Thanks Tony. I'll be OK and so will Kim." Joe turns to find Sarah and her husband Marc standing at his side.

"Thanks Tony, you did a great job with the service." Sarah hugs him and gives him a kiss on the cheek.

"It's the least I could do for my friend," Anthony replies as his eyes close, feeling so helpless to aid his friend. "Take care of Joey," Anthony whispers as he reaches out to shake Marc's hand.

"Thanks Tony, we will," Marc says shaking hands with Anthony. Anthony walks toward the road and then turns back to wave goodbye to everyone. Only Joe, Sarah, Marc and Bill remain as they all stand motionless for a moment quietly staring at the caskets. Sarah puts her arm around Joe and pulls him to her slightly, then rubs his shoulder. She looks at him as a tear runs down her face. She sniffles softly then Joe kisses the side of her head.

"Do you want to stay for a little bit? We can take as much time as you want," Sarah says as a tear escapes from her brother's eye, running down his face. Sarah wipes the tear away with her bare hand.

"I feel like I can't leave my girls here by themselves. I can't walk away," Joe cries desperately as tears flow freely from both eyes. Sharing in his pain and distress, Sarah cries with him. They stand together, holding each other for what feels like an eternity. Marc and Bill turn and walk away to give Sarah and Joe some space.

"Joe, take as much time as you need," Sarah says faintly. Joe nods, closes his eyes and takes a deep breath.

"OK, I'm ready," he says opening his eyes and looking to the ominous sky above. "I'm going to say my final goodbyes. I will meet you at the car in a few minutes." Sarah is looking deep into Joe's eyes with worry. "It's OK. I'll meet you at the car."

"OK." Sarah rubs Joe's back then walks over to the caskets. She kisses her hand and touches both caskets with her fingers. She meets up with Bill and Marc, interlocking her arms with theirs as they walk towards the car in silence. Joe pulls two flowers off the arrangement next to him, walks over to the caskets and stands in between them. Tears again stream down Joe's face as he begins the final process of leaving his babies forever.

"There are so many things that I didn't have a chance to teach you as a father." Joe's voice cracks as he looks back and forth at both caskets with the girl's names engraved on them. "There are so many amazing places that I didn't have the chance to show you. There were so many opportunities to hold you tightly and tell you how much I loved you that I didn't take advantage of." Joe looks up to the sky as tears continue to flow down his cheeks.

He looks back down at the caskets and wipes his face, taking in a deep breath. "I hope you are both at peace and that you're not scared because I can't take care of you anymore. I pray that you are comforting each other wherever you are and that you will always remember how much your Daddy loves you. I promise that we will see each other again someday." Joe looks up to the sky one more time. "Take care of my babies for me." Joe places a single rose on each casket then turns and walks away. As Joe walks away he turns to look at the caskets one more time. As if they are giving him a comforting sign, Joe sees an image of Calie and Talia standing next to the caskets in beautiful white dresses, holding hands and waving goodbye to their Daddy. Joe smiles.

"Joe, do you want to get dropped off at home or do you want to come home with us?" Sarah asks from the front passenger seat. Joe sits in the back seat of Sarah's SUV looking out the window while Marc drives. "Joey?" Joe closes his eyes for a moment then opens them.

"Can you bring me home, Marc? I'm just going to go home and be by myself for a while. Thanks anyway, Sarah," Joe replies as he continues looking out the window.

"Sure, Joe. We understand," Marc replies as he looks at Sarah sitting next to him clearly worried about her brother. A few minutes later Marc pulls into Joe's driveway. Joe gets out of the back driver's side and stops at Marc's open window.

"You sure you don't want any company?" Marc asks as he looks at Joe's face filled with pain and exhaustion.

"Thanks Marc, but I need to do this. I appreciate the ride." Joe turns and walks around the front of the SUV towards the front sidewalk, as Sarah meets him and walks him to the house.

"Please call me if you need to talk, have a beer or just sit and watch TV. You can't do this alone. I'm here for you Joe."

"I know you are Sis. I just need to be alone for a while and maybe take a nap. I have to get back up to the hospital to see Kim at some point this evening." Joe grabs his sister and hugs her tight. "Thanks for everything today. I love you!"

"Love you too Joe!" Sarah walks down the sidewalk while staring at Joe then turns and gets into the SUV.

Joe opens the front door to a quiet and gloomy house. He waits at the entryway hoping that everything up to that moment was just a horrible nightmare and Calie and Talia will come running around the corner to greet him as they have always done. Joe stands motionless and glum as the girls and Kim don't come. He steps into the house and closes the door behind him. The house is eerily quiet and cold. Joe slips his shoes off and makes his way upstairs for a short nap.

It's nighttime as Joe enters Kim's hospital room and stops short of the bed. He looks at his wife, who's wearing a blue hospital gown under the white blanket and stares for a moment. He turns slightly as he thinks about walking out and going home. How does he tell her that their life has tragically changed forever? That he just said goodbye to their daughters? He turns back towards Kim then walks over to the chair on the side of her bed and sits down. Joe sits expressionless, looking around at all of the machines with tubing attached to his wife as she fights for her life. She has no idea that the hardest fight of her life is yet to come.

"I buried our girls today," Joe whispers as he continues sitting motionless and looking straight ahead. He turns his body, his eyes finally looking at his wife who is still wearing a breathing tube but looks as if she is sleeping peacefully. Joe stares at Kim as his emotions take over. Suddenly overwhelmed with anger and resentment he lashes out. "You should have let me pick them up." He stands up, his hands tightly gripping the bed rails staring at his wife, getting angrier by the moment that she is able to sleep peacefully, unknowingly, as he's struggling to just exist. Joe turns his head away from Kim and walks out of her room, not looking back.

CHAPTER 4

It's been three weeks since the tragic night that forever changed Joe's existence in this world. Joe walks into Kim's room at the hospital as he has done now so many times the past few weeks. He stops at the doorway and looks wearily at his wife lying there motionless except for the rise and fall of her chest. She's now breathing without the help of the ventilator but is still heavily sedated. The doctors have decided that it's time for Kim to be taken out of her medically induced coma.

Over the past few days, they have been cutting back on the amount of sedatives used to keep her in the coma. Her body looks skeletal. Her cheeks are sunken and her skin looks grey. If he didn't know better he wouldn't believe that this lifeless figure in the bed was his wife. She is a woman who was so full of life, always smiling and singing and whose very existence centered on being a mom and wife.

Joe slowly walks over to her and takes her limp, cold hand in his. He rubs her fingers trying to bring them some warmth and life as he ponders how he will tell her that their daughters are gone. How do you tell a mother that she is no longer a mother? He has asks himself that very question over and over. "Who am I without my daughters? Am I still a father? What is my purpose in the world if not to be a father?"

The doctors have told Joe that once Kim wakes from her coma, she will know nothing of what happened. She may not even remember being in an accident. The nurse comes in and unplugs the IV supplying Kim with the anesthetic. It's time.

"Joe it's going to take Kim an hour or so to wake up from the anesthesia. She will be groggy and confused at first then she will slowly become more aware and coherent," the nurse informs him.

"OK, thank you." Joe sits on the side of the bed next to Kim, holding her hand. He takes a deep breath, his stomach in knots as the realization hits him that he will have to tell her soon. He decides to go get a cup of the tasteless, bitter coffee he has become accustomed to from the hospital cafeteria. He needs to clear his head and put his thoughts together about how to tell his wife that their daughters have died.

Two cups of coffee later, he returns to Kim's room. After what seems like an eternity, she starts to move her head slightly and struggles to open her eyes. "Hi sweetie," Joe whispers softly. "I'm here babe," he says coaxing her to wake up. Kim struggles to move her dry lips and open her mouth. The effects of being in a coma for three weeks show in her inability to move and talk.

"Hi," she finally gets out in a groggy and raspy voice. Kim's eyes fluttering as she attempts to open them. Her eyes finally open as she gazes around the room, taking in her surroundings. "Where am I?" she asks.

"You're in the hospital. You were in a very serious car accident," Joe tells her. Kim opens her eyes wide looking around the room. She is looking for something or someone. As she continues searching, confusion and panic sets in.

"Where are the girls?" Kim asks in a panicked voice. Joe says nothing and continues to look at her. He looks down at the bed. Kim's eyes become wild with terror. "Joe, where's Calie and Talia?" she says in a stern, demanding voice that pains and exhausts her. "Are they OK?" Joe looks at her with tears in his eyes as his lips tremble with anguish.

"No, they're not OK Kim. They didn't make it," he tells her softly while tears shoot down his cheeks. Kim begins to cry and wail uncontrollably, ripping the tubes from her arm. She tries to get up, but her weakened body won't let her.

"No! My babies! I want my babies!" she howls, reeling from this new pain that overtakes her entire being. Joe grabs Kim and holds her tightly as they sob in anguish together. She pounds her fists on Joe's back as she continues to cry and scream. The nurse and doctor rush into the room hearing the heartbreaking cries and pull Joe away. They quickly reinsert the IV despite her protests and shoot her with a sedative. Kim fights the drowsiness, but it eventually overtakes her as her body and mind succumb to the numbness once again. As she slowly drifts off, she stares at Joe with a look of despair, as if begging Joe to help her. She reaches for Joe as her eyes close. Joe breaks down, lamenting violently as one of the nurses wraps her arms around him.

CHAPTER 5

Joe pushes Kim in a wheelchair towards the main entrance to the hospital. It's been two weeks since Kim was taken off the medication removing her from the coma and now she is going home. Joe's looking straight ahead at the double sliding doors he's approaching as a nurse follows them out. On the other side of the doors, his car is parked in the driveway under the carport. The doors open and Joe slows the wheelchair and pulls up to the passenger side door. Joe helps Kim to stand and supports her as she hobbles with her good leg towards the passenger side of the car.

"Watch your head," Joe says to her as he sits her down on the seat. Joe starts to grab Kim's left leg to help her.

"Don't!" she snaps. Joe stops moving and puts his hand up and away from Kim. "I can do it!" Joe stands up, takes a step back and glares at her. Kim doesn't make eye contact and lifts her cast covered leg into the car, then puts her right leg in. The car door slams with a slight attitude as Joe walks around to the driver's door after placing the crutches and wheelchair in the trunk. Joe pulls out of the parking lot and heads home. The silence in the car during the ride home is brutal.

"I want to stop at the cemetery," Kim says stoic while glaring out the passenger window.

"OK," Joe answers without hesitation. A few minutes later, the large grey stone arch encompassing the entrance to the Jacksonville Cemetery becomes visible in the distance. Joe pulls in and drives under the arch, past the maintenance building and towards the back of the cemetery. He pulls to the side of the road next to a large oak tree. As the car shuts off, Kim looks at Joe. Joe points out Kim's window as she looks to see what he is pointing to.

"The gravestones are on the left side of that small white birch tree. It's about a fifty foot walk." With a slam of the trunk, Joe wheels her chair next to the car and opens her door. "Do you want me to help you?" he asks contemptuously.

"Please," she says remorsefully.

Joe reaches his hand in to help her as she looks up at him. Kim takes Joe's hand as he pulls her up and helps her into the wheelchair. The wheelchair, pushed by Joe through the grass, stops as Kim puts her good leg down on the ground.

"I can do it. Thanks," she says.

Joe allows Kim to get to the site first, trailing behind in case she needs help pushing the chair, or at least that's what he tells himself. In truth he feels like this woman is a stranger to him now. Their interactions with each other over the past two weeks, while Kim was still in the hospital have vacilated between desperately clinging to each other in order to survive this nightmare that no one but the two of them can possibly understand, to sitting with each other in silence for hours, at a loss for conversation. Both Joe and Kim are unsure how to move forward in this new harsh reality. Joe stands back as she approaches the site. He can see her body start to quiver as she cries openly touching her hand to each headstone that now marks her children's new resting place. Joe sits down in the grass and rests his head in his arms with his eyes closed.

"Joe," Kim says suddenly appearing next to him. Joe pops up realizing he has somehow dozed off while waiting for her. His body and mind are so fatigued that he grabs 15 to 30 minute increments of sleep anywhere he can. Joe jumps up to see Kim's face laced with an emotion he is unsure of. Is it anger, resentment, or just plain defeat?

"Are you ready to go?" he asks.

"Yes," she responds in a barely audible voice. She allows Joe to wheel her to the car this time as he helps her into the passenger seat. The wheelchair is dropped into the trunk with a thud as patience start to run thin. Joe looks in the direction of Talia and Calie's headstones as he stands motionless for a moment. Feeling so sad and empty inside, he walks to the driver's side and gets back in the car. As they drive home together for the first time since the accident, Joe takes in a deep breath. He feels the now familiar pangs of anxiety and desolation as they head home, except this time he's not alone. He's not sure if this comforts him or if in some crazy way Kim now feels like an intruder in his misery.

"You did a good job with the gravestones, and they're in a nice spot," Kim says, breaking the awkward silence with pleasantries.

"Thanks," Joe says as he turns to look at her while she dabs her eyes with a tissue. He knows he should offer her something but realizes that he's just too numb to comfort her and too empty to offer her any reassurance that they will be OK. He doesn't even know how or if that will ever be possible again. Every time he looks at her all he sees and feels is the pain of being a family that no longer exists.

CHAPTER 6

A month and a half have passed in a blur. It's 10:30 p.m. and Kim is sitting in an oversized chair reading and wrapped up in Talia's favorite fleece blanket. The cozy and warm faded pink blanket with daisies on it was used by Talia ever since she was two years old. Kim has made remarkable progress during her rehabilitation and physical therapy sessions and is able to get around on her own now. Joe enters the house through the front door after being out for the night again as a cool burst of air blows into the living room from the open door.

Joe's drunk again. He staggers into the living room while mumbling to himself as he tries to maneuver around the coffee table. He looks at Kim with his bloodshot and puffy eyes and gives her a surly smile as he falls onto the couch. Kim breathes a heavy sigh as she looks at this man she thought she knew better than herself. She struggles to work through the pain of their loss every day, trying to figure out how to move forward. Always feeling she is only inches from drowning in her grief.

She knows Joe blames her for the girl's deaths. She sees it in his eyes every time he looks at her. As painful as it is, she understands. She blames herself too. Maybe if she reacted faster or stayed focused on the road instead of looking back at Calie and Talia in the back seats, then maybe the girls would be here today. Kim could go crazy with these thoughts, which is why she keeps her brain busy. Busy with rehabilitation, reading, spending time with her family, and trying to find a way to make Calie and Talia's deaths meaningful. Joe is mentally in a very dark and dangerous place. Kim closes her book and sets it down on her lap, clearly disturbed by Joe's presence. She has tried to accept Joe's need to handle his grief in his own way and empathizes with him emotionally. She has tried to give him time, but she has slowly become intolerant of his drinking and coldness towards her. It only continues to get worse. She feels the anger and resentment building in her as he begins to snore on the couch.

"I can't take this anymore, Joe," Kim says in a low angry tone, slamming the book down on the coffee table. The thump of the book on the wood table briefly gets Joe's attention more than her angry manner. He pops his head up and opens his eyes momentarily then drops his head back into the couch. "You are drunk every single night. You don't talk to me anymore. You're drowning your sorrows with a bottle and I can't live like this anymore!" She pushes herself up off the chair and limps out of the room.

As she starts to hobble up the stairs to the second floor, she stops and looks at Joe briefly, tears welling up in her eyes. Her heart is broken to see what he has become. She continues up the stairs to her bedroom and slams the door behind her. The message Kim sent is clear. Joe's not welcome. He stands up and meanders over to the fireplace and leans on the mantel to support his unstable body.

On the mantel there's a picture of a smiling Talia and Calie hugging Joe cheek to cheek. Joe starts to cry. He knows he's falling apart and letting his wife down at a time she needs him most, but he doesn't know how to stop the agonizing pain he feels every second of the day. He doesn't know how to help himself, never mind be there for Kim. Then there's the anger. He tries to fight it. He knows that the accident was not Kim's fault, but he just can't seem to get past the gnawing anger and resentment he feels towards her. The only time he feels some relief from the constant conflicting thoughts and paralyzing pain is when he drinks. The alcohol numbs his brain and his emotions if only briefly giving him the respite he desperately seeks.

"I miss you girls," Joe said softly. He turns and walks upstairs.

It's early morning and still dark out. Kim rolls over and looks to the other side of the bed hopeful to see Joe. His spot is empty and Kim's heart sinks. She runs her hand over his cold pillow realizing that he never made it to bed. She has never felt so alone. She rolls back over remaining still with her eyes open. Kim slowly gets out of bed and trudges down the end of the hall to Calie's bedroom. The door is open and Kim peeks inside. Joe, still in his clothes, is passed out snoring on Calie's bed as he clutches her favorite brown puppy stuffed animal. Kim's eyes water as she drops her head. She turns and finds her way back into her bedroom and climbs into bed. She has never felt more alone.

Later that morning Kim's in the kitchen making breakfast in front of the stove. Joe methodically steps down the stairs and into the kitchen. Another night of heavy drinking has taken a toll on his body. He stops and stands a few feet behind her. She senses his presence and freezes. Kim turns her head to catch a glimpse of Joe standing behind her. He looks at her, undoubtedly with something on his mind.

"I'm calling the lawyer this morning and telling him that he can sign the settlement with the trucking company," Joe says as Kim stands motionless then turns to look at him. "He said the money would be in the account the next day."

"OK," she says softly. Kim looks tired. She has bags under her eyes and her hair is dull and lifeless. Kim used to take great pride in her appearance, but that hasn't been a priority of hers lately. "Joe," she calls to him as he turns to walk away then stops with his back to her. "We need to talk."

"What do we need to talk about, Kim?" Joe says with a disinterested tone as he looks at her. She tilts her head slightly with a look of resignation on her face as she searches for some flicker of the old Joe.

"Us, Joe. Our family," her voice starts to rise. "You, your drinking, everything that's going on right now!" Kim replies angrily. "We can't keep living like two strangers!" Joe steps closer to her, his eyes now alive and wild with rage. His rancid, day after a drinking binge breath, on her face.

"What family? What family are you talking about? Not sure you're aware of recent events, but we have no family anymore!" Joe's anger builds as tears form in his eyes. The edge of his mouth starts to foam like a rabid dog. "And my drinking? That's funny Kim." Joe's face turns dangerously evil. "I wouldn't have to drink if it wasn't for….!" The muscles in Joe's face are tight and quivering with anger. He stops himself before finishing the sentence. He glares at Kim, points his finger in her face, and then backs off. His face starting to loosen and relax as he realizes that he's unraveling. At first his anger scares Kim, but her fear quickly turns to her own rage and she lashes out back at him.

"What Joe? Say it! If it wasn't for me the girls would still be alive! Is that what you were going to say?" Kim steps towards Joe and closes the space that he created. Her face is filled with her own fury. "You think I don't know that you blame me? I see it and feel it from you every second that we're together. Don't you think I blame myself?" Tears stream down Kim's face. "For the past month and a half, I've had to live with the fact that I was driving the car that killed our girls! I'm sorry Joe." She sobs uncontrollably as she continues to yell. "I'm so sorry that they're gone. I would trade places with them in a second if I could." Joe leans against the counter with his head down. Part of him wants to go to her, wants to wrap his arms around her and make everything better. Her pain is so raw and in need of healing.

"Why couldn't you have let me pick the girls up? If only you hadn't insisted on driving them," Joe says softly then slowly lifts his head and looks at Kim who is now standing motionless looking back at him, her face wet with tears. Joe's eyes are completely red, almost demon like, from crying. "I told you I wanted to pick them up." Joe walks towards her slowly. He is now within a foot of Kim. For a brief moment, she thinks he might hug her. She's aching for the Joe that would have cried with her and would have done anything to relieve her pain. But she can see in his eyes that he's not able to give that to her. Kim accepts confirmation from him of what she already knew. He blames her for the girl's death. Her posture droops and she falls silent as she looks at her husband.

"I don't know what to do. This is killing me too Joe." Tears stream down his cheeks as his face is awash with red.

"You live as if nothing happened!" Joe snaps. "I can't do that!" Joe takes a few steps back. "You're able to keep your emotions inside and keep them in check," he said as his voice gets lower and lower. "I can't do that." Kim cries and stands motionless. Joe turns away from her and walks into the foyer.

"You're not the only person that lost their daughters, Joe!" Kim yells as Joe stands stationary in the hallway with his back to her and his hand on the door knob. "I lost my babies too and it rips my heart out every single day that I'm not with them! You can't just hide from this by drinking every day. We are supposed to be a team," Kim cries in desperation. "We are supposed to help each other through this, not turn our backs on each other and go to war.

You're turning to a bottle for comfort and not to me." Joe turns looking at Kim as her eyes plead with him. His eyes well up again as tears overflow and drip down his face.

"I miss my girls! I can't live without them and I can't keep doing this," Joe says now openly crying, his voice cracking. He turns and walks out the front door. Kim backs up against the counter and sinks to the floor in uncontrollable sobs.

CHAPTER 7

It's 1:30 in the morning, and Joe returns home for the first time since the fight. He takes a deep breath and walks into the house through the front door. When the door opens, he stumbles into the house and drops a bottle of vodka on the hard wood floor. The bottle smashes into pieces as liquor flows into multiple pools. Unaffected by the sound of the glass breaking, Joe attempts to steady himself by reaching for the bannister but misses it. Joe falls to his left, into the wall then face first onto the floor with a loud crash. With his lip busted open, he bleeds unsuspectingly all over the hallway floor. Joe's completely wasted and feels no pain. Blood and saliva spill from his open mouth, as he tries unsuccessfully to lift himself off the floor.

"Kim," he mumbles barely audible. With every bit of strength, he pushes himself up and sits leaning against the wall. Joe's hand bleeds profusely from pushing himself up in the broken glass. He rubs his bloody hand on his shirt then rubs his hand over his forehead to push his sweat drenched hair back. Blood covers his face and shirt as he looks at his hand while trying to catch his breath.

"Ha Ha," Joe laughs at the site of the blood all over his hands, but his laugh quickly tapers as he starts crying uncontrollably. "KIM!" he yells. "Kim," he says softer as his eyes close for a moment, but there's no response. Joe slowly picks himself up by pushing himself off the wall, leaving a long blood smear behind him.

Water flows from the kitchen faucet as Joe rests his arms on the counter and lets the water flow over his blood covered hand. After wrapping his hand in a dish towel, Joe finds a note on the counter. Picking it up with an unsteady and bloodied hand he hesitates then reads:

Joe,

We are both dealing with the unbearable loss of our daughters. You have chosen to deal with this loss in a way that I can't nor want to be a part of. You have chosen to shut me out of your life. Sitting by and watching you drown yourself in alcohol every night isn't an option for me. I cannot look at you and see the blame and anger in your eyes and still try to heal myself. I don't know what to do to fix this or to fix us and I don't even know if we can, but I do know that I cannot live this way any longer. I am staying with my sister for now. Pease do not try to contact me. I feel that we need to take some time and give each other space away from one another. I love you Joe.

Love

Kim

Joe crumbles to the ground crying and wailing. He screams and starts punching at the floor, over and over again leaving more blood spatters. The black framed picture of Talia and Calie on the counter draws his attention as he stands up and stares at it. He remembers the day this picture was taken. It was their last family vacation together. It had been a perfect summer day with the sun blazing and not a cloud in the sky. Joe and the girls had just finished building a sand castle and he asked Kim to take their picture. They were so proud of the castle they created and were grinning ear to ear with pride.

Grabbing the framed photograph of the two girls standing side by side at the beach, he holds it close as he sets out for the long arduous trek up the stairs. Halfway up, he falls into the banister and lands on the stairs, then crawls the rest of the way. At the top, he stands and opens his bedroom door and flicks on the light, smearing blood on the switch. The bed is empty and still made. Joe cries into the photo, reliving the memory as he walks into Talia's room. He kneels down on the floor and leans over the bed. Joe stares at the girls with their vibrant smiles and feels like they are looking right back at him.

"Daddy misses you so much." Joe sobs as his tears drip onto the glass. Exhausted and spent, Joe eventually stops crying. He turns his head and looks toward his bedroom when a thought suddenly enters his mind. "Girls, I know how we can be together again." He stands up and walks to his room, after bouncing off the hallway wall. In his closet he uncovers a small safe on the shelf. He opens the safe and finds what he's looking for, a silver handgun sitting at the bottom. Joe stands motionless staring at the gun. His breathing increases and his heart starts beating rapidly in his chest. He looks like a man possessed. He pulls the handgun out and walks back into Talia's room. With his body shaking violently he cries wildly. "I'm sorry girls, Daddy will be with you soon. I love you!" His sobbing briefly subsides as he gets down on his knees and pushes the handgun against his right temple. His finger is on the trigger as tears flow from his eyes. "I love you!" Joe cries out. His eyes are closed tight and the muscles in his face tighten as he prepares for the bullet's impact against his head. "RRRRR!" He growls as he tries to pull the trigger.

He pulls the gun away from his head and puts the barrel of the gun in his mouth. He holds the gun with both hands and contorts his body straight up while on his knees. Lifting his head, he looks directly across the room. Joe's eyes are wide open, his hands shake violently, and just as he is about to pull the trigger, he looks down at the girls picture on the bed. He pulls the gun from his mouth and throws it to the floor as he cries out. "NOOOO!" He grabs the picture and hugs it as if it were the girls themselves. Falling to the floor in the fetal position, he howls louder and louder. "Girls, I'm sorry, I'm sorry!"

The next morning Talia's room is bright with sunshine. Joe, still in the fetal position and clutching the picture frame, slowly wakens. He starts to sit up. With his head pounding in agony, he looks at the picture he clutches in his hands. Attention is now focused on the pain he feels in his hand as he looks at his dried blood covered palms. Large blood stains cover the rug where Joe's mouth had rested and another where his cut hand oozed blood. He squeezes his cut hand and makes a fist then releases it.

"Ow," he briefly grimaces in pain. As he spots the handgun on the floor, he suddenly remembers the night before. At that moment, he realizes how close he came to doing the unthinkable. He stands up and walks into his bedroom and sets the gun back in the open safe before closing the door.

In the bathroom, Joe looks at himself in the mirror. Shame overtakes him. He can't believe what he's seeing in his reflection and what he has become. He runs his right index and middle finger over his busted lip then looks down at his cut hand as he slowly shakes his head in disgust. Joe's hair is matted on the side of his head and his face is unshaven and covered with dried blood. His skin looks ashen and his eyes are red and swollen. As the vanity drawer opens, Joe removes a pair of tweezers and lifts his bloodied cut hand near his face. A small shard of glass is pulled from his palm as he growls in pain.

"AAAAOW!" Joe barks as he pulls the glass out. Joe looks at the nearly quarter inch long, triangular shard of glass he just removed from his hand. The small hole left in his hand starts to bleed all over again from the absence of the glass. He throws the shard in the garbage then starts taking his bloodied clothes off. As he steps into the shower and turns the water on, the cold water hits him like an arctic blast.

"Ahhh!" Joe screams as the shower floor becomes awash in red while blood runs down his legs. He turns the water on as hot as he can tolerate and lets the water run over him for a long time before finally cleaning the remnants of last night off his head and body.

Thirty minutes later Joe is out of the shower and sitting on the side of the tub wrapped in a blue towel. He begins the delicate task of super gluing his cut and wrapping his hand with a bandage. Gingerly, he attempts to pull his jeans up but stops midway and looks at his left hand. The pain in his hand prevents him from pulling his pants up, but he presses on and bears the pain. A dark green tee shirt is pulled over his head with his uninjured hand. His thirty-seven year old body screams in pain from the results of the fall.

As Joe walks down the stairs, he begins to slow his decent as he nears the bottom. He can't believe what he's seeing. The foyer at the bottom of the stairs is a mess. Broken glass and dried blood covers the floor and blood is smeared on the wall. It looks as if someone was finger painting the wall with red paint. He again shakes his head and sighs hard as he looks down in disappointment. Joe carefully walks around the broken glass and goes to the kitchen where he is relieved to see that nothing is destroyed. On the counter, he finds the note that Kim left for him and reads it again.

With a clear head, Joe finally understands the pain he has caused the woman he has loved since high school. A tear rolls down his face, but he fights to keep his composure. He places the note back on the counter and looks around him. His home once filled with the love and warmth of his family is now cold and unfamiliar. The sounds of his girls laughing and singing come back to him. He remembers the way they would run shrieking and yelling to jump into his arms to welcome him home. After a moment, he turns his head and sees an open bottle of vodka on the counter. Joe walks over and picks up the vodka. He looks at the bottle in repulsion and pours it down the drain. After putting the empty bottle in the garbage, he goes through the cabinets and clears out two more bottles of liquor and pours them down the drain.

Joe turns around and leans up against the counter in front of the sink. He takes a moment to collect himself then heads to the basement where he gets a bucket and large sponge. Back in the kitchen, he fills the bucket with water and soap and begins the process of cleaning up the mess that he created the night before. His final task is to clean up the blood in Talia's bedroom. He finishes up by wiping the blood from the girls' picture and putting it back on the kitchen counter. As Joe walks through the house, he stops in the hallway and looks at his wedding photograph. A small smile comes out but quickly falters and gives way to the frown he has come accustomed to having since the girls died. In the kitchen, he picks up the cordless phone and begins to call Kim at her sister's house but stops before completing the number. The handset is slowly lowered to the counter as Joe glares at it. At this point, he isn't sure he wants to call Kim. Joe isn't sure of anything right now.

CHAPTER 8

The drive into downtown Jacksonville is filled with anxiety as Joe parks the car in front of his business. He sits in the car for a few moments looking into the front windows at Bill, who is sitting at his desk talking on the phone. As he exits the car and walks up onto the sidewalk, Bill sees him and hangs up the phone. They meet in the reception area as Bill greets his friend with a big smile.

"Hey, look whose back!" Bill walks over and embraces Joe in a hug. "It's good to have you back buddy. I've kept your office clean and squared away just like you like it." Bill walks towards Joe's door excited to show him his organized office. What Bill didn't realize was that Joe wasn't following him. Bill stops and looks at Joe. "What's going on buddy?" he says with a look of a concern as he slowly walks back towards Joe. Joe looks at Bill, stoic and cold.

"I'm leaving town! I'm going away for a while and at this point I don't know when or if I will be back."

"What are you talking about?" Bill said softly.

"I have to leave and get away from this place for a while. I'm sorry Billy."

"OK, maybe you and Kim could use some time away together. That's a good idea. I understand. Take all the time you need. I can keep the business going for a while by myself."

"Kim isn't coming with me, I'm going alone." Bill's shoulders drop in disappointment at the news.

"Joe, I know you're hurting inside but think about this for a while. Where are you going? Why isn't Kim going with you?"

"I don't know where I'm going Bill." Joe is reluctant to make eye contact with Bill and turns away from him.

"Joe, in a strange way I feel like I lost my own kids. I loved those little girls like they were my own and I'm hurting too. We are all hurting, but you can't just run away and forget about the life you still have and the people that love you." Joe looks out the window and says nothing. "Joe?"

"I know you loved them Bill. They loved you too, but as far as me leaving, I don't have a choice. I have to clear my head or else I'm going to go crazy." Bill glares at Joe and nods his head slightly. "You've seen what I've been doing. I'm barely surviving in a drunken fog for the past month and a half. I can't keep going like this," Joe says as he turns and takes a few steps with his back to Bill.

"Joe, you have a lot of people who care about you and support you. What do I tell them?"

"I don't have any idea what you're going to tell them."

"Does Kim know?" Joe looks to the floor. "No, she is staying with her sister Sydney. I left her a note."

"Oh shit," Bill says softly as he grabs his head with both hands and rubs his face. He reaches out with his left arm and touches Joe's right shoulder. "Joe, you can't do this to her! She lost those girls just like you did and now she is going to lose you too. Don't do this to her." Joe looks up at Bill. "We will pull through this Joe, I promise. Just stay."

Joe shakes his head. "Keep an eye on Kim. Can you do that for me?" Joe asks. Bill's face shows his displeasure.

"Will you at least promise me that you will keep in touch and tell me how you're doing and where you are? Please," Bill begs as he grabs Joe and they hug each other with nothing left to say. Joe has made up his mind.

"Take care buddy and good luck with the business." Joe turns and walks out the door. Bill slowly follows Joe to the front door and watches as his partner gets into the car. Bill can't believe that his lifelong friend is leaving. He steps out onto the sidewalk as Joe looks at him one more time, then pulls out and disappears into traffic. Bill stands motionless and stunned by the complete breakdown of reality he thinks Joe is going through.

CHAPTER 9

It's a warm sunny afternoon, the day after Joe abruptly walked out of the business and out of everyone's life. Bill is driving his car with the window down listening to his favorite music trying to calm his nerves. He turns off the road into a short paved driveway and shuts his car off. As he steps out and closes the car door, he glances around at Sydney's house and yard. It's a beautiful old white remodeled farmhouse, built on the outskirts of town with plenty of land surrounding it. Years ago Sydney and Kim's parents owned the farm and grew orange trees before retiring and handing the farm down to Sydney and her husband.

Sydney's two black labs run up to greet Bill and begin barking to alert the presence of a stranger. As he attempts to make friends and invite the dogs close for a rub, Sydney and a little boy come out onto the front porch. The dogs go running to the back of the house while Bill slowly walks to the front porch to meet up with Kim's sister. He has no idea what he's going to say or how he'll even begin to explain to Kim that Joe has left town. The forty-five minute ride to Sydney's house should have given Bill plenty of time to think of something to say, but how do you tell your best friend's wife that the love of her life just up and left.

"Hi Bill," Sydney greets him warmly then gives him a quick hug. Sydney is tall with long dirty blonde hair and the same deep blue eyes as her sister. The resemblance between Kim and Sydney is mind blowing. "Come on in, I'm so glad you came to see Kim. That was very nice of you."

"Thanks Sydney. It's good to see you again." Bill steps into the house and immediately feels his body heat up as the inevitable delivery of bad news draws closer. For the first time, he actually feels anger towards his friend for putting him in such an awkward position. He looks around nervously like he's trapped in a corner.

"You OK?" Sydney slants her head slightly as she looks at Bill as if she's peering right though to his soul. He stares back at her, and looks away unnervingly. "Something happened with Joe. That's why you're here to see her, isn't it?" Sydney continues glaring at Bill with dismay.

"What makes you think something happened?" he replies as his forehead creases from sneering at the thought of being read by Sydney.

"Because, you're cracking under pressure Bill. You have a bead of sweat starting to form at the top of your forehead and you're obviously uncomfortable."

"Syd, I just need to talk to her for a few minutes." Sydney nods slightly, then sighs and shakes her head in disappointment.

"She's in the back yard on the patio." Sydney walks Bill to the kitchen where she points to her sister in the backyard. "Go on out, but just so you know, the past hour is the only time she has stopped crying since she showed up at my door." Sydney's anger at the prospect of Bill disturbing the recent calmness in the house is showing by the tone of her voice.

"This isn't easy for me either Syd. The last thing I want to do is upset her even more than she already is, but I have to talk with her." He looks at Kim through the window as Sydney joins him in watching her.

"Can you tell me what's so important that it can't wait until she's in a better state of mind?" Sydney and Bill make eye contact with each other then he looks out the window again.

"Joe left town yesterday," he says without any hesitation or empathy in his tone. Sydney sighs deep and closes her eyes.

"Oh my God. Are you fucking kidding me," Sydney says angrily but quiet enough that Kim didn't hear her. Bill shakes his head while looking at Sydney as she turns her body and rests her backside against the counter and covers her face with both hands. "How could he do that to her?"

"Syd, since I've known Joe I have never seen the look in his face that I saw yesterday." Sydney glares at Bill. "It's like he wasn't even there. He had no emotion, almost expressionless." Her eyes widened in panic. "I'm really worried about him. He wouldn't tell me where he was going and said he didn't know if he was ever coming back." He looks out the window at Kim. "I have to tell her. She has a right to know that her husband is gone and may never come home." Sydney nods with a hopeful look of approval and gives Bill a half smile.

"OK, I will be in here if you need some assistance or if she breaks down." He nods back at her. "Good luck."

"Thanks Syd." Bill looks out the window at Kim as he takes a deep breath and starts for the back door.

"Hi Kim." Surprised to see Bill, she immediately stands up and starts walking towards him.

"Hi Billy, It's good to see you." They meet up and give each other a hug.

"It's nice to see you too. How are you?"

"It's been a rough couple of days. Come sit down. I'm sure you didn't come all the way out here just to say hi." Kim offers a small smile. The vibrant twinkle in her eyes that she was famous for having was nowhere to be found. Her smile that was once a staple on her face now only appears in rare moments and without the lightness and laughter that used to accompany it.

"When was the last time you slept?" Bill asks with concern.

"I can't remember the last time I had a good night's sleep." Her eyes close for what appears to be longer intervals every time she blinks. "So what brings you here?" He hesitates a moment while staring at Kim and thinks to himself that maybe it isn't a good time to share this news.

"Joe came into the office yesterday and told me he was leaving town." She looks at Bill confused.

"Where did he go?"

"He wouldn't tell me. All he said was that he needed to get away to clear his head and he doesn't know when he will be back." She struggles to comprehend what Bill just told her. Her sleep deprivation and emotional state is playing tricks with her mind. She smiles as her chin quivers then attempts to pull herself together.

"Well, Joe and I had a big fight four days ago about his drinking. That's when I left to come here. I told him not to call me," she explains. Her hands wring her skirt and her eyes well up with fresh tears as she begins to take in what Bill just told her. Joe has left her and she is now truly alone.

"I'm worried about him, Kim. I'm not sure what he is planning to do. He said he left you a note. Did you get it?" She shakes her head.

"No, I haven't been back to the house since coming here. Joe blames me for what happened. He couldn't even stand to be in the same room with me anymore," she pauses, considering if she should go on. "Part of me understands because I blame myself too but…" Kim's voice trails off as she looks to the ground.

"That's crazy. The accident wasn't your fault." He leans towards Kim taking her hands in his. "Look at me. It wasn't your fault!" Kim looks into Bill's pleading eyes.

"I know that to some degree, but he's just so angry and so messed up from drinking. I feel like we are two complete strangers." Her bloodshot eyes stream more tears but she doesn't attempt to wipe them.

"You both suffered a terrible loss and I know that part of you will never get over it, but it's you guys, Joe and Kim. You guys are going to get through this. I think he just needs some time to clear his head. Maybe it's a good thing that both of you take some time away from each other. Take a break and heal your own way."

"I hope your right Billy, I miss him. I miss us." Bill hugs her as she softly cries in his arms.

After sitting together for a while longer, Sydney walks out and joins them. "I should probably get going. Bill stands as Kim follows. "If you need anything just call. Please?"

"I will. Thank you Billy." They all hug goodbye before Bill gets into his car and heads down the driveway. Sydney walks over and puts her arm around her sister.

"Hey, you OK?" Sydney asks as she and Kim watch the car pull out onto the main road.

"I think so. I don't know." Kim looks at Sydney. "I'm going home, Syd. I need to be in my own house." Sydney nods as she stares at her little sister.

"I wish you would stay a little longer, just a few more days?" Kim shakes her head no and smiles.

"You are the best sister anyone could ask for, but I'll be fine."

"I know you'll be OK. What did Bill say?"

"He said that Joe left. He needed to get away to clear his head. He doesn't know where, when, or even if Joe will be back." Sydney holds her in silence. Kim rubs her sister's arm. "I'll be fine," Kim says, not so convincingly.

Kim pulls into the driveway later that night and parks in front of the two car garage. Her house is void of life and black with darkness. A momentary pause is held longer as she looks intently at the empty house before opening her car door. Kim's wearing a grey pull over sweatshirt and jeans and removes her duffle bag from the back seat. Using the light from the street lamp to find the keyhole, she inserts the key into the lock. After taking a deep breath and letting it out, she unlocks the door and slowly pushes it open. She doesn't really know what to expect when she enters the house.

As the front door swings all the way open, she reaches into the doorway and turns the hall light on. The bright light illuminates the foyer and adjacent rooms. Apprehensive about entering the strangely quiet house, she looks inside but doesn't step in. It feels like a stranger's home, not the warm and busy house full of life and promise that it once held. Hesitantly she steps inside the foyer and closes the front door behind her. Looking down at the hard wood floor, Kim finds a deep scratch in the center of the floor then finds a small hole in the wall to her left. After exploring further, she walks into the kitchen and turns the light on. The kitchen appears clean and orderly. On the counter the answering machine blinks a neon green 10 to indicate the number of messages on the machine. She pushes "PLAY" on the machine.

BEEP "First Message Friday 2:15 PM." "Hi Kim and Joey, it's Sarah. I haven't heard from you guys in a while and I just wanted to see how you were doing. I figured I would give you some time by yourselves, but I just can't stop thinking of you. Please call me when you get this message. I love you both."

Kim stops the next message from playing and turns to see a note on the counter. Next to the note is Joe's cell phone. She walks over to the counter and picks up the hand written note from Joe as she holds his cell phone in her other hand.

Kim,

I'm sorry for the pain I have caused you these past few months. I never intended to hurt you, but I am now realizing that I'm doing it again. When we had children my life with you was complete in every way. Having Talia, Calie and you by side made me the happiest man in the world. I don't have that anymore and I'm miserable because of it. I am so lonely and dead inside and feel that I have nothing to live for. I feel like I'm in a nightmare that I can't wake up from. Don't worry I'm not going to hurt myself. I am however leaving and don't know when I'm coming back. I have been a terrible husband in a time when you needed me most to be strong and support you. For that I am truly sorry. I have failed you as a husband and I am ashamed to look at myself in the mirror. I have to get away from here until I can come to grips with what happened and move on. This is something I have to do alone. I took half of the settlement money and have transferred it into an account for me. I don't expect you to wait for me for any length of time and I hope you find peace and happiness someday. I have and will always love you.

           Love,

             Joe

Kim begins crying and slowly falls to her knees.

CHAPTER 10

Two months have passed since Joe left home. He's been traveling across the country, wandering aimlessly from city to city. Currently he is staying in a cheap bayside hotel in a small town outside of Tacoma, Washington until he decides it's time to move on. Besides some clothes, the only thing he has with him is a box of photographs. The pictures of Kim, Calie and Talia are the closest thing to a family he has. A full beard has found Joe's face and his hair is unkept and longer than it's been in years. It's a rainy Saturday night in June and Joe is sitting at the hotel bar drinking. Hunched over the bar and staring down at his tequila on the rocks, he ponders his next sip. Before Calie and Talia died, Joe detested hard liquor and would only drink an occasional beer. Now, liquor is his soul mate.

"Hey Joe, you OK?" the bartender asks. Joe looks up at the stocky young bartender with great dark hair and a killer smile. Unfortunately for Joe, the bartender has come to know him by name over the past few weeks. He gives him a nod then goes back to starring at his drink and thinking about the life he had. "I'm here if you want to talk."

"Oh man if you only knew what I have gone through in the past four months," Joe finally says with a slight slur from his intoxication.

"Well I have all night buddy, as you can see there aren't many people in the bar tonight." The bartender slides Joe another drink. "This ones on the house. So where do you want to start? My name is Tim." The bartender encourages conversation. Joe looks at the tequila Tim just slid across the bar. Before picking up the glass and taking a drink, he looks at Tim and scowls.

"Look Tim, no disrespect to you, but I'm not looking for a friend to tell my life story to. I'm just looking to sit here and mind my own business while I drink. That's it. Thanks for the drink though. I appreciate it," Joe says in a raspy voice.

"OK man, no pressure, it's just obvious you're in a bad place. I have heard everything there is to hear from patrons. From, I just got fired or my wife is cheating on me to, I just lost my life savings in a card game. I've heard it all and it never surprises me." Joe looks up from his drink again, looks at Tim and chuckles for a moment out loud.

"Four months ago I had a great life," Joe starts as he continues to look down at his drink. "I had a big house, owned my own business, was a father of two beautiful daughters and had an amazing wife. Then my two daughters and my wife were mowed down by a box truck while on the way to meet me for a Father-Daughter Dance. The two people that meant more to me than anything in the world died and I never even got to tell them how much I loved them. My wife, who was severely injured in the accident, lived. I chose to deal with the death of my children by leaving the last person I cared about most in my life because I was too fucked up in the head." Joe's voice is starting to get louder and angrier. "I have been drinking for four months straight because the alcohol lessens the pain. I don't sleep anymore because every time I close my eyes and fall asleep, I have violent nightmares of my children getting hit by a truck then begging me to save them as they are covered in blood."

Tim stares at Joe, his eyes wide open and shocked by what he is hearing. "How about this Tim? Every time I wake up in the middle of the night drunk and covered in sweat I think of ways to end my life so I don't have to spend another God forsaken day on this earth without my kids. How about that for a fucking story Tim! Heard that one before?"

Tim stands motionless with a bewildered look on his face staring at Joe along with a patron two seats down. Joe stands up and reaches into his pants pocket and pulls out a handful of crumpled 20 dollar bills, all the while staring at Tim. He angrily throws the money on the counter, not even bothering to count it. He walks towards the front door of the bar and exits into the night, slamming the door behind him.

"Daddy help me!" Calie's covered with blood screaming and reaching for Joe. He's running after a doctor that's pushing Calie's stretcher towards large doors that say operating room on it. He can't catch up to Calie and suddenly the stretcher crashes through the operating doors with a thunderous crash. The sudden burst of bright lights from the operating room blinds Joe momentarily. He slowly approaches the double doors to the operating room and gently pushes them open. The operating room is filled with bright lights, but there are no doctors in the room.

Joe walks over to the stretcher in the middle of the room. A white sheet covers something on the stretcher. Joe delicately pulls the sheet off to reveal both Calie and Talia, lying still, wearing their Valentine dresses. They open their eyes and look at Joe.

"You said you would protect us," Calie says softly.

"You said you would always be there for us," Talia whimpers. Joe reaches his hand out to touch them but is being pulled backwards and can't reach the girls. "Daddy please don't leave us!" Calie and Talia plead desperately reaching their arms out for Joe as both girls scream.

Joe shoots up in bed, sweating profusely. It's the middle of the night and the room is pitch black except for the light of the moon shining through one window. Struggling to catch his breath with sweat and tears running down his face, he throws the covers to the side and rolls off the bed onto the floor. He curls up in the fetal position on the floor and begins sobbing.

"I'm sorry," Joe yells. His emotions take over as he rocks himself, still curled up on the floor. "Please forgive me. I'm sorry." Eventually, Joe's breathing starts to slow down. He rolls over onto his back and lies still with his eyes wide open. Tears are running down his face sideways and his mouth is quivering slightly. He closes his eyes and shakes his head. The nightmares follow Joe everywhere, they just won't stop. After pushing himself up off the floor, he sits with his knees in his chest. His face is buried in his hands then he rubs his face to wake himself up.

Joe stands up. Unsteady on his feet, he gets himself to the bathroom and turns on the light. Looking in the mirror, he realizes that he is still wearing the same clothes he was wearing from the day before. As the faucet pours cold water, he bends down to splash the water on his face. He stands up and looks in the mirror, his face dripping water, he sees a man he doesn't recognize. Without looking, he reaches to his left, pulls a blue hand towel off the holder and covers his face with it. Back in the room, Joe removes a bottle of water from the hotel refrigerator and takes a long drink. He drops into a soft chair in the corner of his room and turns the television on with the remote. His head falls backwards and Joe slowly drifts back to sleep.

There is knocking at the front door. "Joe? Hello," a man's voice calls through the door. Joe wakes groggily and lifts his head. The daylight streams through the window as he tries to block it with his hand. He listens for a moment, then his head goes backwards again resting on the back of the chair, hoping whoever it is will go away. The knocking on the door continues. "Joe! Are you OK in there?"

"I'm fine Mr. Dewey, I'm fine," Joe mumbles. Skip Dewey is the nosey hotel manager who retired from his job as a hedge fund manager to run his own business. Joe begrudgingly pushes himself up off the chair and walks toward the front door. As he opens the door, a grey-haired short, stocky man with glasses and wearing a blue baseball cap with the Seattle Mariners logo on it, stands in front of Joe.

"Hi Joe."

"Hi Mr. Dewey, what can I do for you?" Joe yawns while squinting at the sunlight. "What time is it?" Joe asks while looking back and forth across the hotel parking lot.

"It's about 10 a.m. Mr. Walker, one of the neighbors upstairs called me this morning and said they heard some loud noise coming from your room early this morning. They were concerned about you and wanted me to check on you."

"Oh, thanks Mr. Dewey, I fell out of bed last night. It's nothing big. I'm fine. Please apologize to them for me."

"Alright Mr. Walker. Have a good day." Joe closes the door and falls back on the chair he awoke from.

As Joe yawns again he looks at the TV intently. The morning show from one of the major network stations is on. Joe sits up suddenly as he sees a scientist being interviewed. This is the same scientist that he saw on TV while he was in bed with Kim talking about cloning. The scientist was introduced as Dr. Steven Marxx. He is the chief scientist in charge of the Life Science Division of Gene Tech in San Francisco. The interviewer asks Dr. Marxx if there have been any breakthroughs in human cloning.

"There have been major advances in the cloning process over the past few years. As scientists, we are discovering that the cloning process is not as easy as we once thought it would be," Dr. Marxx replies.

"How close are we to cloning a human being?" the interviewer asks.

"As a scientist, I have to be very careful about what I say. There are strict laws governing cloning that the United Nations wants to enact and those very laws could hinder the progress we have made in the area of cloning, over the past few years. I am happy to say that the United States has passed legislation to protect the scientific research of cloning in hopes that one day we can prevent diseases even before a human is born." Joe continues to watch attentively to the broadcast. The interviewer asks the question again.

"Dr. Marxx, in your professional opinion, how close are we to cloning a human?" Dr. Marxx smiles while looking at the interviewer.

"We are ready now," Dr. Marxx says with controlled enthusiasm. "I believe that my team of scientists will be the first group to clone a human being, once we get through the government red tape. Gene Tech will be the leaders in this field." Joe's mouth is open and looks as if he has just seen a ghost. He reaches towards the back of his pants and pulls out his wallet then removes the picture of his daughters. The picture is held up in the light as Joe sees their faces. Joe hurriedly puts his wallet down on the table and begins packing what belongings he has.

CHAPTER 11

Its 5 p.m. on a Friday afternoon, more than four months after Talia and Calie died. Joe stands in front of a tall building in downtown San Francisco as people are shuffling out of work and onto the streets. In front of the building there's a large courtyard with cement benches with the name Gene Tech on the back rests. Next to each bench is a large cement planter with a well pruned maple tree growing in them.

Joe leans up against a large metal sign that reads Gene Tech as he stares at the front doors. He looks like the old Joe. He shaved his face and trimmed his hair and is wearing a gray suit. His mind flashes back to the night that he was lying in bed with Kim, watching the news, after putting the kids to bed. The story about the scientist in San Francisco who claimed to have the ability to clone a human was replaying in his head. He stares at the front doors to Gene Tech, just waiting for something or someone.

He turns slightly as to not make eye contact with a man that just exited the building. The middle-aged man with thick grey hair and silver rimmed glasses is wearing a black suit and carrying a briefcase. The man walks past Joe, completely oblivious to the fact that he is being watched.

As the man walks by him and continues down the sidewalk, Joe begins to follow from about fifty feet away, allowing people to get in between them. As Joe continues walking downtown, he never takes his eyes off the man he's following.

As the crowd between Joe and the man break up and thin out, Joe begins closing the gap until there is no one between them. Joe extends his right arm in an attempt to grab the man as he makes a sharp right turn and walks down a ramp into an underground garage. Joe stops at the entrance to the garage and watches the man for a moment.

"Good afternoon," the man said to the garage attendant as he walks by the booth.

"Afternoon sir! Have a good weekend," the attendant replies.

"You also, see you on Monday," the man said. As the man strolls through the garage, he stays to the right, close to the back of the cars so vehicles can get by. The man pulls the keys from his coat pocket and pushes the button on the remote. BEEP, BEEP, echoes through the garage like a loud speaker as the lights flash two times from a car up ahead. As the man picks out his black four door BMW, he also makes eye contact with a man standing at the back of his car.

"Hi! Can I help you with something?" the man said as he slowly approached Joe.

"Hello Dr. Marxx. My name is Joe Walker." Joe nervously extends his right hand out to shake Dr. Marxx's hand.

"Hi Mr. Walker, how do you know my name?" Dr. Marxx asks as he extends his right hand out and grips Joe's hand.

"Dr. Marxx, everyone knows you in the science community. Hell you're practically famous."

"Well, I'm flattered, but I wouldn't call myself famous by any stretch of the imagination. You're a scientist?" Dr. Marxx asks.

"I am. I work for a small company in New York City. My company works on regenerating cells from a dead host, similar to your work with cloning. You see, unlike cloning where you need live cells to recreate a living organism, we can take a dead cell and recreate that cell through the manipulation of the gene make-up." Joe's been doing some reading about cloning and cells but was winging the whole conversation.

"Wow, that's extraordinary," Dr. Marxx says with an apprehensive smile. "What company do you work for?" Joe wasn't expecting this question.

"Oh ah, Celldyne," Joe said with a relieved sigh. "It's a very small company compared to Gene Tech. You most likely have never heard of it."

"It's not ringing a bell. What are you doing here in San Francisco?"

"I actually had a job interview at Gene Tech."

"No kidding. How did it go?"

"Hopefully I will know very soon, Dr. Marxx. I would love to sit and talk with you further about your work. Can I buy you a drink?" Joe asks.

"Well it just so happens to be Friday and I usually go to my favorite watering hole after work. Jump in!" A few minutes later, Dr. Marxx pulls to the side of the road and parks in front of a small tavern with a lighted neon beer sign in the window. Joe and Dr. Marxx exit the vehicle and push open the large wooden door to the tavern. It's dimly lit inside and the dark wooden bar stretches 30 feet along the wall. Opposite the bar, a row of booths line the wall. The ceiling of the bar is covered with metal beer mugs with the names of beer club members engraved on them. A few patrons occupy a couple stools, but the bar is mainly empty this early on a Friday evening.

"Hey Steve," the bartender yells from the end of the bar as he pours a beer.

"Hello Isaac," Dr. Marxx shouts back. "That's Isaac Decklen. He's the owner. Every Friday afternoon I come in here for a few drinks and Isaac here gets to hear all about my trials and tribulations of the week." Dr. Marxx smiles and motions towards two seats at the end of the bar. "Is this OK?" Dr. Marxx asks.

"Sure, this is fine."

"The usual Steve?" Isaac asks while walking towards them.

"That would be great." Isaac pours a dark beer from the tap and slides it a few inches towards Dr. Marxx. "Thanks. Isaac this is Joe." Isaac extends his hand to Joe.

"Good to meet you, Joe. Any friend of Steve's is a friend of mine especially if it means I am saved today from having to solve all of his problems," Isaac grins.

"Thanks Isaac. Good to meet you too."

"What can I get you to drink?"

"How about an IPA on draft?"

"Coming right up," Isaac replies.

An hour or so has passed by while sitting at the bar and both Dr. Marxx and Joe have had a few beers each. The conversation has gone from working at a major pharmaceutical and science research company to now talking about family.

"Do you have any kids Dr. Marxx?"

"Joe we have known each other for about an hour now, please, call me Steve."

"OK, Steve," Joe says with a smile.

"No I don't have any children, but I have an ex-wife who acts like a child. Is that close enough?" Dr. Marxx says with a grin while looking at Joe.

"Huh. Doesn't sound like things worked out too well between you guys?"

"Oh it was great for the first few years, but then it all fell apart. I was always working and she was always out with her friends. We were coming and going." Dr. Marxx looks straight ahead at the beer taps.

"That sucks. I guess the good thing is that you are very successful at what you do and you have probably made a lot of money over the years so you can move on and still be very happy and financially secure," Joe says giving him a quick sideways glance to see what Dr. Marxx reaction is.

"I caught Darlene having an affair about a year ago, but I couldn't prove it. When I confronted her, she lashed out at me and asked for a divorce. I agreed to sign the papers just because I didn't have the time to deal with the divorce proceedings."

"Wow, I'm sorry Steve."

"You haven't heard the kicker. The morning we were meeting at the lawyer's office to finalize and sign off on the divorce, Darlene withdrew all the money from our three savings accounts and also bought a new luxury SUV on my credit card. I have practically nothing left and I stand to lose everything.

"I'm sorry to hear that," Joe remarks. "That's tough." Joe considers for a moment how to proceed.

"How about you? What's your family story?"

"I left my wife two months ago. We had the perfect marriage and family, until one day everything changed."

"What happened?"

Joe hesitates. "Isaac," Joe calls to the bartender. "Can we get another round?"

"Thanks," Dr. Marxx says sensing that Joe is not going to offer any further information about the demise of his marriage.

"Tell me about this ape you cloned!" Joe inquires with enthusiasm, getting the topic of conversation away from his past. "Is this classified information? Can you get in trouble for telling me this?" Joe asks.

"Are you a spy for another company or do you work for the Federal Government?" Dr. Marxx asks kiddingly.

"I can assure you that your secret is safe with me," Joe replies with a smile. "Is the ape healthy? How old is it?"

"The ape is 16 months old and it is as healthy as can be. I named her Hope," he said with a little chuckle and a smile.

"There were no side effects from the cloning process to Hope?" Joe asks.

"None, at this point anyway. But there's so much we don't know about cloning, we just have to keep a close watch and keep testing."

"Do you foresee something going wrong in the future?"

"Not at all, everything looks great."

"So if this ape is so healthy and everything worked perfectly, why isn't your company giving you money to keep your research going?"

"That's what I don't understand," Dr. Marxx replies somewhat frustrated.

"Maybe it's a very lengthy process and the company doesn't want to waste the time," Joe pushed.

"No, that's not it. The process from extracting the DNA of the specimen to implanting the DNA into an egg takes a few weeks. From there it's just the natural process of pregnancy and birth. Honestly, I think the company is scared to go forward."

"Scared? Why?"

"The United States is the only country in the naturalized world that hasn't banned human cloning. Although there are tons of regulations, there's no law that bans the actual cloning process."

Joe continues to listen intently as Dr. Marxx goes on. "For most countries, the technology just isn't there, yet. The moment a scientist perfects the sequence to human cloning and it becomes a reality and known to the media, every country in the world will be pushing the US to ban it until it can be regulated." Joe is more and more interested by the minute.

"The company heads believe we are about to complete the sequence and they believe that once this is out in the public, the government will cut funding to most of the programs my company is involved in. That means billions of dollars in research gone. Shareholders losing millions of dollars, job cuts, hell maybe even bankruptcy," Dr. Marxx says with a disappointing look on his face while drinking his last big sip of beer. Joe motions to Isaac for another round.

"Wow," Joe says. "I never thought about it that way." Joe looks forward sorting out his thoughts. "If you can clone an ape then you should be able to clone a human in the near future," Joe says with a slow methodical voice. Dr. Marxx and Joe stare intently at each other as Dr. Marxx grins sheepishly.

"I already have," Dr. Marxx proclaims.

"What?" Joe says with surprise. The doctor looks at Joe and nods his head, saying yes silently, with a smile. It's clear the doctor is probably sharing more information than he would have, had he not had multiple beers. Joe looks forward with a glimmer of hope in his eyes and a slight smile. "Isaac, we need a shot of tequila to celebrate!" Joe yells. "That's amazing," Joe says quietly. His eyes widen and a smile blooms as he lifts his drink to toast with Dr. Marxx. Dr. Marxx raises his glass and the mugs touch with a little clink.

"Congratulations Doc. That's amazing." For the first time in four months, Joe smiles.

CHAPTER 12

It's morning and the sun is shining through the window in Dr. Marxx's face. He starts to move around and wipes his face with his bare hand. A loud moan bellows from his insides thanks to the hangover he now has from drinking all night in the bar. Dr. Marxx is still clothed and lying on top of his bed with no shoes on. He lifts his legs over the side of his bed and touches them to the floor. He slowly sits up on the side of the bed, anguishing in pain as his head pounds harder and harder with every breath. As Dr. Marxx sits up straight and stretches his arms, he blinks rapidly to clear the cobwebs.

"Good morning Dr. Marxx," a cheery voice from behind him says.

"Holy Shit!" Dr. Marxx shouts as he turns and jumps off his bed. His throbbing head immediately reminding him not to make such sudden movements. "How did you get in my apartment?"

"I used your key. I had to make sure you got home safely," Joe says calmly. "How's your head?"

"It hurts," Dr. Marxx tells Joe while staring at him as his memory of the night before slowly returns. He starts to feel a sense of dread and panic as he vaguely remembers sharing too much information with this man the night before. "Well, thank you for getting me home safely and it was nice meeting you, but I think it's time for you to go now. I don't even know you and now you are in my home. Please leave."

"OK. I will, but there is something I need to talk with you about first. Just give me five minutes of your time. Please. Then I'll leave," Joe begs. Dr. Marxx ponders Joe's request as he stands quietly for a moment.

"You have five minutes," Dr. Marxx replies. "But before you start talking, I need some coffee. Would you like a cup?" Dr. Marxx asks as he starts walking out of the bedroom and into the hallway, glaring at Joe.

"I would love a cup. Thank you." Dr. Marxx walks down the stairs as Joe follows. Dr. Marxx looks back at Joe briefly with an inquisitive look then turns and enters the kitchen. Gesturing towards the kitchen table he motions for Joe to have a seat.

"It's Joe right?"

"Yes. Joe Walker."

"What was it that you do again?" Dr. Marxx asks as he fills the coffee maker with water while his back is to Joe.

"Actually, nothing at this point. I was a security consultant and private investigator about four months ago in my hometown just outside of Jacksonville, Florida."

"So that story about you being a scientist and regenerating dead cells was just a line to get me interested in having a beer with you?"

"Yes, sorry about that," he replies with a somber and apologetic tone.

"That's good, because I've never heard of such a ridiculous thing and I've been doing this type of work for thirty years." Dr. Marxx looks at Joe, smirks and slightly shakes his head. Dr. Marxx walks over to the table and places a coffee cup down in front of Joe. "Cream and sugar?" Dr. Marxx asks.

"No thanks, I like it black."

"Huh, me too." Dr. Marxx sits down across from Joe as he contemplates kicking this stranger out of his home or giving him the few minutes he asked for. "OK, Joe Walker from Florida. So what was so important that you traveled thousands of miles to talk with me in person, before getting me drunk and watching over me all night?"

"I believe I can help you with your funding issue so you can continue your work. In return, I need your help."

"I'm listening, but your time is ticking away rapidly," Dr. Marxx replies, almost dismissing Joe's comment.

"You told me last night that you have already cloned a human." Dr. Marxx stands up and becomes angry. He slams his hands down on the table as he leans over staring at Joe.

"I told you that last night?"

"Yes." Dr. Marxx turns around with his back to Joe and takes a few steps away from the table. He looks out the kitchen window then looks down and closes his eyes.

"That information is strictly confidential and could get me fired, sued and could even get my license stripped from me. God Dammit!" Dr. Marxx yells as he turns around and looks at Joe. His breathing increases suddenly as he glares in discontent at Joe.

"Doc this information is safe with me. I promise you."

"This is where you blackmail me right?" Dr. Marxx's disgust for the information he divulged is evident by the frown on his face and crunched eyebrows.

"No, I'm not here to blackmail you. I'm here because I'm looking for your help, that's it. Please sit down and I will tell you what happened and how you can help me." Dr. Marxx starts to calm down as his breathing slowly returns to normal. "Please Doc." Dr. Marxx sits down and takes a sip of coffee. Joe takes a deep breath and lets it out slowly. "Six months ago, my two young daughters, Talia and Calie were killed in a car accident while my wife was driving them to meet me at a dance. My wife Kim survived and in the months after the accident, I slowly went into depression. I began drinking daily and attempted suicide numerous times. I was a complete mess, and because of my drinking, I lost everything. I quit my business and left my wife. I took money from a settlement we received and moved away. I didn't even talk to my wife. I just left her a note. At some point, I saw you on TV talking about being able to clone humans and here I am." Dr. Marxx glares at Joe.

"I'm sorry Joe, it sounds like a horrible ordeal, but I'm still not sure why you are here."

"It was the worst thing I ever had to endure. I couldn't go on with life without my girls and I found a way to get my girls back." Dr. Marxx looks puzzled as he stares at Joe looking for more information. Then the doctor closes his eyes.

"You want me to clone your daughters," Dr. Marxx replies condescendingly then snickers.

"Dr. Marxx, You can clone my girls and bring them back to me." Dr. Marxx's eyes close while he shakes his head in disbelief then slowly stands up.

"Joe, I can't clone your girls for you. I'm sorry."

"Why not, you told me that you've done it before. Dr. Marxx, you are the only shred of hope I can grasp onto right now. Please help me." Joe's eyes begin to well up as he wipes his face to catch the tears. He stands up and looks at Dr. Marxx with dejection in his face. His eyes are now bloodshot and glassy.

"Joe that was a different circumstance. It was all controlled in a lab and I had the child's DNA already. I can't just stick a needle in your arm, draw some blood and recreate your children for you. I would need both your daughter's blood to clone them and I'm sure you don't have that. I'm sorry to disappoint you Joe." Joe looks down in defeat and sits back in the chair. He bends forward and buries his face in his hands. Dr. Marxx walks over and rubs his back slightly. Joe stops then perks up.

"I do have their blood!" Joe pops up from his chair and grabs Dr. Marxx's arms. I do have their blood, when the girls were born we saved the cord blood and stored it in a blood bank in case the kids became sick and needed it."

"You have blood from both girls?" Dr. Marxx asks shockingly.

"We banked both girls cord blood," Joe says enthusiastically. The doctor shakes his head as if he's trying to clear the cobwebs from his mind. "Joe even if I wanted to help you, I don't think I could do this. There are so many procedures involved from start to finish and I'm trying to get additional funding right now. I'm sorry Joe. I can't do this for you."

"Doc, I can help you with your funding problem. I can ensure that your research can continue for another few years."

"How can you do that? It would take a lot of money to keep the program going for two years," Dr. Marxx chuckles.

"I will give you five hundred thousand dollars to clone Talia and Calie. With that kind of money, you can continue doing what you love to do and put some money aside for yourself." Dr. Marxx is in shock at the thought of Joe's proposal. Joe grabs a napkin and pen from the table and writes on it. "I'm staying at the Heritage High Rise in room 203. Think about my proposal. If I don't hear from you in two days, I will take that to mean you're not interested and I will be leaving town. If that's the case, I wish you good luck in the future. Joe reaches out to shake Dr. Marxx's hand and Dr. Marxx reciprocates.

"You too, Joe."

CHAPTER 13

It's Sunday afternoon and Dr. Marxx is sitting at the kitchen table looking through a stack of bills. Dr. Marxx is wearing his usual Sunday grey sweatshirt, sweatpants and black slippers. His traditional routine on Sunday is to sit on the couch while trying to catch up on his favorite TV shows on demand. It's been twenty four hours since Joe made the proposal to Dr. Marxx to clone his daughters and he hasn't been able to concentrate since. "Bill after bill after bill! This is madness! I will never get caught up with these bills at this rate," Dr. Marxx grumbles. He stands up and drops the bills on the counter next to the cordless phone handset sitting in its cradle. Dr. Marxx stares at the phone for a moment then turns and starts pacing.

His laptop turns on and he pulls it close to him from the other side of the table. The internet browser is open and Dr. Marxx types something in the search bar and taps enter on the keyboard. Appearing on the screen is a list of search results. Looking intently at the screen, he slowly backs his head away from the computer in horror. He reaches for the mouse and clicks on one of the search results. Big bold letters emerge at the top of the screen. **"Two Children Die In Horrific Valentine's Day Accident"** Dr. Marxx reads the article from the Jacksonville Sun Newspaper. A few minutes elapse as he finishes the article with shock in his eyes and closes the page. He was hoping that this was all just a terrible dream, but he just confirmed the legitimacy of Joe's story. He begins to type again in the search bar and clicks the mouse. Instantly, the web site for the Heritage High Rise Hotel pops up on the screen. Dr. Marxx reaches for the telephone handset on the counter and dials a number after looking at the screen again.

"Thanks for calling the Heritage High Rise, this is Carol. How can I help you today?" the female voice asks.

"Hello, can you connect me with room 203 please?"

"Sure, one moment sir." Dr. Marxx suddenly starts to shake uncontrollably. Panic sets in as he takes a deep breath then suddenly pushes the off button on the phone to end the call. Sitting motionless looking at the phone, he tries to catch his breath. His head resting against the back of the chair as his eyes are fixated on the ceiling fan. "I hope you know what you're doing Steve," Dr. Marxx says softly to himself. He sits up in the chair and dials the number again and slowly puts the phone to his head.

"Thank you for calling the Heritage High Rise, this is Carol. How can I help you?"

"Hi can I have room 203 again please?"

"Sure, I'm sorry did I hang up on you sir?" Carol asks.

"No, no, that was my fault," Dr. Marxx assures the operator.

"OK sir, hold on one moment please."

The phone rings once, twice, three times. "Hello." Dr. Marxx closes his eyes for a moment and thinks about hanging up. "Hello?"

"Joe, its Steven Marxx."

"Hi Doc."

"Can you meet me at the tavern tomorrow at noon?"

"Yes, absolutely," Joe agreed enthusiastically. "OK, Joe, I will see you tomorrow."

Monday at noon Joe enters the tavern and makes eye contact with Dr. Marxx, who is sitting in the back of the tavern in a booth. Dr. Marxx is facing the front of the bar as he waves to Joe. "Hi Steve," Joe says as he approaches the dimly lit back corner of the room.

"Hello Joe." Joe sits down in the booth across from Dr. Marxx. A waitress comes over to the booth and pulls out a pad and pen.

"Hi gentlemen, can I get you anything to drink?"

"I will have an ice water with lemon please," Dr. Marxx requests.

"Tonic water would be great, thanks," Joe replies as the waitress walks off.

"Joe there is no guarantee this will work. I don't want you to get your hopes up then be disappointed if this fails."

"I understand Steve. Tell me about the person you cloned," Joe asks. Dr. Marxx looks at Joe for a few moments without a saying a thing, then nods his head slightly.

"My brother Sam and his wife, Elizabeth, had a daughter, Meghan. She was the most beautiful child you have ever seen. She was funny and kind and so friendly to everyone she met," Dr. Marxx explains with an intense smile on his face. "When she was four, two months from her fifth birthday, she got out of her bed during the middle of the night. Dr. Marxx face turns to a frown as he stares at his napkin that he's ripping into little pieces.

Sam and Elizabeth woke up to the sound of Meghan screaming then they heard her tumbling down the stairs to the first floor." Steve's eyes fill with tears. "By the time they got to the bottom of the stairs, Meghan had already stopped breathing. She suffered massive head trauma and died instantly. Meghan was their world, and they couldn't accept the idea of life without her." Steve looks at Joe for a moment. "I'm assuming much the same way you feel." Joe nods slightly.

"What happened?"

"Two years ago, without telling anyone in my team, I completed the sequence of implanting living human cells into an egg. I had inevitably completed the cloning process from cell to egg and then to embryo." Joe's eyes open wide as this was exactly what he wanted to hear. "I didn't tell anyone for fear that it would have leaked to the company executives and they would use it to make money for the stockholders and then the media storm would have been next." Joe listens intently. "You don't understand what kind of hysteria that kind of discovery would create."

"So what did you do with that knowledge?"

"I created Hope. Once Hope was deemed a success, the only thing left to do was test the research out on a human and that's when Meghan died. I needed to test my research and make sure I did everything correctly. I destroyed the first human embryo and completed the sequence again and again and again. Every single time I completed the sequence, an embryo was created from the cells and the cloning process was complete. The only thing left to do was to implant the embryo into a host, who would carry the fetus through the normal gestation period."

"You needed to find someone who wanted a baby, and you found Elizabeth," Joe answers his own question. Dr. Marxx looks at Joe and chuckles.

"I went to my brother and asked him a simple question. If I could bring Meghan back for you, would you be happy again. What do you think he said?"

"I haven't got a clue."

"He asked me if she would be five years old again."

"Ha, ha," Joe laughed.

"Sam was on board from the start. Elizabeth on the other hand took some persuading. They both wanted to try and have another child after Meghan died so they agreed to the procedure. After I pulled living cells from Meghan's cord blood and removed the nucleus from Elizabeth's egg, I fused Meghan's cells to the egg with electricity. This method only works in one out of two hundred attempts, but when I inject more living cells from the blood of the person to be cloned, around the fused center of the egg, it works ninety-nine percent of the time."

"Wow, that's incredible Doc," Joe says softly with excitement so no one in the bar can hear him.

"Meghan is now 11 months old and she is identical to the first Meghan except a small birthmark is missing from her right hand. Other than that, she is the exact same child."

"It's amazing to think about," Joe says astounded and pondering the idea of having the girls back. "Can I meet her?"

"I don't see why not. I will call Sam and see if he is busy this afternoon." Dr. Marxx stands up and pulls his cell phone from his pocket as he walks toward the front door. A few moments later, Dr. Marxx taps Joe on the left shoulder. "Sam and Elizabeth are home and free for a little while. I just paid the bill so let's get going." Joe follows Dr. Marxx to the front door as they exit the bar. They get into Dr. Marxx's car parked on the side of the road in front of the bar.

"How far away do they live?"

"They live over the river in a rural area called West Lake. It will take us about 20 minutes to get there," Dr. Marxx says as he pulls out into traffic. Both of Joe's legs are bouncing and shaking nervously as Dr. Marxx takes notice. "Why are you nervous?"

"I don't really know. I think the fact that this is starting to become a reality is scaring me," Joe says while looking out the window. "Maybe I'm more excited than nervous." They drive through a few neighborhoods off the busy highway as Joe scans the area in amazement at the tightly packed homes. The houses in the suburbs of San Francisco are packed together tightly with structures practically touching one another. A few minutes later, Dr. Marxx pulls into Sam and Elizabeth's driveway.

"Here we are. Now Joe, don't say anything about your daughters or what you are doing in San Francisco. For all they know, you're an old friend that dropped by for a few days."

"Got it." As they exit the car, Sam and Elizabeth open the front door to the large brick two story house. Elizabeth is holding a toddler in her arms and pointing to Dr. Marxx to get Meghan to see him.

"Hi guys," Dr. Marxx calls out to Sam and Elizabeth as he walks up the sidewalk to the front stairs.

"Hi Steve," Elizabeth says as he greets her with a hug and a kiss to her cheek. Sam reaches out and shakes his brother's hand.

"Joe this is my brother Sam and my sister in-law Elizabeth."

"Hi, it's very nice to meet both of you." Joe reaches out and meets Elizabeth's hand to shake. Elizabeth is a thin woman at about five foot tall with short dark brown hair. Sam is also thin built with a brown crew cut.

"Please Joe, call me Liz."

"OK, Liz." Sam reaches out for a shake and hooks up with Joe. Dr. Marxx gently takes a hold of Meghan and lifts her out of Elizabeth's arms and gives her a hug. Meghan has brown hair with small curls and is wearing a pink summer dress.

"This is my beautiful niece, Meghan. Can you say hi to Joe?" Dr. Marxx says to Meghan in a soft voice. Joe reaches out and gently takes Meghan's little hand with his index and thumb then shakes it.

"Hello Meghan, it's very nice to meet you," Joe says with a smile and a twinkle in his eye.

"Come on in, can I get anyone a drink?" Sam asks as Joe and Dr. Marxx follow Sam and Elizabeth into the house.

"Sure, I will have some ice water," Dr. Marxx replies.

"I will have the same, thank you," Joe responds.

"Sam it's a beautiful sunny day. Take the guys and Meghan to the back patio and relax. I will get the drinks and some snacks," Elizabeth says. As Dr. Marxx and Joe lag behind a few steps, Dr. Marxx points out a baby picture on the wall.

"This is a picture of Meghan when she was a year old," Dr. Marxx says quietly so Sam and Elizabeth can't hear him. Dr. Marxx holds Meghan up close to the picture on the wall so Joe can see the resemblance.

"Oh my God," Joe says softly. "They are identical." The picture on the wall appeared to be the same child, Steve was holding.

"So, Steven tells me you guys are buddies from years ago," Sam remarks as Joe, Sam and Elizabeth are sitting on the deck. Dr. Marxx is holding Meghan and walking around the yard pointing to the trees.

"That's right. We have tried to stay in touch over the years, but it's been very difficult," Joe replies. "You have a very nice family and Meghan is beautiful," Joe says to change the subject.

"Thanks Joe. That's very nice of you," Elizabeth says. "Do you have children?" she asks.

"No, but I hope to have children very soon," Joe says with a smile on his face as he looks at Meghan and Dr. Marxx. Dr. Marxx walks over to the patio with Meghan in his arms then gently hands her to Sam.

"We should get going. Joe has to get himself checked into the hotel. I just wanted to stop by to see Meghan and say hi."

"Oh, OK. Well it was great meeting you Joe," Sam says as they all stand up simultaneously.

"Thanks Sam. It was nice to meet both of you also," Joe says as he reaches out to shake both their hands. "And it was extra nice to meet you Meghan," Joe says as he gets down to eye level with Meghan, who is still being held by Sam, and softly pokes her on the tip of her nose. Dr. Marxx gives Elizabeth a kiss on the cheek and turns and shakes his brother's hand.

"Bye guys. I will talk to you soon." Joe and Dr. Marxx walk across the small back yard towards the side of the house and onto the driveway.

"So when do we get started?" Joe asks while continuing to look forward as he opens the passenger side door. Joe and Steve make eye contact and smile, before getting into the car.

"So I think you should move in with me. Now that we have decided to go forward with the project, we are going to need to spend time putting this together logistically. If you are living somewhere else, it's going to make this process much more difficult," Steve says as they drive down the street.

"That's a good idea."

"Good."

CHAPTER 14

"I hate flying," Dr. Marxx comments. Joe and Dr. Marxx are sitting side by side on a plane as Dr. Marxx fidgets in his seat. He looks out the window and gets rattled even more. "Oh God!" His head slams back against the seat and he closes his eyes as he somehow believes that will calm the intense anxiety coursing through his body.

"You have to try and relax Steve. We will be up in the air for about six hours so you should try to take a nap." Joe is calm and closes his eyes and puts his head back against the head rest.

"I'm just not good with planes. How much longer until we are on the ground?"

"Six more hours," Joe says with his eyes closed as he cracks a smile.

Six hours later, the plane lands at Jacksonville Airport and Joe and Dr. Marxx exit the jet bridge and start walking towards the exit. Dr. Marxx isn't feeling well due to his less than entertaining flight. "There's a car rental desk on the first floor. We should be able to get a car for one day," Joe tells Dr. Marxx.

"I can smell the ocean from here," Joe says taking deep breaths of Florida air through his nose with his window rolled down. "I love the smell of Florida ocean air." Joe's driving the rented white sedan as Dr. Marxx looks over the paperwork he downloaded from the internet. The paperwork is information about the Jacksonville Blood Bank. The window on Dr. Marxx door rolls down as he sticks his head out slightly and breathes in through his nose.

"Smells like the same ocean from San Francisco," Dr. Marxx replies sarcastically with a grin as his window goes back up.

"It's nothing like San Francisco ocean. When you breathe here, the air is clean, almost pure."

"Whatever! All I know is that it's ridiculously hot here. Roll your window up and turn the air on. Not sure what we were thinking coming to Florida at the end of June. Our appointment is in a half hour. This should be a fairly straight forward withdrawal from the bank. Looks like identification is all they will need from both of us. You will have to sign some legal documents that eliminate the blood bank from liability," Dr. Marxx explains as Joe focuses on navigating the busy highway.

"Good, so we should be in and out of there quickly?" Joe asks as he glances back and forth between the road and Dr. Marxx.

"It's not that easy. If it's anything like it was when we made the withdrawal for Meghan, they will have many questions for us. They also have to take the blood out of cold storage and document everything. We will be here for at least three to four hours." Joe makes a right turn into the hospital's driveway and parks the car in the visitor parking section.

"What kind of questions?" Joe asks inquisitively as he raises his eyebrows.

"Well they are going to want to know why we are making the withdrawal, where it's going, and who will be utilizing the blood. So obviously we can't tell them we are using the blood to clone your children because they would throw us out and call the police. We need to get our story straight."

"What are we going to say?"

"I haven't thought that far ahead," Dr. Marxx says as they both exit the car and start walking towards the main entrance. "I will think of something. Just let me do all the talking when we get in there though," Dr. Marxx says. As they enter through the large automatic glass double doors, Dr. Marxx points to a sign, hanging from the ceiling that reads, "Lab and Blood Bank with a left arrow." They take a left at the sign and walk down the hallway to a counter with a secretary sitting in a chair.

"Hi can I help you?" the female receptionist says, setting down the clipboard she was writing on.

"Hi. My name is Dr. Steven Marxx and this is my client, Joe Walker. We have an appointment to make a partial withdrawal from two accounts."

"OK, I just need the name of the person the samples came from."

"Calie and Talia Walker," Dr. Marxx replies.

"If you want to have a seat, I will have our accounts director come out and escort you to his office."

"Thank you," Dr. Marxx says as they sit down in the waiting room. They are the only people sitting in the small waiting room with six chairs. The walls are lightly colored with black framed pictures of newborn babies. Joe removes a pamphlet from the display holder on the side table and begins to read it. A few minutes later, a tall man wearing a black suit with a name tag clipped to the breast pocket, comes out into the waiting room from a side door and approaches Dr. Marxx and Joe.

"Hello! I'm Dr. Plankey. I'm your account director." Dr. Plankey extends his hand out to Joe.

"Hi I'm Joe Walker and this is Dr. Steven Marxx."

"Hi gentlemen, it's nice to meet you. If you would just follow me, we will go to my office where we can talk about this process." They follow Dr. Plankey through the door that he came out of then to a large open office with brown leather chairs. Dr. Plankey closes the door behind Dr. Marxx. "Please sit down." Joe and Dr. Marxx sit down in the chairs in front of the large light colored wooden desk.

The desk has a few pictures on it facing Joe and Dr. Marxx and there is a large window behind Dr. Plankey that overlooks a courtyard.

"So you are here to make a partial withdrawal of two specimens today. The specimens are cord blood taken at birth of Calie Walker, and let's see, oh here we are, Talia Walker." Dr. Plankey flips through the pages of documents from two different folders. "Is that correct, Mr. Walker?"

"Yes that's right," Joe says before attempting to swallow. His mouth feeling like Plaster of Paris as his tongue sticks to the roof of his mouth. Joe's starting to unnerve and sweat as he sits in front of Dr. Plankey. He knows that if he messes this up, he will have no chance to retrieve the blood.

"OK." Dr. Plankey pauses for a moment while he is looking through the folders, as Joe and Dr. Marxx glance at each other. Dr. Marxx gives Joe a slight nod as to say, "Everything is fine." Dr. Plankey looks up from the file and looks at Joe then goes back to flipping pages. "I'm very sorry Mr. Walker." Joe looks at Dr. Marxx with concern.

"Sorry Dr. Plankey?"

"There's an entry in the file here from seven months ago." Joe's nervousness subsides as he grows more serious and glares intently at Dr. Plankey. "I'm so sorry for your loss, Mr. Walker."

"Thank you Dr. Plankey. It's been a very long road since the accident."

"I'm sure it has sir. Something like that isn't an easy thing to deal with. Everything seems to be in order and your account has been paid until the contract date which doesn't expire for another fifteen years. Since you're only making a partial withdrawal, the remaining specimens will remain in the bank until such time the contract is extended or the account expires. That's per the contract."

"That's fine Dr. Plankey, I understand."

"The hospital, for liability purposes, needs to know what the reason for the withdrawal is." Joe takes another deep swallow, this one more pronounced than the first. He wipes his forehead with his sleeve as his brow starts to bead with sweat. Joe opens his mouth to say something but Dr. Marxx kicks his foot softly and speaks up.

"I was hired by the Walkers to analyze their daughter's blood for signs of hereditary disorders." Dr. Plankey looks perplexed.

"You're checking the girl's blood even though they are deceased?" Joe senses the plan is starting to fall apart.

"Well, the Walkers have been contemplating having more children before they get too old. They just want to be sure there are no problems down the road."

"You are a licensed physician I assume?" Dr. Plankey asks skeptically.

"Of course I am. I have been a licensed pathologist for the past twenty years. My license number, on file with the American Medical Society, is SM45037192." Dr. Plankey writes Dr. Marxx's license number on a piece of paper in the file.

"As part of our procedure, I have to check your license and I need to make a copy of your license too Mr. Walker. Then all this paperwork will be combined and attached to the account withdrawal forms." Joe pulls his wallet out of his back pocket and opens it. As he opens the wallet, he sees the picture of Calie and Talia that he's had for years.

Calie and Talia are sitting on an examination table at their doctor's office. "Daddy, why do we need to get a check-up?" Calie asked. Calie is five and Talia is three years old.

"Well we have to get check-ups so the doctors can make sure we are healthy and growing strong. We wouldn't want to get sick now would we?" Joe is hugging both the girls together as Calie answered no.

"Joe!" Dr. Marxx nudges Joe slightly.

"Sorry Doc. I was just daydreaming." Joe hands Dr. Plankey his Florida license. Dr. Marxx is looking at Joe then looks at Dr. Plankey again.

"Mr. Walker, I will just need your signature to withdraw from the account then it will just be a matter of taking the blood out of cold storage and preparing it for transport. That should take about two hours and then you can be on your way."

"Do I need to stay here for that process or can I take off for a while and come back when it's ready?"

"Sure, there is no reason that you have to sit around and wait. I will have Dr. Marxx work with the staff and prepare the amount of blood required for his research and you can come back and sign before you leave."

"That sounds great," Joe replies. Joe and Dr. Marxx stand up.

"I will walk you out Joe," Dr. Marxx says. Joe and Dr. Marxx walk out of the office and into the lobby. "Are you OK?"

"I'm good. I just got a little unsettled there for a moment."

"Where are you going?" Dr. Marxx asks as they walk through the double doors and outside.

"I'm just going for a little drive to clear my head."

"You're not thinking of visiting anyone while you are home, are you? I don't think that would be a good idea. We should think about not having any distractions and get what we need and go back to San Francisco."

"I'm just going for a drive Steve, that's it. I will see you in a few hours. I'm going to go somewhere and read this pamphlet." Joe pats Dr. Marxx on his shoulder and walks away towards the parking lot as he slides the pamphlet into his inside coat pocket. Dr. Marxx watches him walk away as Joe turns and gives him a thumbs up then gets into the rental car.

A short time later, Joe pulls to the side of the road at the intersection of First St and Central Ave. Joe stares across the street at the storefront with a large sign above the window that reads Target Security. He's back at his business for the first time in five months. Looking out the window for a minute, he smiles as he sees Bill and his secretary having a laugh together. Life is going on without him and he feels good about that. After driving for another thirty minutes or so, he's looking around at all the familiar sights and feeling nostalgic. A smile shines on Joe's face as if he was home for good and ready to be reunited with his family. He pulls onto Williams St. and immediately pulls to the side of the road two houses down the street. With his window up, he gazes across the street at the large white colonial house. Joe is home.

Joe pulls into the driveway and gets out of the car. "Daddy, Daddy!" Calie calls out to Joe as she runs out the front door and down the porch stairs. Talia follows Calie out the front door, also calling for her daddy. As he walks up the front walkway and bends over with his arms out, he grabs both girls as they run to him. "Mommy, Dad's home!" Talia yells. Kim walks up to the open front door and smiles at Joe as Talia and Calie mob him in the front yard. The smile remains as he stares at the front of the house remembering what an amazing life he had less than a year ago.

As he continues to reflect about his storybook past, Kim walks around from behind the house pushing a wheelbarrow. Joe takes a deep anxiety filled breath as his heart begins pounding faster and faster. Kim has her hair up in a ponytail and she's wearing dirty tight jeans. She dumps the wheelbarrow of dirt in the flower garden on the right side of the house. "Wow, she looks amazing," Joe says faintly to himself. She looks in the direction of the car and Joe moves his head back slightly. The windows in the rented car are tinted so Kim can't see inside, but Joe takes no chances. He senses that Kim can feel his presence while she grows more curious about the strange car across the street. Joe's heart pounds against his chest and his breathing rapidly increases.

Kim begins slowly walking towards the road as she feels something more than curiosity. The door handle in Joe's hand is gripped tight as he pulls on it slightly in a bid to end this crazy idea of bringing his kids back to life. Suddenly, Kim's attention is diverted to her vibrating cell phone that she pulls from her pant's pocket. Still staring at her, he yearns to hold her. She holds her cell phone in her hand and looks down at it. Suddenly she looks up at the car again as Joe pulls tighter on the handle. As she stops walking and puts the phone to her ear, she turns away momentarily. Joe releases the door handle and puts his head back against the head rest as his heart beats out of control. He takes a few deep breaths and tries to regain his composure. A tear forms then flows from his right eye, down his cheek.

"I have to go. There's a car in the road in front of my house and I need to see who it is," Kim says to the person on the phone as she hangs up. When she turns eagerly to walk towards the road, she takes a deep breath and her eyes open wide. Her body stops abruptly as if she hit an invisible wall. The white car parked in the road is gone. She exhales as a great sadness comes over her and her body slumps in defeat. "No," she says faintly to herself.

With a slight turn of the key the engine powers down as Joe sits in the parking lot static for a few moments. He looks up at the entrance and sees Dr. Marxx waving to him to come in. Joe exits the car and starts walking towards Dr. Marxx. "What's going on, Steve?"

"We are all set. They just need your signature to finalize the withdrawal then they will escort us out of the building." Dr. Plankey meets them at the desk with the paperwork attached to a clipboard.

"Joe, I just need your signature on this form, right here." Dr. Plankey points to a spot on the form where Joe signs his name then hands Dr. Plankey the pen. Dr. Plankey reaches over the desk and grabs a small blue cooler with a clear plastic tube sticking out of the top. "I gave Dr. Marxx all the information about the samples and how to thaw them for use. With the cooler packed with dry ice, you have about twenty-four hours to get the samples in a refrigerator at the lab. Good luck and thanks for choosing the Jacksonville Blood Bank."

CHAPTER 15

"This is mind blowing. This process from extracting the DNA, to implanting the egg into the host takes about a week," Joe says to himself with astonishment. He's sitting at the kitchen table reading some of Dr. Marxx notes and research papers. The front door to Dr. Marxx's apartment shuts and Joe stands up and walks into the foyer. "Hi Steve," Joe says while holding some of the papers in his hand.

"Hey Joe. What are you reading?" Dr. Marxx walks past Joe towards the kitchen with a brown paper bag as Joe follows him.

"I was just looking at some of the research you have done on cloning. You've been working on this for a long time." Dr. Marxx puts the bag down on the counter next to the refrigerator and turns towards Joe.

"I have indeed. That's interesting reading material, don't you think?"

"I never realized how fast this whole process is." Dr. Marxx takes a few steps toward Joe and looks at him.

"Hold on Joe. That research talks about the cloning procedures and turnaround time under the most ideal conditions. I don't think it will be that fast for this situation, but I could be wrong," Dr. Marxx replies optimistically as he shrugs his shoulders.

"I was reading some of the material where you talk about the host. How do we find a host?"

"It's funny you ask that. I was going to talk with you about that as soon as I got home so I grabbed a six pack of beer on the way. Do you want one before we talk?"

"Sure, sounds like I might need it." Dr. Marxx reaches into the paper bag and pulls out a six pack. He pulls two bottles out and twists the tops off and hands one to Joe then raises his bottle for a toast.

"Let's go sit in the living room and figure this out," Dr. Marxx says.

Joe follows Dr. Marxx into the large open living room with high ceilings. There is natural dark mahogany wood trim throughout the whole apartment and the living room looks more like a library. The twenty foot ceiling in the living room is finished with a large, dark wood fan. The open grand staircase flows to the second floor and four large bedrooms. They sit down on the brown leather couch and Joe drops the paperwork between them.

"When we started this research, the project started to progress quickly, and we had to line up surrogate mothers to carry our embryos to term. I had some connections with the local university and found some students who wanted to donate and help with our research."

"You found women who were willing to become pregnant for your research?" Joe asks with a wince of his eyes.

"Actually, we did. The power of money has a great influence on people, especially young women trying to pay their own way through college. We had a strict set of criteria that we were looking for in a host. The host played the most important role in this whole project." Joe takes a swig of his beer while listening intently. "To maximize the chance of carrying a fetus to full term, the host had to be healthy and physically fit, couldn't be a smoker and had to eat right."

"How were you going to monitor them?"

"We were going to observe and scrutinize their every move and oversee their lives for nine months. We had established a pool of about twelve women who signed up to be surrogates. We also figured that through attrition we would lose a few women because they graduated and moved on or whatever. I still have five women, between the ages of 22 and 25 years old, that are willing to become surrogates, but it will cost about eighty thousand dollars for two hosts."

"That's OK, I have the money for that," Joe answers.

"Because we have to monitor them and make sure they are taking care of themselves, we will have them move in here until the girls are born. I have two extra bedrooms upstairs where they can stay."

"Sounds good Steve, but I have a question about the hosts. When you initially sought these women out, did you or members of your staff tell them in detail what the project was? Do they know they will be carrying cloned fetuses?"

"No. We couldn't tell them about the cloning process. That would compromise the research and the project in general. The hosts were told that they would be carrying a child for a set of parents that could not have children. They were told that the research we were doing was part of a federal grant to make the process of in-vitro fertilization safer. Therefore it's paramount that during the pregnancy the hosts know nothing about this."

"What are we going to tell them about my role in this project?"

"You are going to be the client that has contracted me out to implant the fertilized eggs into the surrogates. That's it. If things get skewed along the way, we will improvise as we go. OK?"

"I'm good. Let's get started," Joe says with enthusiasm as he claps his hands and rubs them together.

"I have the contact information for the five women we would be picking from. They all still meet the criteria since I last had contact with them four months ago."

"Did you keep regular contact with these women?"

"When it looked like my company would be going forward with the project, five months ago, I was in touch with the twelve women we were going to use as hosts, but all but five were disqualified for various reasons. I think I have a good idea which two women I will call first."

"I'm getting excited about how this is coming together. When can I meet the hosts?"

"I will arrange a get together tomorrow evening," Dr. Marxx replies.

It's 6 p.m. the following day and the doorbell rings twice.

"Sounds like one of the girls is here Joe," Dr. Marxx shouts upstairs.

"I'm coming," Joe says as he hurries down the stairs to the foyer. Dr. Marxx opens the door. Standing in the hallway is an attractive woman with dark brown shoulder length hair, wearing glasses.

"Hi Steve," the female says.

"Hello Danielle, come in." Dr. Marxx closes the door as Danielle steps inside the foyer.

"Danielle this is my friend, Joe Walker. Joe this is Danielle Wallace."

"Hello Danielle, it's nice to meet you."

"It's nice to meet you too."

"Danielle, have a seat and get comfortable. Here let me take your coat." Danielle hands her coat to Dr. Marxx and he hangs it in the closet next to the door. "Can I get you something to drink while we wait for Tara?"

"Tara's coming too?" Danielle asks as she sits down on the couch.

"She is. I asked both of you to come over tonight."

"That's awesome! I can't wait to see her again."

"Danielle and Tara met about five months ago when we first proposed this idea to the twelve women we selected to be hosts," Dr. Marxx explains to Joe.

"Oh, no kidding! So you guys haven't stayed in touch?" Joe asks.

"No, I think we were both so busy with school that we just didn't have time to get together."

"I have a feeling you may be seeing quite a bit of each other," Joe says with a chuckle. Dr. Marxx clears his throat as a way to interrupt.

"Sorry. Danielle how about that drink?"

"Sure Steve. How about a seltzer and if you don't have that then water would be fine. Thank you!" Dr. Marxx walks into the kitchen as Joe sits down next to Danielle.

"So are you Dr. Marxx's assistant?" Danielle inquires.

"I guess you could say that."

"This is a little awkward for me. I have to admit that I'm a little nervous about the idea of becoming pregnant. I mean I'm only 23 years old so I'm just not ready to have children right now. I mean my own children anyway. If my family ever knew I was doing this, they would kill me."

"So your parents don't know anything about this?"

"No. Not yet anyway," Danielle replies.

"Don't you think it's something you should talk with them about? I mean after all, you'll be showing after five months and I would assume you see your parents often."

"I do. I see them about every three to four months. I guess I didn't think of that." Danielle looks down and goes silent for a moment, then looks up at Joe. "I will deal with that when the situation comes up." Dr. Marxx enters the room holding a tray with some glasses of water and some pretzels and crackers on a plate.

"Here we go guys!" He places the tray down on the coffee table and hands Danielle a glass of ice water. "Sorry Danielle, I didn't have any seltzer."

"That's fine. Thank you."

"So what are we talking about?" Dr. Marxx asks.

"We're talking about the fact that Danielle didn't, nor was she going to tell her parents about being a host.

"Hmm," Dr. Marxx mumbles.

"That's not a problem is it?" Danielle asks.

"No, I don't see a problem with it. After all, you're an adult. You can make decisions for yourself," Dr. Marxx says as he sits on the chair opposite Joe and Danielle.

"I had mentioned the idea that her parents would possibly see her while she was pregnant. I'm just wondering what kind of confrontation that would create?"

"I promise you, it will be fine," Danielle explains as someone knocks at the front door.

"That must be Tara," Dr. Marxx says as he gets up to answer the door. Joe stands and walks towards the door as Danielle follows. Dr. Marxx opens the front door. "Hello Tara, it's nice to see you again," Dr. Marxx says as Tara walks up to him and gives him a hug.

"Steve, I'm so glad you called me yesterday. I've been looking forward to tonight ever since you called." Joe and Danielle walk over to the door to meet Tara. Tara, a tall 25 year old with long blonde hair, is very friendly and bubbly.

"Joe, this is Tara Gaston. Tara, this is Joe Walker." Joe extends his right hand to Tara and reaches out and shakes her hand.

"Hi Tara it's great to meet you," Joe replies as Tara smiles back.

"Hello, nice to meet you."

"Tara, you remember Danielle," Dr. Marxx says. Danielle is smiling and walks up to Tara and gives her a big hug.

"It's so nice to see you again Tara."

"You too Danielle, I'm sorry we didn't stay in touch."

"Why don't we all sit down and get started?" Dr. Marxx asks. Tara and Danielle sit on the brown leather couch together as Joe pulls up a chair and sits next to the couch. Dr. Marxx sits in the large leather chair across from the girls. "So ladies we talked briefly yesterday about the process. Since Joe is here now, I will just go over it again and we can talk about any problems or issues when I'm done." Both Tara and Danielle give a nod to Dr. Marxx.

"I have to ask both of you a personal question."

"OK," Danielle says.

"Sure," Tara replies.

"I need to know when your next menstrual cycle will start. I have to work around your body's clock.

"My period ended last week," Tara replies.

"It must be a coincidence, because mine ended last week also," Danielle adds.

"That works out perfectly then," Dr. Marxx said excitedly. "Are both of you available tomorrow afternoon?"

"I am available after 2:30," Tara explains.

"I'm also available anytime," Danielle replies.

"Good. Danielle, you be at my office at 3:00 and Tara you be there at 4:00. I will take you to our lab's medical room for the procedure and I will have to sedate you and give you something for the pain. A doctor, the lab hired, will be performing a quick procedure on you, which should take about an hour. I also need you to halt any further sexual intercourse for the next nine months."

"So what is this procedure you are doing?" Tara asks while looking at Danielle with a confused look.

"It's called a trans-vaginal ultrasound aspiration. Without going into detail about the procedure, the doctors are going to remove eggs from your ovaries. It's a common procedure and is harmless to you. You may have some discomfort after the procedure, but that should only last for a day or two. Your role in this entire procedure is that you are a donor and a surrogate for this baby." Both Tara and Danielle are listening intently to Dr. Marxx as Joe stands up and walks around the room. "You will hear me use the word host many times. That is what you are being paid for. To be a host," Dr. Marxx explains.

"How much are we getting paid to do this?" Tara asks.

"You will each be compensated forty thousand dollars after the babies are delivered." Danielle and Tara look at each other and smile. "You will also be required to live in this apartment so Joe and I can monitor your progress and your health along with monitoring the baby's development. All you're medical care, clothing and food will be provided for you during the course of the next nine months."

"This is a lot to think about," Tara explains. Joe is pacing from one side of the room to the other.

"They are going to back out of this, I know they are," Joe says to himself silently.

"Ladies, this will not be easy. You will be pregnant and carrying a baby for nine months. You will gain weight and be sore and miserable at times. You will go though many emotional changes because of the pregnancy. This could be a difficult nine months," Dr. Marxx explains. Danielle looks at her hands as she nervously picks at her fingers while Tara is staring at Dr. Marxx. "Not to mention that after all that, you will then give up the baby you carried and nurtured as your own. I'm going to administer some medications to you in the next week or so before the procedure. I am also going to ask you to do many things during the next nine months. Some may be uncomfortable, like this procedure tomorrow. But there are only a few procedures that we need to do before we insert the fertilized eggs and attach them to your uterus. After that, it's the normal process of pregnancy."

Thinking that Tara and Danielle may have just been scared enough to back out, Joe speaks up.

"But at the end of it all, you will be responsible for fulfilling the dreams of two people that don't have the ability to do what you are doing for them! And that is something that you will feel good about for the rest of your life," Joe says from behind the girls as he walks towards the front of the couch. "You don't yet realize what this means for my family. Someday you will understand how you changed our lives for the better. For that I will be forever grateful to you." Tara and Danielle look at each other and smile.

"I'm in," Tara says enthusiastically as she stands up and looks down at Danielle. Danielle looks scared as her breathing increases rapidly. She looks at Dr. Marxx then at Joe.

"Please Danielle," Joe says softly. Danielle looks up at Tara. Tara extends her hand down to Danielle.

"We will do this together, you and me," Tara says to Danielle with an assuring tone. Joe stands next to Dr. Marxx watching the girls intently. Danielle takes Tara's hand and stands up. Her eyes are locked onto Tara's eyes.

"We will do this together?" Danielle asks Tara softly. Tara nods.

"Together," Tara says as Danielle looks at Dr. Marxx and Joe with a smile.

"I'm in!"

CHAPTER 16

"Watch your hands going through the door, Joe," Dr. Marxx says as Danielle follows Joe through the front door. Joe and Dr. Marxx are moving Danielle's dresser and clothes into Dr. Marxx's apartment. It's been one week since the eggs were removed from Tara and Danielle's ovaries and placed into cold storage. For the past week, Dr. Marxx has been very optimistic about the cloning process and being able to fulfill Joe's dream of reuniting with his children.

"Tara just sent a text. She will be here in a few minutes with her stuff too."

"That's great Danielle. I hope her stuff is lighter than yours," Joe says jokingly while struggling with Danielle's dresser. A blue sports car pulls up to the front of Dr. Marxx's apartment building as the horn beeps twice. Tara gets out of the car, then reaches in the back seat and pulls out two black garbage bags filled with clothes. The apartment building has a flight of stairs in the front of the old brick structure going up to the first floor entry way. Joe comes out of the main door and runs down the flight of stairs to meet Tara as she struggles to carry both bags. "I got these Tara." Joe takes the bags from Tara and walks up the stairs to the front door. Joe stops at the top of the stairs and shouts down to Tara. "How much more stuff do you have?"

"Not much. Just a small bag of shoes and some pictures. I've got them though."

"OK. I will put these bags in your room."

That evening Joe, Dr. Marxx, Tara and Danielle are sitting in the living room, eating pizza.

"Steve, how did the tests results on Tara and Danielle's eggs go today," Joe asks.

"Everything is on schedule and the eggs look good. If everything goes as planned, we should be ready for implanting in the next few days."

"That's good to hear," Joe replies. "How are you guys feeling? Any after effects from the egg removal?"

"I don't know about Tara, but I felt fine a day later."

"I was good about two days later," Tara responds.

Joe and Dr. Marxx clean up the coffee table and put the left over pizza in the refrigerator, while Tara and Danielle are sitting on the couch watching a video about childbirth.

"Joe, I didn't get a chance to tell you earlier because the girls were around."

"Tell me what?"

"I fused the cells to the eggs today. It took me two attempts with Tara's eggs and four attempts with Danielle's eggs, but both eggs accepted the cells."

"Wow, that's great news." Joe grabs Dr. Marxx and gives him a rough bear hug. "Good job Steve!"

"It was a big hurdle, but we aren't in the clear yet. I'm hoping that when I go to the lab tomorrow morning, the transformation to embryo will have started. If that transformation has begun then the embryos can be transplanted the following day. Then we have to get the girls bodies to accept the eggs."

"What are the chances their bodies will reject the embryos? I thought you said that every time you did this in the lab, the eggs were accepted?"

"That was getting the eggs to accept the cells. We have to hope that the girl's bodies accept the embryos instead of rejecting them. I will start the girls on progesterone tonight. The progesterone will make the lining of the uterus more receptive to the embryos," Dr. Marxx says as both of them walk into the living room and sit on the couch.

"Girls, we have some things to discuss. I have two fertilized eggs and once those eggs are ready, I will implant them into your uterus. If all goes as planned, I should have you both in and out of my office within four hours. I'm hoping that when I go to the lab tomorrow, the transformation from egg to embryo will have started. If that's the case, I will call you immediately and let you know." Tara and Danielle look at each other and give each other a hug.

"Oh my God, this is really happening," Tara says giggling.

"I have something for you two that I need you to take tonight and tomorrow. I will be right back," Dr. Marxx says as he walks to the foyer and upstairs to the second floor. Danielle looks at Joe.

"Aren't you excited about this?" Danielle asks.

"I am very excited for this whole process to start. It's been a long road and I just hope that everything works out." Tara and Danielle stand up and walk over to the other side of the couch and give Joe a hug.

"We are happy for you Joe," Tara says with a smile. Dr. Marxx comes back down the stairs and sits next to the girls. He opens an orange pill bottle and shakes two pills out into his hand and gives one pill to both Tara and Danielle.

"Girls, this is progesterone. This medication will help the lining of your uterus accept the embryos much easier when implanted. Go ahead and take them." The girls pick up their drinks, put the pills in their mouths and swallow them. "Good," Dr. Marxx said. "I have a long day ahead of me tomorrow and I will probably stay at the lab tomorrow night to monitor the specimens so I am going to bed. Girls, if I don't see you tomorrow morning, try and spend the day just relaxing around the apartment. Goodnight everyone."

"Goodnight Steve," Danielle, Tara and Joe say in unison as Dr. Marxx makes his way upstairs.

CHAPTER 17

A cell phone vibrates and rings in the living room and echoes throughout the apartment. Tara runs down the stairs from the second floor in hopes of answering the phone before the caller hangs up. "I got it, it's my phone." Tara grabs her phone off the coffee table. "Hello."

"Tara, it's Steve."

"Hi Steve. What's up?"

"Is Joe and Danielle there with you?"

"Um, yeah they're upstairs in my room. Why? What's going on?"

"Can you go upstairs and put me on speaker, please."

"Sure, hold on a minute." Tara hikes back upstairs into the bedroom where Joe and Danielle are hanging pictures. "Hey guys. Steve is on the phone and he wants to talk with all of us," Tara explains. Tara sets the phone down on the bedside table and pushes the speaker button. "OK Steve. You're on speaker."

"Can everyone hear me?"

"We can all hear you Steve," Joe replies.

"I have great news," Steve says enthusiastically. "The eggs accepted the cells and they were successfully fused together. The cells and eggs are forming into an embryo."

Joe and the girls are high-fiving each other then they group hug. "That's awesome news Steve!" Joe says while directing his voice towards the phone.

"I need to spend the night here tonight so I can monitor the embryos. I will touch base with you guys in the morning. Girls, be prepared to come to my office tomorrow afternoon. We will implant the embryos then. Tara and Danielle, this is very important. As soon as we hang up, I want you both to take another progesterone pill."

"I will get those now," Danielle says while looking at Tara.

"We will all be there tomorrow. How is three o'clock?" Joe asks.

"Great, see you then," Dr. Marxx replies as Danielle hangs up. Dr. Marxx hangs up the phone then looks into a microscope at the fertilized egg.

"Wow these eggs are evolving much faster than the last ones," Dr. Marxx says out loud. He lifts his face away from the microscope and looks at paperwork on the desk as he writes some numbers down. "These numbers are off the charts!"

The following day at 3 p.m., Joe walks into the main entrance to Gene Tech with Danielle and Tara. The girls are excited but nervous about their new purpose for the immediate future. At some point it wasn't about them and the sacrifice they were about to make. The girls have talked about this over and over. What they were doing for Joe was about giving back to society and paying it forward in a way that no one could dream about. It was about the opportunity to bring a family together, or so they were led to believe. Dr. Marxx escorts the girls into examination room one at the lab.

"Girls, I need you to get into these surgical gowns for me when I leave the room." Dr. Marxx sets down a set of gowns and socks on the table in the room. "When you are ready, come out of the room and take a left and we will be waiting for you in the lab's operating room."

"Got it, we will be right out," Danielle says. After a few minutes, Danielle and Tara emerge from the dressing room and enter the bright white operating room.

"Are we ready?" Dr. Marxx asks as he walks over to the girls after they close the door to the operating room. Tara looks at Dr. Marxx with a panicked look on her face. "Tara, everything will be fine. This will be a short procedure and you will be done," Dr. Marxx says reassuringly. If you girls can lie down on the beds here, we will get started. As they take their places on the beds, they both turn make eye contact and smile at each other. Dr. Marxx gives Tara a wink and smile as Tara nods her head back to Dr. Marxx. The two anesthesiologists walk over to Tara and Danielle and hook up the IV to the girl's left arm after giving them some brief instructions. Danielle looks at a small red box on a table next to Dr. Marxx. The red box is marked with a caution label and human embryo specimen.

"What is that?" Danielle asks, pointing to the box as her eyes start to flutter. Dr. Marxx turns away briefly towards the red box on the table.

"Those are the embryos that will be transplanted into both of you in the next hour. Dr. Marxx looks at Danielle who is now deep in sleep and pulls a tube from the red box marked "Talia."

CHAPTER 18

"Girls, can you come downstairs please," Joe shouts up the stairs while standing in the living room. Dr. Marxx is sitting on the couch looking over some paperwork from Tara and Danielle's most recent check-up. The girls are four months into their pregnancy and all indications are that both babies and hosts are healthy. Tara and Danielle have been planning and talking about the day they give birth and how special that day will be. Unfortunately, a few of these conversations between the girls about shopping for clothes after the babies are born have been overheard by Joe. Concern mounts as Joe believes the girls haven't fully understood their role in this arrangement.

"Are you sure you want to have this conversation with the girls?" Dr. Marxx asks as he looks at Joe then raises his eyebrows.

"We have to talk about this with them. We need to be sure the girls understand what happens when the babies are born," Joe says as the girls come walking down the stairs. Tara has gained about five pounds and Danielle has gained a little less than that. Both girls are in great spirits and are looking forward to the next few months.

"What's up Joe?" Danielle asks as she stops half way down the stairs and leans up against the banister. Danielle grabs Tara's hand and stops her so she doesn't have to walk down to the bottom of the stairs if it's not needed. Throughout the past four months, Danielle has been the leader and the spokeswomen for the two girls and Tara has been the shy and reserved one.

"Come down girls and have a seat on the couch. Steve and I would like to talk with you for a few minutes." Joe stands at the bottom of the stairs, watching the girls walk slowly down to the bottom. As the girls get to the bottom of the stairs and walk over to the couch, Joe follows and sits down across from the girls. The paperwork on the coffee table, Dr. Marxx was reading, gets cleaned up and shuffled into a pile as everyone prepares to listen to Joe.

"We wanted to talk with you about the day you give birth. We are still five months away from your due dates but we need to talk about the day you give birth and about our contract." The girls look at each other with a look of concern then look back at Joe.

"Is everything OK?" Danielle asks. "I thought everything was going smoothly." Danielle says as Tara nods her head, agreeing with Danielle.

"Everything is fine and we couldn't ask for the situation to be any better than it is. What we want to talk with you about is how you girls are going to deal with..." Joe pauses for a moment and looks at Dr. Marxx, clearly uncomfortable with where he is going with the conversation. Expecting bad news, Tara's eyebrows rise as she stares at Joe attentively. "Shortly after giving birth, I'm planning on taking custody of my girls and at that point, our relationship will be over and our contract will be fulfilled." There is a moment of awkwardness and silence as Danielle looks at Joe and tilts her head slightly. Danielle turns her head and glances at Tara then back to Joe. "Danielle, please tell me what you're thinking."

"Danielle, we talked about this when we interviewed you. This shouldn't be a surprise. This is what the contract outlined," Dr. Marxx says after interrupting.

"I get it," Danielle replies as she looks at Tara, who's stoic and unaffected by Joe's forwardness, then back at Dr. Marxx again. "I think we both get it. I think we were under the assumption that it wouldn't be immediately after the girls were born. We, or at least I, thought we would be able to spend some time with the girls before we just walked away." Joe looks at Dr. Marxx and takes a deep breath. Joe was spot on with his prediction and now has to do damage control before it's too late.

"Danielle, this is exactly why we needed to have this conversation. It's important for you guys and me to move on with our lives after the girls are born. Can you understand the emotional and physical attachment you will feel if you spend weeks with the girls before separating from them?" Tightly grabbing Danielle's hand, Tara glances at Danielle then takes over the conversation.

"He's right Danielle. We need to let go immediately when the girls are born. We are getting paid to carry these babies for nine months. They're not our babies." Danielle stares deeply into Tara's eyes. "Joe, we understand what our role is here, we do. I think Danielle is very emotional right now because she's carrying a baby she knows will never call her mom. We accept the idea that we are carrying your children and after the girls are born, we will not have any part in raising your daughters." Tara looks back at Danielle, who is still staring at her. "Right Danielle?" Danielle dejectedly nods and lowers her head in defeat.

CHAPTER 19

"Hey Tara," Danielle says as both girls sit on the couch in the living room.

"Yeah."

"I just thought of something."

"Danielle everything will be fine," Tara says as she's looking at her phone.

"No, seriously Tara." Tara stops playing with her phone, and pays attention to Danielle.

"What are you thinking about?" Tara asks.

"Have you wondered why we haven't met Joe's wife?" Tara stares at Danielle for a few seconds.

"I guess I haven't really thought about it, but now that you bring it up. If Joe and Kim are doing this together, why hasn't she come around and met us or why isn't she visiting Joe?" Tara asks. "I mean we are five months pregnant with Kim and Joe's babies, why wouldn't she want to meet us or talk with us?"

"I don't know, but we should find out," Danielle says as she jumps up off the couch and starts walking towards the kitchen with Tara following. Dr. Marxx and Joe are sitting at the kitchen table talking and looking over documents when Danielle and Tara enter the room.

"Hi girls," Joe says as the girls stop in front of the table. "You girls look like you're on a mission."

"We were just thinking about your wife, Kim." Joe and Dr. Marxx look at each other then look back at Danielle and Tara.

"Why were you thinking about her?" Joe says slowly as if he's shocked by the statement. "Well, how is it that we haven't met her. We are having her babies and she has never even bothered to come meet us and check on our progress. We are finding this rather odd," Danielle replies.

Dr. Marxx and Joe again look at each other in an attempt to read each other's thoughts. "Joe, you might as well tell them why Kim doesn't come around." Joe's face crunches as he thinks quickly to avert a disaster.

"The truth is that Kim isn't very comfortable with this situation. Wait, that's not the right term. She's very supportive of you and she is concerned about your progress and your well-being, and the babies' well-being too."

"Then why hasn't she come around or even wanted to meet us and why is she uncomfortable about this arrangement?" Tara asks with a slightly less accusatory tone as Danielle's.

"It's upsetting to her that she can't have children naturally and she almost feels like she's letting me down. But she isn't and I've told her that. The funny part about this is that I just talked with her yesterday and she was actually asking if she could finally meet you guys." Joe looks at Dr. Marxx and grins as Dr. Marxx gives him a half-hearted smile back.

"Huh, that's such a coincidence," Danielle says.

"I will call her later today and we will set it up."

"Sounds great, we can't wait to meet her," Tara replies as she and Danielle look at each other in approval then head upstairs.

"I can't wait to hear how you are going to pull this off," Dr. Marxx comments quietly with a smirk as he picks up the paperwork he was looking at.

"I'm not sure how I'm going to pull it off either, but we have to think of something," Joe replies as he looks at Dr. Marxx. "How about using one of the women at the office? You must be friendly with someone there that would help you out?"

"Joe, I can't ask anyone at the office to lie for me and play your wife. We don't want anyone to know what we are doing. Besides, some of those people in the office have met most of the women that volunteered for this experiment. Something like that could backfire on us and have detrimental consequences."

"OK, so that's not a good idea. Think," Joe barks.

Dr. Marxx stands up and starts pacing with Joe. He opens the refrigerator and pulls out a bottle of water then closes the door and turns to continue pacing but stops abruptly. Dr. Marxx leans over and looks at a picture on the refrigerator and smiles. "I have an idea," Dr. Marxx says quietly as Joe stops pacing and smiles at him.

CHAPTER 20

It's Saturday night, one week after Tara and Danielle asked about Kim. "I'm really nervous about this Steve."

"Don't worry about it Joe. You need to just stick to your part and everything will be fine," Dr. Marxx says to Joe as they prepare snacks in the kitchen. Dr. Marxx looks down at his watch. "She will be here any minute. Grab the pretzels." Dr. Marxx turns and walks into the living room with a platter of cheese and crackers and a bowl of chips. Joe follows Dr. Marxx with the pretzels and sets the large silver chip bowl down on the coffee table.

The doorbell rings. "She's here girls, come on down," Dr. Marxx calls out to Tara and Danielle from the hallway as he walks toward the front door. Tara and Danielle come down the stairs and meet Joe at the bottom as Dr. Marxx opens the front door. "Hello Kim, come in. It's great to see you again." Dr. Marxx takes a step forward and gives Kim a hug, but the door is blocking Tara, Danielle and Joe's view of Kim. As Dr. Marxx steps aside and begins closing the door, Kim steps into the hallway and into view.

"Hi Honey," Joe says to Elizabeth Marxx and gives her a big hug. "I've missed you." Joe gives Elizabeth a kiss on her cheek and gives her another hug.

"It's good to see you too Joe." Danielle and Tara are standing at the bottom of the stairs with smiles on their faces as they wait to be introduced to Kim.

"Kim, I want you to meet Tara and Danielle." Elizabeth steps toward Tara and Danielle as they do the same. They meet and hug each other as Joe and Dr. Marxx glance at each other.

"Oh my God, I'm so excited to finally meet you girls. How are you both feeling?" Elizabeth leads the girls to the living room as if she rehearsed this in her head over and over again. Joe and Dr. Marxx follow the girls to the couch as they give each other a fist bump.

"We are both doing really good. We were sick for a few months, but that has all passed," Tara replies as Danielle nods her head and agrees with Tara.

"Let's all sit down, relax and get to know each," Elizabeth says as she sits down between Tara and Danielle on the couch. Joe and Dr. Marxx take a seat across from the girls on the other couch. "So Tara, tell me about yourself." Danielle looks at Kim for a few moments and tilts her head slightly while she is talking with Tara. Danielle senses that something isn't right.

"Can we get you girls something to drink?" Joe asks while pushing himself off the couch and standing up.

"I would love some lemonade. It's in the fridge," Tara says.

"Me too," Danielle yells.

"I guess I will have the same," Elizabeth replies. Joe and Dr. Marxx head to the kitchen as Danielle, Tara and Elizabeth get to know each other.

"So Kim. It's great to finally meet you. You must have so many questions that you want to ask us? I mean, since we are carrying your children," Danielle says with a soft but unmistakable annoyed tone.

"I do Danielle," Elizabeth replies as Danielle puts her hand up to stop her before she says anything else.

"But before you ask us questions, I just wanted to ask you a few first."

"Oh, sure," Elizabeth says as Tara looks at Danielle perplexed.

"How long have you and Joe been married?" Elizabeth takes a moment then looks to the kitchen in hopes that Joe and her brother in-law would be coming back in. "Oh, many years. It's been so long I can't even count how many years it's been."

"I'm sure." Tara stares at Danielle, as she's not sure what's going on. "Oh, I just wanted to tell you how sorry I am about your cancer surgery you had five years ago."

"Cancer surgery?" Elizabeth asks.

"Yes, Joe said that you had ovarian cancer and that's why you couldn't have children. That's why Tara and I are carrying your babies. Right?" Danielle asks before throwing on a huge fake smile.

"Oh yeah the cancer. I have been trying to forget that," Elizabeth replies. Agitated with Elizabeth, Danielle glares at her, while Tara looks on.

"Danielle, are you OK?" Tara asks.

"Not really Tara! Not really!" Just in the nick of time, Joe and Dr. Marxx walk back into the living room from the kitchen.

"How is everyone doing?" Dr. Marxx asks as he glances at Danielle and she stares back at him.

"Danielle, is something wrong?" Joe asks.

"What's going on?" Danielle asks with a tone to her voice as her eyebrows crunch together. Joe looks at Dr. Marxx then back to Danielle. Elizabeth sits uneasy still looking down as Tara looks at Joe for some guidance. Danielle jumps off the couch quickly and walks upstairs to the second floor. Joe and Dr. Marxx look at Elizabeth then at Tara.

"Steve, what's wrong with Danielle?" Tara asks as she sits up and leans forward toward Steve.

Danielle then appears from the second floor walking down the stairs with a purpose as Joe, Dr. Marxx, Tara and

Elizabeth are watching from the couch. She walks over to Joe clearly upset and holds a picture out in front of his face.

"Who's this Joe? You must not have remembered the conversation we had about Kim two weeks after our procedure. Do you remember showing me this picture of your wife?" Joe stands motionless looking at the photograph of Kim then closes his eyes in defeat. "That isn't your wife!" Danielle shouts at Joe as she points to Elizabeth.

"I'm going home Steve. I'm sorry," Elizabeth says as she stands up and walks toward the door.

"Elizabeth, hang on. I will walk you out," Dr. Marxx replies as he follows Elizabeth out the door.

"Elizabeth?" Danielle says as she turns and looks back at Joe. "What the fuck is going on Joe?"

"Can you please sit and try to calm down a little. I will tell you everything when Steve comes back in." Tara sits quietly caressing her belly on the couch. "Tara, are you OK?" Joe asks.

"I am. I'm just very confused right now," Tara replies calmly.

"I know. Everything will be clear in a few minutes."

Danielle's pacing back and forth in the living room when Steve walks back into the foyer from walking Elizabeth out. "Danielle, please sit down next to Tara," Dr. Marxx asks as he walks back into the room. "Joe, do you want to tell them or should I?"

"I will. Girls, I'm sorry we lied to you about Kim, I mean Elizabeth. Elizabeth is Steve's sister in-law and she lives here in the city." Still visibly angry, Danielle sits down on the couch next to Tara. "This is my wife, Kim." He holds up the picture of himself and Kim that Danielle brought downstairs. "She meant the world to me one year ago and she still means the world to me today. Today she lives in Florida by herself because I left her." Tara and Danielle look at each other then look back at Joe.

"10 months ago, my wife was bringing my two daughters, Calie and Talia, to meet me at a Father-Daughter Valentine's Day Dance. They didn't make it to the dance. A truck swerved into my wife's lane and struck her car, sending it rolling over and off the road. Both of my daughters died shortly after the accident at the hospital." Danielle and Tara both begin to cry while Dr. Marxx looks down to the floor. As much as he tries to keep his tears in, Joe's eyes fill and tears flow down his cheeks. "My wife survived the crash and after recovering at the hospital from her injuries, she came home. Deep down inside, I blamed my wife for the death of my girls and my life soon fell apart without them." Danielle's wrathful and furious posture has completely flipped, as she becomes remorseful and docile. Tara holds Danielle as if they are being terrified in a scary movie as they listen to Joe's heartbreaking story.

"I left home a few months later and somehow found Steve. Steve was the answer to what I was looking for." Danielle, beside herself with guilt at becoming angry with Joe, grabbed his hand and held it tight as she silently mouthed the words, "I'm sorry," at Joe who was now looking down at her on the couch.

"What were you looking for?" Tara asked.

"Calie and Talia."

"I don't understand. I thought you said they died?"

"They did Tara. They died 10 months ago, but when I found Steve I discovered a way to get my girls back."

"I still don't understand," Tara pleads. Danielle looks at Tara with shock.

"Calie and Talia are inside of us," Danielle says with a smile as she gazes at Tara.

For the next four months the babies continued to grow and all check-ups showed the babies to be healthy. Danielle and Tara vowed to do everything they could to support Joe during the pregnancy. They had many nights together just sitting around the apartment talking about Calie and Talia and the life Joe had before the girls died. Over the course of the next few months, Danielle and Tara visited their families and explained the work they were doing for Joe and his family. The majority of their families were supportive.

CHAPTER 21

"Everything is going as planned and we will begin administering the Pitocin in the next few minutes. The Pitocin will help to initiate the contractions and soon after you should have two baby girls in your arms," Dr. George says with optimism to Joe and Dr. Marxx in the delivery room. Joe looks at Dr. Marxx with a big smile as Dr. Marxx pats Joe on the back. The delivery room is separated into two rooms by a curtain. Danielle and Tara each occupy a side of the room and each has a team of nurses and doctors to assist in delivering the babies. Dr. George is an Obstetrician hired by Gene Tech and works closely with Dr. Marxx on the cloning project.

"This is very exciting, Joe. I'm very happy for you," Dr. Marxx says to Joe softly as the two are standing in the middle of the room watching both girls.

"I owe it all to you Steve. Thank you for everything you've done." Joe reaches out and shakes Dr. Marxx's hand and looks him in the eye. Dr. Marxx gives Joe a smile back. "Let's go see the girls."

"How are you doing Danielle?" Dr. Marxx asks softly as he leans over the bed slightly towards her. Joe's on the opposite side of the bed.

"I'm OK, I think. It's starting to hurt a little during the contractions." Danielle looks at Joe. "How are you doing Joe?" she asks as she smiles then takes a deep breath. She nods her head at Joe to convince him that he's good.

"I'm nervous but very excited," Joe says as he leans over and kisses Danielle's sweaty forehead. "You're doing great Danielle. I'm very proud of you." Joe gives Danielle a big smile and she smiles back at him. "I'm going to check on Tara." Danielle nods her head quickly as she takes another deep breath and grimaces in pain.

"Ow, Ow, Ow," Danielle blurts out as she takes faster and shorter breaths. Joe turns back to look at Danielle as he walks towards Tara.

"Danielle, you OK?" Tara shouts to her.

"No, it hurts Tara. It hurts like hell!" Danielle shouts as she turns her head towards the curtain. "Can we open this curtain? I can't see Tara."

"Sure we can." Dr. Marxx walks over to the curtain and pushes it back towards the wall. "How's that girls?"

"Much better, thanks. Hi Danielle," Tara says as she waves across the room to Danielle. "We are going to have babies today." Danielle is looking at Tara, with an evil eye while she breathes heavy.

"Looks like you're faring better than Danielle right now," Joe says to Tara as they both look over to Danielle.

"This is easy. I'm not sure why she is having so much pain, but I'm ahhhhh!" Tara grabs her stomach, throws herself back against the bed, and looks up as she opens her mouth and takes a deep breath. "OH MY GOD!"

"Guess we talked too soon," Joe says with a slight smirk on his face. Tara takes a deep breath and looks at Joe. "Does it hurt?" Tara nods her head quickly as she holds her breath in between contractions.

"You have to keep breathing Tara, don't hold your breath," the nursing assistant said softly. Tara begins taking short breaths and once again grabs her stomach in pain. "AAHH!" Tara screams again. The doctor rushes over to check Tara as Dr. Marxx joins Joe.

While labor continues for the girls, Joe and Dr. Marxx pace back and forth in anticipation of Calie and Talia's arrival. Tara has been having contractions for about an hour and Danielle has been in full labor for an hour and a half.

"Tara is moving along slowly. Her cervix is dilated six centimeters and Danielle's is about eight centimeters," Dr. George says out loud.

"Well Joe, it looks like Talia will be born first today and the way it looks right now she will be here soon," Dr. Marxx said to Joe but loud enough for everyone to hear.

"Looks like we're going to have a baby very soon so I'm going across the hall to scrub in. The nurses are going to be bringing in some equipment so try not to get in the way," the doctor says. "Joe if you are going to assist with delivery then you will need to scrub in too."

"I'm going right now Doc," Joe replies as he looks at Danielle. "Are you OK with me delivering the baby?" Danielle disheveled and sweating profusely smiles at Joe while she rests briefly.

"She is your daughter Joe. You should be the one to bring her into this world." Danielle grimaces in pain but then tries to smile.

Meanwhile, Tara continues to go through labor, reeling in pain from the constant cramps and tightening. Pain is coursing through both of the girl's bodies as Danielle readies herself to welcome Talia into the world. Nurses give Tara a shot of medicine to ease the pain slightly but not enough to slow down labor. Dr. George and the nurses rush in with equipment as Dr. Marxx moves to the side of the room. The doctor lifts Danielle's legs and looks to see if the baby is crowning while the nurses begin to secure her feet in the stirrups. Dr. George pops up with a smile.

"Good news Danielle. The baby has crowned and now it's just a matter of a few pushes."

"Thank God!" Danielle shouts as her rapid breathing and pushing is replaced with short breaks. Joe runs into the room after scrubbing up across the hall.

"Joe, I need you right here with me at Danielle's feet. Once the baby comes out, I'm going to hand her to you and we will suction her nose out and get her breathing on her own. Then I will have you cut the cord."

"I'm ready Doc." Joe peeks up over the sheet at Danielle and Dr. Marxx who is standing next to her. "Danielle, you're doing a great job. Keep it up," Joe says as he gives her the thumbs up.

"Danielle. I need a couple of good pushes and we will be done. Ready?" Dr. George asks.

"Yup!" Danielle screams as she begins to push. "AAHH!" She pushes then takes a break and lays her head back on the pillow.

"That was good. Two more like that and we will have a baby."

"Come on Danielle, push," Tara yells from her bed as she pushes too. Danielle holds in her scream as she holds her breath and pushes with all her might. She stops and remains still on the bed while shaking her head.

"I need to rest, I can't push anymore, it hurts way too much," Danielle says utterly exhausted.

"One more time Danielle and I think that should do it," Dr. George encourages, as Talia's head is halfway out. Joe stands in awe at the sight of his daughter emerging into the world.

"Come on Danielle, one more big push," Joe shouts encouragingly. She uses all of her remaining power and gives one more mighty push. She breaks down in exhaustion and stops pushing as she can feel the baby slide out of her body.

"Ha Ha!" Joe shouts with joy. "Oh my God Danielle, you did it." The doctor wraps Talia in a warm blanket and hands her to Joe as she begins to screech from the trauma of her birth. Unable to holdback his emotions any longer, Joe starts sobbing with an incredible smile across his face as his eyes flood with tears. The last time he held Talia in his arms was when she died in the accident. A nurse rushes over with a suction and cleans out Talia's nose and wipes her face off. Joe cuts the umbilical cord then kisses Talia on her forehead as he cradles his daughter. Talia has stopped crying and for the first time looks at her father. A rush of emotions and a sense of euphoria take ahold of Joe right now with his newborn daughter in his arms as she gazes into his eyes.

"Hi Princess, welcome back," Joe whispers softly to Talia as tears fall from his eyes onto her blanket. He's oblivious to the sounds and mayhem around him as the doctors prepare for the arrival of Calie. All is silent with Joe as he takes in the moment with his newborn. While cradling Talia, Joe walks over the head of the bed and shows Danielle the amazing life she brought into the world.

"Here she is Danielle. This is Talia." Danielle is exhausted and still trying to catch her breath.

"She's beautiful Joe." Danielle looks at Joe and smiles. "Congratulations Joe. I'm so happy for you." Joe bends over and gives Danielle a kiss on her forehead.

"Thank you Danielle." Joe says as he stares into her eyes and smiles. "Do you want to hold her?" Danielle shakes her head and whimpers slightly. She doesn't want to get attached to Talia and feels it's easier just to let her go immediately. Joe looks at Danielle intently and crunches his lips together. He also remembers the conversation he and Dr. Marxx had with the girls.

"Joe, the nurse has to take Talia and start her examination then get her on a bottle," Dr. George says. Joe gives Talia a kiss on her forehead then hands her to the nurse. A second nurse comes in and pushes Danielle's bed out of the room and into recovery.

Meanwhile, Tara is still breathing and taking her contractions with stride. Dr. George cleans up, changes his gloves and comes back in as Joe and Dr. Marxx assist Tara. Twenty minutes later Calie is born into the world with a dramatic entrance similar to Talia's. Calie was taken for her examination as Joe holds Tara, who is fatigued and mentally drained.

"Thank you Tara. Thank you for bringing Calie back to me." Joe stares into Tara's eyes then gives her a kiss on her forehead. "I'll be down to see you guys in recovery in a little bit."

"OK Joe," Tara says, barely getting it out of her mouth as her eyes close. Joe watches as Tara's bed is pushed into the hallway. He turns to Dr. Marxx as both make eye contact and smile. They walk towards each other and hug tightly.

"You did it Steve," Joe says in the embrace. "I'm a father again."

CHAPTER 22

Joe rolls in an attempt to get comfortable in the dimly lit hospital room. The narrow fold up cot in the corner of the girl's recovery room, that Joe has made his bed, hasn't afforded him much sleep. Feedings every two to three hours has put Joe on a crash course with his love bugs that he can't wait to wake up for. All the excitement of the past twenty four hours hasn't presented Joe with the opportunity to sleep much. As the morning sun filters in through the windows, Tara slowly wakes to see Joe in the overstuffed chair feeding one of the babies. Tara watches Joe for a few moments, trying not to alert him to her gawking stare, as he smiles at Calie and whispers to her while holding the bottle. Calie stares back at Joe, listening to the sound of his soothing voice. Joe holds his cell phone in his hand and dials a number.

"You look so happy," Tara says quietly so she doesn't wake Danielle. The phone suddenly gets tossed to the side before he looks up at Tara.

"Hi," Joe replies just as softly, as he stands and walks over to Tara's bed. "How are you feeling?"

"I'm a little sore, but I'll make it," she says looking at Calie wrapped in a white blanket cradled by Joe then glancing over at Joe's cell phone on the chair. "Did you call someone?" she asked inquisitively. He glances back at his phone for an extended moment.

"No, I don't know what I was doing with that. It's nothing." Tara smiles and looks at Calie while softly rubbing her head.

"You're a good dad, and Calie is beautiful." Tara looks over towards Danielle. "Where's Talia?" Joe looks over to her bassinet next to Danielle's bed.

"She's still sleeping and so is Danielle. Thanks Tara." Joe looks back at Tara. "Really, I can't thank you and Danielle enough for everything you did for me." Tara smiles at Joe as he smiles back.

"We are both happy that we could make your life whole again."

"And you did," Joe nods his head slightly, agreeing with Tara.

"I'm very happy for you Joe. I really am." The nurse comes into the room and interrupts the conversation.

"How are you feeling? Do you have any pain?" she asks as she scans the heart monitor.

"I have some pain in my lower stomach. It's slowly getting more intense," Tara replies.

"I will bring some medicine for you in a minute. Do you want some breakfast or something to drink?"

"I would love some water. Thank you."

"No problem. Joe, how about for you?" the nurse asks as she walks closer to Joe and takes the empty formula bottle from his hand.

"Thanks, I'm all set," Joe replies without looking up at the nurse or taking his eyes off of his beautiful daughter. He walks slowly around the room. The purposeful slow motion dance extends the time he gets to hold his sleeping daughter. Peacefully rocking Calie back and forth until her eyes close, she receives a loving and gentle kiss on her forehead before being lowered into her pink ruffled maternity bassinet. More than seven years has elapsed since Joe last held Calie in his arms as an infant. It's all come back to him as if it were only yesterday.

<hr />

"Good morning everyone," Dr. Marxx says quietly as he enters the room holding a shoebox. Danielle and Tara are awake and having breakfast in bed while Joe performs for them, dancing around the room with his sleeping girls in his arms. Calie and Talia are wrapped in blankets like a cocoon and only their faces are visible. Everyone turns to look at Dr. Marxx as they greet him hello. "Girls, how are you feeling today?" Dr. Marxx asks as he walks over to Danielle's bed. He leans over and gives her a kiss on her forehead. Tara isn't left out of the greeting and offers Dr. Marxx a hug with her arms open.

"We are awesome after getting our dose of pain killers. Right Tara?"

"Oh yeah," Tara replies as she takes a spoonful of food and giggles as she tries chewing her gorged mouth. Dr. Marxx stands next to Joe and admires the babies.

"They are precious," Dr. Marxx says to Joe as he stands close to watch the girls. He steps to the side and places the shoebox on the rolling cart. "Here's the box you wanted me to bring in," he says to Joe.

"Thanks Steve. Tara, can I borrow the end of your bed for a minute?" Tara nods and pulls her feet up. "Thanks." Joe gently sets the sleeping girls down on the bed next to each other then grabs the shoebox off the cart. Sifting through the box, he suddenly stops. "Here they are." Joe pulls out two baby photographs. "These pictures were each taken one day after Talia and Calie were born."

"I know what you're doing," Dr. Marxx says as he approaches Joe at the end of Tara's bed. Joe has Talia's picture in his left hand and Calie's in his right. He glances at Dr. Marxx.

"Are you ready?" Joe asks.

"I think so." Joe moves the two pictures close to Talia and Calie's faces and compares the pictures to the baby's faces.

"Wow," Joe whispers with a smile on his face as Dr. Marxx pats him on the back.

Tara and Danielle were discharged from the hospital and spent the next two weeks back at Dr. Marxx's home recovering from the birth of Talia and Calie. Over the course of the following two weeks, Danielle and Tara spent very little time with the babies, but spent the majority of their time preparing to move out of Dr. Marxx's apartment. Bank accounts were set up for the girls, and Joe deposited forty thousand dollars into each of them based on the signed contract. Dr. Marxx completed all the legal paperwork with the help of an attorney friend, and both Tara and Danielle moved out of the apartment.

CHAPTER 23

Six years has flown by in the blink of an eye for Joe and his daughters. One year after the girls were born, Joe rented a two bedroom apartment a few doors down from Dr. Marxx, who was also known as Uncle Steve. Joe found work in San Francisco during the day as a security guard just to occupy his time while the girls went to preschool then on to kindergarten. Dr. Marxx continued his research with Gene Tech with a new government grant and he also shored up his personal finances with the money Joe gave him. Life was great for Joe and the girls, but there was still something missing in Talia and Calie's lives.

It's a warm, sunny Saturday afternoon in August and Talia and Calie are having fun on the swings at the park. The girls now six years old, are healthy and happy and visit the park regularly with their father. Freedom Park is down the street a few blocks from his apartment building so it's a quick walk for him and the girls to visit regularly. The girls jump off the swings and run away from Joe as he chases them around the park. Suddenly the girls stop running and stare across the playground. Joe walks up behind them and gets down on one knee and stares in the same direction at a mother and father playing with their two daughters. The girls aren't talking, just staring.

"Hey, let's get out of here and go get some ice cream." Both girls look at him as Calie nods. The ice cream truck is a regular stop on their park visit before they leave for the day, so Joe takes their hands as they walk towards the entrance of the park. He takes one more quick glance at the father and mother then looks down at Calie and Talia as they smile up at him. He returns the smile and gives their hands a gentle squeeze.

⊲⊳⊲⊳⊲⊳

As the big purple hair brush slides through Calie's long wet blonde hair, she sits in front of her father patiently waiting for him to finish. Talia, sitting next to Calie on the bed, is waiting for her turn. The girls are in their matching pink robes after taking a bath and getting ready for bed. They haven't talked much since coming back from the park and that's not like them.

"Girls, is something wrong? You two haven't said much in the past few hours." Talia looks at Calie and gives her a little nod as Joe tends to Talia's wet hair.

"Daddy, was that lady in the park, the little girl's mommy?" Calie asks.

"I don't know sweetie, probably." Calie was silent for a few moments then she turns around along with Talia and they both look at Joe. "Girls, what's going on?" They look at each other, unsure if they should be asking about this. "Talk to me," Joe encourages gently.

"Why don't we have a mommy?" Calie asks softly. The girls have never asked about their mother before and the question catches Joe off guard.

"Um, that's a great question." Joe takes a deep breath and lets it out slowly while looking down at the brush in his hand. "Talia, lets finish your hair and we will talk about it another day."

"We always see kids with their mommy and daddy, but we don't have a mommy," Talia says as a tear in her eye escapes down her cheek.

"Come here girls." Joe wraps his arms around the girls and pulls them close. He holds them and gives them a kiss on their foreheads then smiles as he closes his eyes and relishes the moment.

"You girls have a daddy that loves you very much and I would do anything for you. You know that right?" Both girls nod slightly while their eyes lock onto Joe's. Come on, let's get into bed. It's getting late." Joe picks both girls up in a bear hug as he walks over to Calie's bed and sets her down softly. She slithers under the firmly tucked covers while Joe lowers Talia onto her bed then pulls the covers over her and kisses her on her forehead. "I love you sweetie."

"I love you too Daddy," Talia says softly with a hint of a whimper. Joe then walks over to Calie's bed and gives her a kiss on the forehead. "Love you honey."

"Love you too," Calie responds softly.

"Sleep well girls. See you in the morning." Joe steps out of the room as he turns the light off in the bedroom. The light from the hallway illuminates the girl's faces as Joe watches them for a moment then walks down the hall.

"Calie," Talia says softly as to not alert her father.

"Yeah?" Calie responds as she rolls in her bed to look at her sister. The faint glow from the hallway nightlight affords them enough luminosity to see each other's faces.

"Do you think Dad will tell us about our mom?" Talia says with a smile.

"I don't know, but I hope so. I wonder what she looks like."

"I bet she's beautiful like a princess," Talia says as she closes her eyes.

"What's wrong Joe?" Dr. Marxx asks as Joe walks down the hallway slowly with something obviously on his mind. Joe invited Dr. Marxx over to hang out after the girls went to bed as he often does. He walks towards Dr. Marxx, who's sitting on the couch reading his favorite science fiction novel. The small shoebox drops onto the coffee table with a gentle thud before Joe sits down on the couch. Even more curious then before, Dr. Marxx closes the book and removes his reading glasses from his face.

"The girls were watching a mother and father in the park today while they were playing with their kids."

"Yeah."

"The girls asked me why they don't have a mother." Dr. Marxx closes his eyes and sighs.

"What did you tell them?"

"I didn't say anything. I skirted around the question and avoided it all together."

"That's probably the best thing for them Joe."

"Is it Steve? Because I'm having a hard time convincing myself of that. I have been thinking about this for a very long time and I don't think it's fair to the girls. They have a right to know that they have a mother. Don't they?"

"But then what Joe? How do you tell your six-year-old daughters that they have a mother and oh by the way she lives in Florida? Then what?"

"I don't know. All I know is that guilt is running through me because of this. The longer I keep this from them and the older they get, the angrier they'll be when they finally discover the truth."

"Joe, whatever you choose to do, I'll support your decision." Dr. Marxx picks up his book and glasses and goes back to reading after glancing at Joe one more time.

The top of the box is lifted off and Joe pulls out pictures of Kim and the girls. A 3x5 glossy color print emerges from the box. It's a picture of Kim and the girls making a sand castle on the beach. A big smile washes over his face as Dr. Marxx looks on.

CHAPTER 24

"Daddy," a soothing voice says into Joe's ear. Slowly waking from his peaceful and tranquil sleep, Joe partially opens his eyes to let some of the morning light in. He looks straight ahead at the window as the early morning sun shines through the tiny space between the shade and the window frame. As he turns his head to see Talia staring at him, he smiles.

"Hi sweetie. Are you OK?" Talia nods her head as she rubs her eyes. Joe looks at his open bedroom door and across the hall to Calie and Talia's room. "Is Calie still sleeping?" Talia nods again. "Come here and snuggle with Daddy." Talia's picked up by Joe as he places her down gently on the other side of him and holds her close. "How come you're up so early?"

"I had a dream," Talia says softly.

"What was your dream about?" Joe asks as he closes his eyes, enjoying the moment snuggled up with Talia and thinking about falling back asleep.

"We were playing at the park and a beautiful lady, who looked like a princess, was playing with us. Then she grabbed me and Calie and picked us up and hugged us."

Joe's eyes open wide as he looks down at Talia. She looks up at him with her big beautiful brown eyes suddenly brimming with a sadness he hadn't seen before.

"That's a great dream sweetie."

"Daddy, then she whispered in our ear and said, 'I'm your mommy.' She hugged and spun us around then put us down and walked away. As she walked away she turned around and said, 'I love you.' Then she disappeared."

"Wow. That sounds like an amazing dream," Joe says as he pulls Talia closer to him and hugs her tight.

"Daddy, I was so excited that I couldn't fall back asleep, but I was sad that the dream ended." As Joe takes a deep breath and looks down at Talia, he comes to terms with the fact that the subject of having a mother is here to stay. His beautiful love closes her eyes as she falls asleep in his arms.

"Pancakes are ready girls!" Joe shouts loud enough that the girls in their bedroom can hear him. Calie and Talia come running down the hallway towards the kitchen like a herd of starving elephants. As they jump into their seats and dig into their favorite Sunday morning breakfast, their dad looks at them and smiles as he sits down. He watches his daughters for a minute, completely enthralled by their pure innocence and beauty when suddenly guilt ravishes his mind as Joe's reminded of what he's deprived them of, the love of their mother. Both girls giggle and smile back at Joe.

"Girls, Daddy has something he needs to tell you." They stop chewing their food to listen. "I have been waiting for the right time to tell you this and I think it's time." The girls stare at their dad, waiting for him to talk. Joe opens the newspaper sitting on the table and pulls out a picture he stashed inside it. It's a picture of Joe and Kim at the beach together. The photo is placed on the table in front of Calie and Talia. "See this woman in the picture?" Joe sits lower in the chair and gets down to the girl's level as the girls gaze at the picture. "This is your mommy." The girls look at each other with confused but happy faces.

"This is our mommy?" Talia asks while her eyes are glued to the photograph while staring in awe. "But I thought we didn't have a mommy." Both girls look up at Joe. "Where is she? Can we see her?"

"When can we see her, Daddy?" Calie asks jubilantly. Joe was barraged with questions from his two excited and confused little girls. "She is so pretty," Calie says with a big smile. Relief and excitement come over Joe now that he's revealed the secret that's been avoided for six years. The girls hug each other then jump out of their chairs and run around the table. They grab Joe and give him a big hug. With tears filling up in his eyes, Joe thinks about all the questions he will soon get answers to. How will Kim react? Will she accept the girls? Will she hate him for what he's done? Could they actually be a family again?

"When can we meet her?" Talia asks.

"I think that we should go find your mommy soon."

"Find her," Talia says. "Don't you know where she is?"

"I know where she is, but she's far away so we should start planning our trip to see her now."

"Daddy, is Uncle Steve coming with us to see Mommy?" Talia asks. Joe pauses for a moment and looks at both girls.

"I don't think Uncle Steve will be coming with us. He has to stay here and work. This is where he lives." Sadness overcomes Talia. He drops his head a little to look into Talia's eyes. "Talia. Look at me honey." When she looks up at Joe the despair in Talia's eyes is evident. "What if I told you that we could visit Uncle Steve if you miss him?" She nods in approval and begins to smile. "OK, high-five." Joe puts his hand up in front of Talia and she slaps it. Calie comes over and slaps Joe's hand too. Joe gives Calie a smile. "Good, you both like the idea. Let's hurry up and finish breakfast so we can start planning the trip." The girls continue eating as Joe stares at both of them for a moment and savors in the idea of his family getting back together.

―――

Its early evening and Joe and the girls walk through the front door of Dr. Marxx's apartment.

"Hello everyone. How was your day?" Dr. Marxx asks.

"Hi Uncle Steve," Calie yells as she runs up the stairs.

"Hi Uncle Steve!" Talia also shouts as she follows Calie. Dr. Marxx stands up with his arms out waiting for a hug, but no hugs come his way. He turns to Joe with a funny disappointed look, then smiles and sits back down on the living room couch.

"They miss their old rooms," Joe says as he walks over to the couch where Dr. Marxx continues reading. "How was your day?" Dr. Marxx looks up at Joe and pauses momentarily as he grimaces. Joe looks up the stairs to make sure the girls didn't stop then sits down next to Steve. Dr. Marxx senses discomfort in Joe.

"My day was good. Thanks for asking. How was yours?" Dr. Marxx flips his reading glasses to the top of his head and sets his paperwork down on the coffee table as Joe looks down at his cell phone. "Joe, what's going on?"

"I'm taking the girls home. I've thought long and hard about this and I owe it to Talia and Calie to bring them home." Dr. Marxx sits motionless, starring at Joe. "Steve we can't stay in San Francisco forever. You have a life here. I have a life back home and the girls have a life waiting for them. They also have a mother who they have never met before." Dr. Marxx stands up and walks around the room slowly then stops. He closes his eyes and takes a moment while taking a deep breath.

"I knew this day would come. When you were talking about this yesterday, I knew it would lead to this. Although, I didn't see it materializing this quickly, but I did see it coming." Joe's hands are cupping his cheeks as he rubs his face slowly. "When are you thinking of leaving?"

"Next week." Dr. Marxx crunches his lips together and nods slightly.

"Do the girls know about Kim? Do they know they are leaving?"

"Yes. I told them about her this morning. They were very excited and still are, to say the least."

"Joe, I'm just concerned that I won't be able to monitor the girl's health."

"Steve the girls are fine! They are doing great and they are healthy. The cloning process was a success." Dr. Marxx turns away from Joe. "It was Steve. There is nothing more you can do for them."

"I hope your right Joe." He turns and faces Joe. "I hope your right." Dr. Marxx says as he turns and walks away. Joe sits motionless, watching Dr. Marxx.

CHAPTER 25

"Come on girls, we're going to miss our plane," Joe yells from the bottom of the stairs towards the open apartment door. The car is parked in front of the building as Joe and Dr. Marxx load the luggage.

"You have everything, right?" Dr. Marxx asks while he paces back and forth thinking of stuff Joe needs. "You have their birth certificates and their latest blood work results?"

"I got it Steve, I have everything they need. Talia and Calie, we have to go! What are they doing in there?" Joe asks. Dr. Marxx shrugs his shoulders then goes back to looking at the checklist.

"Do you have the plane tickets?" Joe stops and looks at Dr. Marxx.

"Yes, I have the tickets," Joe says mildly annoyed as he makes his way into the apartment through the front door. Joe walks down the hall to look for the girls since they haven't responded to him. "Girls, why aren't you..." As he turns the corner to the girl's bedroom he sees Calie and Talia sitting on the floor. Dolls are strewn all over the floor and the girls are crying. "Hey, hey, hey. Why are my girls crying?" Joe says as he sits on the floor between the girls and hugs them both.

"We don't want to leave," Talia says as they hug their dad tightly. Calie pulls away from Joe slightly and looks at him.

"Daddy what about all of our dolls and toys we still have here?" Calie says as she goes back to hugging Joe. Joe chuckles to himself with a smile as the girls continue to cry.

"Girls you're so cute. Uncle Steve will mail all your toys to us when we get settled in our new house." Joe begins rocking the girls slightly then stops. "Hey, look at me girls." Joe backs away as he nudges the girls forward and looks into their eyes. "I promise Uncle Steve will send your stuff to us, OK?" The girls slow their crying down to a whimper as Joe wipes the tears from their faces. "Why don't you each bring a doll and a stuffed animal with you for the ride?" Calie and Talia dash towards the corner of the bedroom where the toys are stacked and they each grab their favorite stuffed animal. "Are we all set?"

"I'm ready," Calie says as she runs back to Joe and picks up her back pack off the floor. Joe put his right hand in the air and Calie high-fives him.

"Me too," Talia says as she walks over to her dad with her head down. Joe lifts her chin up softly to look at her face. Joe smiles at Talia then looks at Calie. Joe takes the girl's hands and starts for the hallway.

"Looks like you guys are ready to go now," Dr. Marxx says at the bottom of the stairs while holding his checklist.

"We are good now. The girls want to make sure you will ship their toys to them." Dr. Marxx kneels on the floor in front of the girls.

"As soon as you get to your new home, call me, give me the new address and I will send your toys to you immediately. How does that sound?"

"OK," Talia says as Calie nods her head. Talia wraps her arms around Dr. Marxx as Calie joins in. Dr. Marxx gives both girls a kiss on the cheek then pulls away from the girls but stays on his knees.

"I love both of you very much and I will come visit you soon. OK?" Both girls nod in approval. Dr. Marxx stands up and looks at Joe. "You ready?"

"Yeah," Joe says as he picks up one of the bags and Dr. Marxx grabs the second. The group walks down the porch steps to the waiting car as Joe loads the last bag then sits Talia in a booster seat in the back seat. Calie straps herself in as she races with her dad to strap her sister in.

"Thank you for everything you did for me and my family," Joe says as they let go and back up from each other after embracing in a brotherly hug. "You are an amazing scientist Steve and I see big things for you in the future."

"Thanks Joe, I appreciate that. Make sure to send me your email address so we can keep in touch."

"I will." Joe turns to walk around the car then stops. "Oh I forgot something." Joe pulls out a small white envelope from his bag. "Here, this is for you." Joe extends the envelope out and Dr. Marxx takes it and starts to open it. "Wait, don't open it now. Wait until we are gone. It's just my way of thanking you and it's kind of emotional too."

"Oh, I get it."

"Take care of yourself, Steve."

"You too Joe." Joe gets into the driver's seat as Dr. Marxx waves to the girls in the back. As the car drives away, Joe honks the horn and Dr. Marxx waves one more time. He opens the envelope that Joe gave him and pulls out an index card with a note written on it;

Steve,
    I can't thank you enough for everything you have done over the past six years for me. I know we have talked about it before, but I feel compelled to tell you again. You gave me a reason to live again when you brought my girls back to me and for that I will forever be in your debt.

The past six years has been an incredible journey for me and the girls. None of it would have been possible if you weren't here to guide me and take care of the girls. My hope is that you can continue the incredible progress you have made in DNA research and that one day you may be able to touch another person's life like you did mine. Thank you again and take care.

                                Your Friend Always

                                    Joe Walker

Dr. Marxx looks up in the direction Joe drove off in then smiles and begins the short walk to his apartment.

CHAPTER 26

"Daddy, whose house is this?" Calie asks. The large brown ranch style house with a small front porch has an expansive yard with big magnolia trees all around the property. Joe stops in front of the two car garage as Calie and Talia look intently out the back window at the unfamiliar house.

"There is someone I want you to meet, but I want you to stay in the car until I tell you to come out?"

"OK!" Both girls reply. Slowly, Joe walks up to the front door while looking around the property. Unsure of what awaits him when he makes contact with someone at the house, he apprehensively knocks on the door. A few moments later a tall female with long brown hair answers the door.

"Joey?" Sarah says in shock at the appearance of her brother on her front porch.

"Hi Sarah," he replies with a big smile.

"My little brother is home!" She screams and grabs Joe, pulling him to her and squeezing tight. "Oh my God, I was so worried about you all these years. I got a few postcards from you and that was it."

"I know, I'm sorry. It's been a crazy six years. I promise to keep in touch with you now that I'm back home."

"Your back?"

"Yeah, I'm home." Sarah grabs her brother again and gives him another tight hug. "It's great to see you again and be home too." Joe looks over at the car, nervously as Sarah glances in the same direction.

"What's going on Joe?"

"Hey can we talk for a few minutes?" Joe asks.

"Sure," she says.

"Can we sit out here on the porch?"

"Sure!" The wooden bench swing on the porch that Joe and Sarah sit on gets used more frequently in the cooler Florida evenings.

"I've really missed you," Joe said as he moves the swing back and forth slowly.

"I missed you too, Joe."

"Have you seen Kim yet?"

"No, not yet. I wanted to stop and see you first. Have you seen her?" The girls are anxiously awaiting a sign from their father as they stare out the window at Joe and the strange woman.

"I saw her a lot after you left, but we haven't been in touch on a regular basis for the past few years."

"How's she been?" Joe asks.

"She was a mess for a long time after you left. She went through periods of anger then depression and isolation. I think losing the girls and you at the same time really did a number on her mentally." Sarah gazes at her younger brother as her eyebrows lower and she looks distressed. "Joey she called me about six months after you left and told me she was going to kill herself. I went to the house and found her on the bedroom floor. There were pills all over the place. She actually tried to take her life." Joe looks down to the floor and sighs as his sister watches a tear trail down his cheek. Joe wipes his face quickly and sniffles. "I was able to get over there before it was too late and we got her some help. She was in a really bad place back then."

"I shouldn't have left her like that."

"You just went through a very traumatic event, Joe. People handle things like that in different ways." Sarah glances toward the car after seeing movement inside. "You should go see her. She isn't seeing anyone if you're thinking about that." Sarah winces as she tries to see long distance toward Joe's car. "Is there someone in your car? I just saw someone moving in the backseat." He grabs his sister's hand quickly and holds it.

"Sarah. I did something while I was gone that a lot of people may not be happy about including you."

"What is it? She looks at Joe with concern as he doesn't reply. "Joey?"

"Come with me." Joe holds on to Sarah's hand and they start walking off the porch. "This is going to be hard for you to comprehend." Although she's Joe's older sister and practically raised him when their mother became sick, she's confused by her brother's sudden arrival in town and now his strange behavior. Joe stops in the middle of the front yard and motions for the girls to come out. Sarah is now looking at the car in the driveway and watches the back door open. Sarah sees two girls with long blonde hair get out of the car and walk towards her and Joe. The smile and jubilance disappears as her expression turns to shock and disbelief.

"Oh my God Joe!" Calie and Talia get closer to Sarah and Joe as Sarah realizes what she's seeing. As she crouches down, she grabs both girls and gives them a hug. Unable to accept what she sees, Sarah pulls away and looks at both girls as she cries. "Talia, Calie?" Sarah says. Her face filled with excitement, concern and confusion all at the same time as she looks at Joe with bewilderment. "Joey! It can't be!" Shocked and confused, Sarah desperately tries to understand what she's seeing and feeling.

"Girls, I want you to meet your Aunt Sarah. This is Daddy's sister."

"Hi," both girls say. "Daddy told us all about you," Calie said with a smile.

"You don't know me?" Sarah asks. Calie and Talia are nervous and slowly creep towards their father and take his hands.

"Why are you crying?" Talia asks as Sarah's amazement and disbelief transforms into tears of joy.

"I'm just so happy to see you girls." She says while touching their faces and running her fingers through their hair. Sarah looks at her little brother, her eyes full of questions. Joe nods, confirming what she's feeling and seeing. He knows he has a lot to explain.

"Sarah, do you still have the swings?" Sarah confirms with a nod.

"Girls, why don't you go play on the swing set in the backyard for a few minutes while I talk with Aunt Sarah."

"I'll race you Talia," Calie says as she takes off running.

"Hey no fair wait for me," Talia yells. Joe and Sarah walk around the side of the house and keep an eye on the girls playing on the swings. Joe looks at the sister that raised him after their mom died, apprehensively, trying to decide how to begin and how she's going to react.

"Joe, how is this possible, I feel like I'm in a dream and I'm going to wake up any minute."

Joe chuckles with excitement. "It's not a dream, Sis. It's all real. That's Talia and Calie, your nieces."

"Joe. Calie and Talia died seven years ago. I don't understand," Sarah says as she stops walking and stares at her brother.

"I told you I did something. I did something that a lot of people, once they find out about it, are not going to be happy with. You have always been like a mother to me. When Mom died, you took care of me when I couldn't take care of myself. It's important that you're not disappointed in me."

"I'm your sister Joe. I will love you forever, no matter how bad it is." She points towards the girls on the swing. "And by the looks of this, it's bad. So tell me how seven years after my nieces died, they are here playing on my swing set."

"I went to San Francisco and met a scientist that has been doing research for the past twenty years on human cell manipulation. I convinced this scientist to clone Calie and Talia." Sarah stops walking again.

"Are you telling me that the two girls on the swings are clones of Talia and Calie? Clones of the same Calie and Talia that died seven years ago?"

"They are identical, beside slightly different personalities, they are the same girls."

"I'm...... speechless. Is that even legal? I've heard of people cloning their pets, but not their kids."

"I'm not sure if it's legal or not to be honest with you, but look at them. I have my girls back and you have your nieces back….."

"And Kim has her daughters back," Sarah cuts Joe off.

"Yeah, Kim has her daughters back. That's the plan anyway," Joe replies not taking his eyes off the girls.

"Joe, I'm not sure this was a good idea."

"What do you mean?"

"It took Kim more than two years to accept the fact that the girls were gone and never coming back, and now their back. How are you going to tell her this?"

"I don't know. I haven't run that conversation through my head yet."

"I love you Joe, but I would think long and hard before you tell her. She's not going to be happy, that's for sure." They stand in silence for a moment.

"Where are you staying?" Sarah asks.

"We just got into town last night and we stayed at a hotel near the airport."

"Well you guys are staying with us for however long you need. Marc will be thrilled to have another guy here with him for a while." Joe grabs his sister, gives her a hug and kisses the side of her head.

"Thanks, Sis." Calie runs over and takes Sarah's hand.

"Aunty Sarah, will you push us on the swings?" Sarah looks at Joe and smiles.

"I would love to Calie." She runs back towards the swings pulling her new favorite aunt by the hand as Sarah turns towards Joe. "It's a good thing we didn't get rid of the swing set," she says as Joe nods with a smile. Happiness shifts to worry as his thoughts turn to Kim and how he will explain this to her.

It's early evening and Marc Landry pulls into the driveway and parks next to the Joe's black four door rental car. His wife opens the door and walks out to greet Marc in the driveway. Marc is an averaged size man with short curly dark brown hair.

"Hi. How was work?"

"It was a really good day today," he says pointing to Joe's car. "Whose car is this?"

"There is something I need to tell you and when I show you who is inside, you may freak out a little."

"Don't tell me your old boyfriend showed up at our house? I told you to stop e-mailing him," Marc smirks.

"No! Marc, it's not Jason Carpenter." The front door opens and Joe walks out onto the front porch.

"Holy shit! Joe Walker?" Joe walks down the front porch steps and meets his brother in-law in the driveway.

"Hi Marc."

"I could have sworn you were dead." Joe extends his hand out and shakes Marc's hand.

"No, I'm alive and well and back home."

"No shit? That's good to hear, bud."

"Joe just got back in town yesterday and I told him that he could stay here until he gets on his feet and figures out where he's going to stay. I hope that's OK," Sarah asks.

"Sure. It'll be fun. Let's go have a beer and celebrate. I want to hear all about your travels." Sarah looks at Joe quickly then back to Marc. "What?" Marc asks.

"There is one more thing we have to tell you before you go into the house."

"Oh my God, what is it?" Marc looks back and forth between his wife and her brother. She takes a deep breath and lets it out.

"Well, while Joe was away he cloned Talia and Calie and they are alive again and inside our house." Sarah blurts out quickly.

"Quit screwing around. Let's go have a beer already." Marc grabs Joe and gives him a big side squeeze as they walk towards the house. "Good to have you back home bro." The three of them start walking towards the front door of the house. Marc is leading the group as Joe and his sister follow behind as a look of concern is shared between them.

Marc walks into the living room where Talia and Calie are sitting on the floor looking at one of Sarah's animal books. Immediately he sees the girls sitting on the floor but can't see their faces yet as he stops abruptly and turns back to Joe and Sarah. "What's going on here?"

"Marc, I want you to meet your nieces, Talia and Calie." The girls turn around and see everyone that just walked in the room. Marc stands in shock of what he is seeing before him. His work bag falls to the ground with a thud as he slowly walks over to the girls and crouches down on the floor in front of them.

"Hi," Marc says barely louder than a whisper. Stunned and unable to speak, he sits for a moment then looks up at Joe and his wife. "Wow, this is incredible." Calie and Talia look at their uncle.

"I'm Calie and this is my sister Talia. What's incredible?" Calie asks.

"It's great to meet you girls," he stammers. "What's incredible is that you two are sitting in my living room, talking to me right now." Marc can't help but stare and eventually stands up and walks back over to Joe and Sarah. "OK, these girls look very much like your daughters, but they are not Calie and Talia. Right?" Marc asks quietly.

"Marc, come on, let's sit and have that beer and we'll talk all about it. Girls. Daddy, Aunt Sarah and Uncle Marc will be in the kitchen talking."

"OK Daddy," Talia responds. They walk towards the kitchen as Marc looks back at the girls sitting on the floor one more time. Over a few beers, Joe tells Marc and Sarah everything that's happened since the girls died seven years ago.

CHAPTER 27

"I love you girls." Joe says before giving them both a kiss on the forehead. They have their favorite stuffed animals wrapped in their arms while getting ready to fall asleep in one of Sarah's two spare bedrooms. Joe closes the door halfway as he exits the room and makes his way down the main hallway into the large family room to rejoin Marc and his sister.

"Joe do you want another beer?" Sarah asks from the kitchen while putting together some snacks for everyone.

"Sure. Thanks." The large beanbag chair on the floor makes a comfortable spot to crash for Joe as he looks at Marc sitting on the couch. The three bottles of beer clang together as Sarah sets them down on the coffee table and sits next to Marc.

"Dude, I never thought anything like this was ever possible. I can't believe that you actually cloned your daughters."

"Marc, there are days that I look at Calie and Talia and I still can't believe it myself," Joe replies as he shakes his head slowly.

"I get the love you have for your daughters, but did you think about this thoroughly before you decided to do it? I'm sitting here thinking about one explanation after another that you will need to come up with when various situations arise," Marc explains.

"Like what?" Joe asks as Sarah follows along and stares at Joe.

"How about school. How are you going to enroll the same girls in the same school they went to seven years ago with the same teachers? How about all the people you know around town and all of your friends that knew Calie and Talia before they died. Oh my God Joe! All these situations are popping up in my head. I haven't even thought about Kim yet and how she's going to react to this." Marc stares at Joe. "Do the girls know that they are cloned from girls that died seven years ago?" Joe sits motionless looking at Marc then dropping his eyes towards the floor.

"Of course not, Marc," Joe says with an annoyed tone to his voice.

"Joe, this is what I'm talking……."

"I haven't thought about any of these things yet, Marc," Joe says cutting him off, clearly aggravated with the line of questions. Joe stands up and begins pacing back and forth in front of Marc and Sarah. "I guess I will deal with those situations as they come up. All I know is that my life feels right again. I have my girls back with me and you're both right. I have to see Kim at some point and somehow explain to her that her daughters are alive. I have to explain to her where I've been and why I left. But I think at the end of all the explanations and yelling and crying, she will be happy to see her daughters again. Who wouldn't be?" Joe asks, looking at Marc and Sarah with a halfhearted smile. "Am I right?" Marc looks at Sarah for guidance on answering the question.

"When the time comes for you to confront Kim, I think it will be a very emotional and stressful time and I'm just not sure how she will handle it," Sarah responds.

"Are you guys still married?" Marc asks while looking at Sarah. She shrugs her shoulders at Marc as they both turn to Joe for an answer.

"I think so. I don't know if she ever filed for divorce, but I didn't. Do you know?" Joe asks as he looks at his sister.

"I don't think she has. She never said anything to me. Joe, can I ask you a personal question?" Sarah asks.

"Of course you can."

"Do you miss Calie and Talia? Because, I can't stop thinking about them," she says as her eyes pool to their breaking point and flow with emotion down her cheeks. "It makes me cry every time I think about them and what they went through that night." The wedding ring on Joe's finger spins around and around as Joe nervously plays with it while Sarah dries her face.

"Honestly. When Calie and Talia were born again, I stopped missing them and now it's almost as if they never died." She looks at Joe in disbelief as that was not the answer she was expecting. "I miss Kim. I get sick thinking about the time we've missed as a family, but I don't miss my girls anymore because I have them back."

"There is something very disheartening and sick about that Joe," his sister says as she wipes the remaining tears from her face.

"I'm going to see Kim tomorrow," Joe says.

"Are you sure you're ready for that?" Marc replies.

"I'm not sure I'd ever be ready for something like that, but I owe her the truth. Anyway she decides to handle this, good or bad, she still has the right to know."

"Do you want me and Marc to go with you tomorrow, just in case it goes bad?"

"Thanks, but this is something we have to do ourselves. After everything is said and done, they are and always will be her daughters. What's done is done and I don't regret any of it." A big sip of beer flows into Joe's mouth as he again looks down at his ring.

"Joe, have you thought about what you're going to do if she rejects you and the girls?" Sarah asks. He looks up as his eyes water slightly.

"I hope that doesn't happen, but if it does and that's her decision, I'll accept it and we'll stay out of her life. We would probably have to move away from here."

"Let's not start talking crazy! You just came back into my life. I'm not losing you guys again," Sarah replies. Marc yawns as Joe and Sarah continue their conversation.

"It's getting late guys. I'm hitting the sack. Some of us have to work around here." Throwing the parting shot at Joe as he walks into the kitchen.

"Yeah, yeah," Joe replies as he stands up and gives his sister a hug and a reassuring smile.

"I'm glad you're home Joe," she remarks with a little giggle.

"Thanks for letting us crash here until we figure out what we're going to do. I knew I could count on my big sister."

"Stay as long as you want. The longer the better." Joe gives Sarah another hug before she turns and walks up the stairs.

"Goodnight. See you in the morning, Sis."

CHAPTER 28

"Daddy, are you OK?" Calie asks as Joe lifts his right hand up in front of his face, watching it shake uncontrollably. His nerves are starting to get the better of him and there's no reprieve in sight. While the girls watch his mannerisms through the rear view mirror, he tries to pull himself together.

"Maybe we will just move away and start over. That would be easy enough to do," he thinks to himself. Now he glances down and sees that his leg is bouncing up and down. "Calm down Joe. Get your shit together," he says silently.

"Girls are you OK back there?"

"Yes, we're fine, Daddy. Where are we going?" Talia asks.

"Girls, I have decided that it's time for you to meet your mother." Talia and Calie look at each other with an excited look and start screaming in the backseat. The girls are hugging each other as the excitement of the moment takes over.

"Daddy, do you think Mommy is going to be happy to see us?" Talia asks.

"I think she will be thrilled to see her little girls again."

"Again," Calie says.

"Sorry honey, I mean she will be excited to meet you." Joe turns onto Williams Street and pulls into the driveway of the large white colonial house. He is astonished at the pristine condition of the house as he turns the car off. Maybe he was thinking that because he was gone, everything would have gone to hell. "Calm down Joe," he says quietly while looking in the mirror at the girls then out the window at the familiar surroundings. He gives the girls another quick glance then turns his attention back to his old house. "Girls you stay in the car for a few minutes."

His blood pressure skyrockets as he leaves the safety and confines of his car. The veins in his neck are fluttering and his heart beats through his chest as he walks up to the front door and stops. As he changes his mind at the last second, he starts walking down the stairs in hopes that he can get away before Kim sees him. The fear of rejection has gotten the better of him. He stops at the bottom of the stairs and stands motionless as he hears the front door open and footsteps on the wooden porch.

"Hello. Are you looking for someone?" A familiar female voice says. Joe closes his eyes momentarily then turns towards Kim's voice. So many emotions are going through his head at this very instant. The vision of Joe freezes Kim as she stands motionless starring at him with her eyes open wide. No one says anything for a few moments.

"Hi," Joe initiates with a slight smile. Kim shows no emotion as she takes a deep breath holds it in with her mouth open, and then slowly lets it out. She is in shock at the sight of her husband who vanished over seven years ago with only a note. "It's great to see you Kim, you look really good." She looks down at the porch then back at Joe as he steps to the top of the porch.

"I didn't think I would ever see you again," she says without emotion.

"I'm sorry Kim. I didn't think I would come back either."

"Then why did you?" she asks with a cross tone.

"Things changed for me. I needed to come back home and see you, and tell you that I was sorry for all the pain that…"

"Pain, Joe! Pain! You want to talk about what you did to me now after seven years. You don't deserve to know anything about my pain," she says highly agitated.

"Kim, I was hurting too. I was in agony every single day after the girls died. I carried anger, resentment, and loneliness around with me to the point that I couldn't function properly." She turns her head to the side to show her disdain for Joe's plight. "When that was too much to bear, I turned to alcohol to ease the pain. At that point, I felt as if the only thing I could do was run away from it all." Kim steps up to Joe and gets into his face while her eyes water as if they were hooked up to a garden hose. She makes no attempt to wipe her tears in front of him.

"And run away from the only other person that needed you more than any other time in my life!" she yells angrily in his face as he stands firm and maintains eye contact. He can't turn away or back up from her. She deserves to yell in his face. He owes it to her to allow her pain and fury to erupt all over him. She backs up a few steps and calms down while looking at Joe then wipes her cheeks with her hand. "I don't give a fuck about your pain anymore, Joe! I was your wife and I loved you more than anything and I needed you!" Anger fills her as her face flushes with red. "Even though I wasn't emotionally wrecked like you were, I still needed you to comfort me and tell me everything was going to be OK." Now Joe and Kim both have tears streaming down their cheeks as she calms slightly. "I thought we were going to cry together, heal together and ultimately be together." Calie and Talia are looking out the window at their father and the woman on the front porch.

"Do you think that's our mom?" Calie asks with excitement.

"It has to be. It looks like the lady in the picture that Daddy showed us," Talia said. Calie reaches for the car door handle and pulls on it slightly. "What are you doing Calie? Talia asks.

"I want to see our mom."

"Get the fuck out of here Joe and don't ever come back again you piece of sh…!" Kim says angrily but stops suddenly as she turns her attention to the car door that just opened and the familiar little girl that stepped out of the car. With the sound of the car door opening, Joe closes his eyes and realizes that there's no turning back now. The girls step out of the car as Kim watches from the porch. Time stands still as Joe witnesses the instant change in Kim's facial expression at the sight of her daughters. This is a make or break moment for Joe and Kim. It could represent a fresh start for the family or this could be a relapse of heartache, torture, and grief for Kim.

Fixated on the two little girls walking towards her, Kim steps off the porch towards them. With Joe following close behind, he sees the happiness in his daughter's eyes at the up close view of their mother. Not sure if she's dreaming or not, Kim continues towards the girls she knows are her daughters. Like any other loving mother that lost her daughters, Kim has never forgotten their faces. She looks back and makes eye contact with Joe as she begins to cry and sob. As she gets down on her knees in front of her daughters, tears pour from her bloodshot swollen eyes. She silently prays and begs for this dream not to end.

"Mommy?" Calie says with an uncertain tone as Kim opens her arms to greet her children. She has a vision from before the girls died as euphoria takes hold of her as she closes her eyes briefly. Believing that she's dreaming, she smiles and takes in the moment, hoping that it doesn't end as exhilaration engulfs her body.

"Are you our Mommy? Calie asks softly. Unexpectedly, Kim snaps out of her fantasy as her eyes blast open hastily. The girls stop two feet in front of her. She kneels motionless as Calie and Talia both stare at the person they believe to be their mother. Kim's lungs are in overdrive as she attempts to catch her breath. Desperately she tries to gather herself as her chin twitches violently while staring at her children.

"Calie?" she says sobbing then looks at Talia. "Talia?"

"Daddy said you are our mommy," Talia says as she breaks down and gives into her emotions with a lone tear. Joe stands behind Kim, trying to fight back his own feelings. She again glances at Joe with uncertainty, looking for some sort of sign that this is real, then back at the girls.

Kim reaches out to touch Talia's face. As her fingers get closer and closer, she cries and sobs even more. The simple touch of her daughter's skin is all that is needed to assure Kim that the girls standing before her are real. Talia is unsure of what is happening and looks at Joe.

"It's OK," Joe says softly as he nods his head slightly to reassure Talia. Kim's fingertips touch Talia's left cheek and Kim smiles slightly then the smile turns to a frown. She looks down to the ground and covers her face with her hands and begins shaking her head violently.

"No, No, No! What is this?" Kim screams into her hands. With an enraged look about her, she jumps to her feet and invades Joe's personal space as she is nose to nose with him. "Why are you doing this to me? How's this possible?" Kim begins pounding on Joe's chest with both arms as Joe grabs her by the shoulders. Quickly but forcefully, he shakes her to snap her out of her incensed state of hysteria then stares into her eyes.

Joe cries with Kim. "Hey, it's Calie and Talia! It's your daughters Kim, they are home."

"No! It's not possible. Why are you torturing me?" Kim is emotionally drained as she rests her head on Joe's chest while her arms fall to her side. Joe pulls her close to him and holds her tight. Just as she's about to succumb to the moment, she pushes herself away from Joe.

"No! This is nothing more than a nightmare!" Calie and Talia are crying and don't know what to make of what their seeing. Only twenty minutes ago, Calie and Talia were about to start a new chapter in their life. The person they had longed for since seeing the happy family in the park back in San Francisco didn't exist.

"Daddy, I want to go, please! Please Daddy!" Calie says while slowly backing up with her sister towards the car.

"Yes go! Get out of here all of you and don't come back." The anger running through her blood allows her to grasp reality and makes her stronger, if only for a few moments. She wipes her face with her hands as she turns and walks towards the house with a purpose. Standing motionless with his back to Kim, Joe looks to the girls for strength then turns towards Kim.

"Kim please," he begs, pleading with her to stop and listen as the front door slams with a thunderous bang. Joe can't believe what just happened as he wipes the tears from his face. Calie and Talia run to their father and embrace him in an emotional hug as they all cry together. With her back against the door Kim cries hysterically as she slowly slides down the door. Her cries stop her breathing for what feels like an eternity as she wails in agony.

"Why is this happening?" Kim yells to herself. Joe gets the girls back in the car as he looks at the house for the last time. He drives down the driveway and out of Kim's life for good.

"Daddy, she doesn't want us." Calie cries as Joe reaches to the backseat and comforts the girls by taking their hands in his. "Daddy, I want to go back home to San Francisco," Talia cries.

"Me too, sweetie. We will start packing tonight."

Kim stands up and looks out the small front door window. She continues to wail out loud as she tries to catch her breath while staring out the window. The front door is thrust open as she runs onto the porch and into the front yard in hopes of seeing the girls again. Kim is a woman possessed. Consumed with anxiety and fury only moments ago, happiness and love has suddenly engulfed her crazed lonely soul. The front yard and driveway are quiet and void of life with only the sounds of passing cars from the road to fill the humid air. With every calming breath she takes, she comes to the realization that what she just experienced was real.

"How is this possible?" she asks herself softly as she shakes her head slowly and walks back through the front door. Kim looks over to the fireplace mantle and gently picks up the glass framed picture of Calie and Talia. Mesmerized by the photo, she touches the girl's faces with her fingers and smiles.

A few minutes later, Joe pulls into Sarah's driveway and turns the car off. He bangs his head backwards off the headrest a few times then sits motionless. His eyes are bloodshot and overflowing with sadness. As the front door opens and Sarah walks out onto the porch, she stares at him. It's all too obvious that it didn't go as planned as Joe looks at her shaking his head. She meets her brother in the driveway and wraps her arms around him.

"I'm sorry Joe."

"I don't get it. Her daughters were right in front of her and she wanted nothing to do with them. She completely freaked out." Heartbreak for Kim fills Sarah's every being. She knows what Kim went through and now fears that she could break down again.

"How bad was she? Do you think she'll be OK?"

"I'm not sure. She didn't take it very well." Shock takes hold of Sarah as she covers her mouth at the news.

"Joey, Sarah wasn't ready for something like this. She moved on. She was at peace with the fact that her daughters were gone and never coming back," Sarah says low enough so the girls can't hear her as she watches the car door opening. Calie and Talia exit the car and walk towards Sarah and Joe. Joe picks up Calie and holds her tight as Sarah picks up Talia and gives her a kiss on the cheek. Talia holds her aunt tight as Sarah rubs her back.

"I was stupid to think that she would have embraced this idea. She hates me more now than she did when I left town. We're going back to San Francisco." Joe and Sarah walk slowly towards the house holding the girls. "I'm sorry to put you through this Sarah."

"Come on Joe. You didn't put me through anything. I'm your sister and we're family. I'm glad you came back home and I'm glad I had a chance to see Calie and Talia again. I'm not really sure what you should do at this point though." Joe nods his head while lost in thought. "Why don't you guys come in and relax. Think about it for the next couple of days and if you want to go back to San Francisco after that, then that's what you should do." Joe looks at his sister and smiles.

"Thanks, Sis!"

The doorbell rings two times. The front door opens as Kim looks out the screen door and breaks down crying. As the door opens, she walks out onto the porch and into the waiting arms of Sarah. An emotional mess beyond comprehension, Kim breaks down, crying hysterically.

"Oh my God Kim. It's OK, I'm here." Kim cries wildly while holding Sarah with no end in sight to her sudden collapse of serenity. This is the reaction that Sarah was afraid of. "Come on, let's go inside." Cradling Kim like a crying child that just fell off her bike, she walks her into the house. They sit down together on the couch and hold each other for a few more moments.

"Is this really happening? Please tell me I just had a terrible dream. Please Sarah." Sarah giggles quickly then stops.

"I wish I could tell you this was all just a bad dream, but I can't. We will get through this together. Believe me I was just as shocked as you are." Sarah stares at Kim with a reassuring smile and wipes a tear from Kim's face as her crying slowly calms. "Are you OK?"

"I think so. Thank you so much for coming over. I really needed someone to be with me after that." Kim gives Sarah a half-hearted smile. "Is that really Calie and Talia?"

"It really is Calie and Talia," Sarah says with a quick happy snicker.

"Oh my God," Kim giggles back with a smile.

"How? How could this be? Calie and Talia died seven years ago and if they didn't die and that was all an elaborate hoax then they would be much older than they are now. So what's going on?"

"If you have a few minutes, I will tell you what I know." Kim nods. "It's a crazy story so prepare yourself."

CHAPTER 29

Kim is driving down the road and looking in the rear view mirror at Calie and Talia in the back seat. Horns blare as the box truck slams into the front of Kim's car with a hideous bang. Darkness is everywhere. Suspended upside down, Kim opens her eyes to see Calie and Talia in her rear view mirror still strapped in their car seats. The white dresses they are wearing to the dance are saturated with blood. As she reaches for the motionless girls with every bit of strength she has, both girls open their eyes and scream. Kim jumps up in bed from her nightmare covered in sweat. Her rapid breathing scares her as she begins crying. "Oh God!" she says as she lies back down and rolls over to her side. "Not again God, please!"

Kim used to have nightmares every night for the first few years after the girls died. She would relive that horrific night in her mind over and over again. These nightmares contributed to Kim's depression and her desire to end her life and now, the nightmares are back. Its 5 a.m. the day after Kim saw her girls again. She hasn't had more than two hours of sleep the whole night. Since Joe and the girls showed up at her door, she hasn't been able to get them out of her head.

Kim sits up in bed again and turns on her bedside light. She takes a deep breath and holds it for a moment before letting it out. As she sits on the side of her bed, a vision of her daughters standing in front of her plays over and over again in her head as she gets up and walks to the bathroom. The blinding bathroom light shines in her eyes as she looks at herself in the mirror. Kim shakes her head to clear the images then looks at herself in the mirror again before turning the light off.

At the end of the second floor hallway, the door to Calie's room opens as the early morning darkness is shattered by the light on the ceiling. Standing in the doorway looking into the pink and sky blue room, Kim smiles as she remembers playing dolls with her oldest daughter. The room is clean, but everything is as it was when Calie died. Kim takes a few steps into the bedroom and sits down on Calie's bed slowly. The girl's bedroom doors have remained closed from the time they died until today.

She reaches for one of Calie's favorite stuffed animals, that is resting against the pillow. The small brown puppy was Calie's favorite animal and every night she would curl up with it before falling asleep. As Kim picks up the puppy and holds it close to her face, she closes her eyes and gives the puppy a long sniff. A smile lights up her face as she holds the puppy for a moment. "I can still smell you," Kim whispered softly to herself then gently sets the puppy back on the pillow.

The door to Calie's room closes slowly as Kim reaches in and flicks the light switch off, returning the room to darkness. Talia's door opens slowly and quietly as if she was sleeping and Kim was trying not to wake her. The light illuminates the bright yellow room with a light orange chair rail halfway down the wall. Talia's room is also clean and in the same condition it was in when she left for the dance. Kim enters the bedroom and walks slowly across the room and stops in front of Talia's dresser. A black framed picture sits on top of the dresser with the word "Family" inscribed in white letters on the bottom of the wood frame. In the picture, Joe and Kim are on all fours next to each other in the grass and Talia is sitting on Joe's back and Calie is sitting on Kim's back. The girls have their arms around each other in the photo and everyone is smiling. She touches the glass with her fingers where Talia and Calie's faces are pictured and smiles. She can still remember the day that picture was taken at the local garden club, one year before the girls died.

The light goes on at the bottom of the stairs in the foyer as Kim slowly descends the natural wood staircase with white railings. She stops at the bottom of the stairs to look at the family pictures on the wall. Seeing Joe and the girls yesterday has brought back all of Kim's memories and emotions. For the past seven years, she has buried her memories in the back of her mind just to relieve herself of the nightmares.

"Calie and Talia, get Daddy!" Kim shouts in the background. A family beach vacation video plays on the television while Kim sits on the couch watching intently. The video was recorded in Key West, two months before the accident. Calie and Talia chase Joe into the ocean and splash him while Kim recorded the action. Kim laughs and cries at the same time while the home movie plays. Kim lies down on the couch while the movie continues as she slowly falls asleep to the sound of her family's voices.

CHAPTER 30

"Aunty Sarah these are the best pancakes I ever had," Talia says. Joe and the girls are sitting at the kitchen table eating breakfast as Sarah stands at the stove, drinking her coffee and watching everyone.

"Thanks Talia. I'm glad you like them."

"Thanks Sis," her brother says with a smile.

"I'm more than happy to make pancakes for my nieces and little broth….." Sarah is cut off by Marc yelling down the stairs.

"Sarah, there's someone coming down the driveway!"

"OK, I'll see who it is." As she walks down the hall and opens the front door, she is shocked at what she sees.

"Joey!" The strain in his sister's voice gets Joe's attention as he meets her at the front door. After opening the front door, he steps out onto the porch with Sarah. Kim gets out of her car and hesitantly walks towards the house. "Joey," Sarah whispers to get him to stop. The emotional trauma Kim sustained the day before makes her a little unpredictable right now and Sarah has a real concern for her brother.

"It's OK," Joe says glancing back at his sister as he continues walking towards Kim. They create a distance of about eight feet between one another as they stop along the side of the driveway.

"Hi," Joe says softly.

"I'm not sure what…." Kim stops and wipes the single tear rolling down her cheek as Joe's face droops slightly at the sight of her despair.

"I'm not sure what I am supposed to say to you or what I should do right now. So many voices in my head tell me to run and stay away from you, but the problem is that somehow you brought our daughters back to me, and I can't run from them. Every day for a year, I would stand by the door waiting for you to come home, but you never did. I was afraid to leave the house because I thought I would miss your phone call, telling me you were OK, or that you loved me and you were coming home, but you never called. I hated you for leaving me, but I loved you so much that I couldn't forget you or the thought of you holding me again. That idea stayed with me for a whole year until one day I stopped looking out the front door and stopped thinking about you needing me."

He stands frozen as he listens to his wife. She has earned the right to tell him what she's feeling and Joe knows enough to allow her that time.

"Joe, I don't know what or how this happ…." Kim stops as the front door opens and Talia and Calie step out onto the porch. Joe turns and sees the girls on the porch and smiles to them.

Sarah crouches down behind Calie and Talia and gives them a hug. The girls want so much to run to their mother and be a part of her life, but they remember what happened yesterday and how scared they were. Kim smiles at her girls as Calie and Talia look at her then look at Sarah.

"It's OK girls. Go see your Mom." Calie and Talia don't move. "Go ahead," Sarah says as she nudges them forward softly until they start walking down the stairs. Joe walks over to the girls and takes both of their hands as they walk together towards Kim.

"Girls, Mommy wants to say hi," Joe tells them as they look up at him then look at Kim. As the girls slowly step towards Kim, their father lets go. Taking a few steps forward slowly, Kim kneels down in the grass. Round salty drops of water stream down her cheeks as she wipes them from her face quickly. Calie stops walking as does Joe, but Talia, who was always the brave one of the two girls, continues towards her mother.

"Hi Talia," she says while crying and giggling slightly at the same time.

"Hi," Talia says softly back to Kim. "Are you our mommy?" With a smile on her face, Kim giggles while wiping her tears from her now soaked cheeks. Tears have also taken over Joe's face as he attempts to catch them before they fall. With an encouraging nod from Joe, Kim's reassured that she can confirm to the girls that she is their mother. Kim's eyes return back to Talia who is about two feet from her.

"I am your mommy." Talia smiles as she steps forward and wraps her arms around Kim tightly. A boisterous and uninhabited cry comes from Kim as her daughter's hug pierces her every being. With her eyes closed, taking in the moment, Kim breaks down and lets the loneliness of the last seven years out in one heart wrenching burst. Joe turns his body away from Kim and the girls as his emotions take him to a place he hasn't seen since the girls died. Joe glances at his sister as she walks over to him in complete emotional euphoria, laughing and crying at the same time. Joe and Sarah embrace and confirm that everything immoral and unethical Joe did up to this point would be forgiven by everyone who questioned him. With Kim and Talia still clinched, refusing to let go of each other, Calie steps forward to meet her mom.

"Mommy," Calie says softly.

"Hi Calie," Kim says as she opens her arms inviting Calie in for the group hug with Talia. Kim hugs the girls and kisses their cheeks. "Let me look at you both," she says as the girls take a step backwards. Talia is standing on the left of Kim and Calie is on her right. Her left hand caresses the cheek of Talia as her right hand caresses Calie's cheek. "You girls are so beautiful. I have missed you both so much. How old are you now?"

"We are six." Kim begins to cry again slightly while trying to keep herself together. She looks up at Joe then back to the girls and wipes under her eyes before the tears fall.

"Well, we have a lot to talk about, don't we? Where do we start?" Sarah shuffles over and joins the reunion.

"Hi Kim," she says as she kneels and hugs Kim tightly, which makes Kim sob and laugh simultaneously.

"Hi Sarah, I'm sorry I can't stop crying."

"How are you doing with all of this?" Sarah says after pulling away from Kim and looking in her eyes while holding her arms.

"I feel like this is a dream and I'm going to wake up any second and I don't want to wake up."

"Kim, this is real. Calie and Talia are right here with us." Kim crouches down to the girls and hugs them again as she weeps loudly. She releases the girls and stands up then takes Sarah's hand briefly before letting go.

The short nerve racking walk to Joe has everyone on pins and needles as he stares at her, not sure of what she's going to do. "Joe, I don't know how we move forward, and forgive and forget. I don't know what to say to you about my feelings or where my head is at right now." Joe nods slightly while listening to Kim as if he understands her feelings. "I can't tell you what any of this means for us or if it even changes what happened. All I can tell you is my daughters need their mother and I need my daughters."

Kim steps closer to Joe and opens her arms and gives Joe a hug. Joe wraps his arms around Kim and closes his eyes and smiles. "Thank you for bringing them home to me," Kim says softly.

"OK everyone. Why don't we all go inside and have some pancakes," Sarah says.

"That sounds great," Joe replies as he looks at Kim. "What do you think, Kim? Do you want to spend the day with us?" Kim smiles at Joe then smiles at Talia and Calie.

"I think that's a fantastic idea." Talia walks over to Kim and takes her hand.

"Can you stay and have breakfast with us."

"I would love to sweetie," she says while looking down at Talia. As they start walking to the front door, Calie runs over to Kim and takes her other hand and looks up at her mom with the biggest smile ever.

As Sarah prepares breakfast, Kim, Talia and Calie are playing a game of tag in the backyard. They are all laughing and having fun as Kim chases the girls around the yard. Joe sits in a chair on the patio watching the girls as Sarah sets two coffee cups down on the table next to him. "What are you thinking about?" she asks.

"I'm thinking that I waited way too long to come back home. I should've come back after the girls were born. She didn't deserve to be left out all these years."

"You can't beat yourself up about this. What's done is done. The important thing is that your home now."

As daylight fades and darkness creeps in, Kim, Calie and Talia are still playing in the backyard as Joe slowly walks over to them. "Girls it's getting late and you need to take a bath. Aunty Sarah is running the water for you now."

"No, we want to keep playing," Calie says.

"Please, Daddy?" Talia begs.

"I'm sorry girls, it's getting late." Kim and Joe look at each other. Joe whispers softly. "I'm sorry."

"It's OK," Kim whispers back with a quick smile. "I should probably get going too," Kim says as she looks down at Calie and Talia while holding their hands. Kim gets down on her knees in front of the girls. "How about I come over early tomorrow and we can play for the whole day again. How does that sound?"

"Yes, Yes," Calie and Talia both shout.

Kim, Joe, Calie and Talia all walk around the house to the driveway. Kim holds Calie and Talia's hand as they walk together towards Kim's car then Calie takes Joe's hand and swings her arms. With a smile on her face, Kim gazes down at Calie then glances at Joe with the same happy grin.

"Thanks for playing with me today, girls. I had lots of fun," Kim says while hugging the girls. "I can't wait to do this again tomorrow."

"I don't want you to leave," Calie says with a whimper.

"I don't want you to go either," Talia says as she hugs Kim again. Kim looks up at Joe, heartbroken by the sadness. Joe, who's in the early stages of tearing up, turns away for some privacy.

"OK girls, I should go." Both girls are on the receiving end of a huge hug and a kiss on their cheeks.

Joe reaches down and takes the girls hands as Kim walks around to the driver's side of the car. As she gets in the car and starts it, both girls wave to her and Kim waves back. She backs out of the driveway and starts tearing up as she wipes her face and looks at the girls one last time before vanishing into traffic.

CHAPTER 31

A few minutes later Kim pulls into her driveway and stops the car next to the garage as she lethargically shifts it into park. Everything feels like slow motion to Kim.

"I know I'm going to wake up. There is no way this is real," Kim says as she looks at herself in the rear view mirror. A grin cracks then blows up to a full smile as she pinches her left wrist and discovers that it hurt.

"So girls did you have fun today with your mom?" Sarah asks the girls in the bathtub as she sits on the floor next to the tub helping the girls.

"Yeah, I had lots of fun with her. My mom is beautiful," Calie replies as Sarah gives her a smile.

"Talia you're kind of quiet over there, did you have a good day?" Talia looks at Sarah while holding a doll.

"Today was fun, but why did she have to leave?"

"Yeah how come?" Calie follows.

"Well your mom has her own house that she has to go to and it was getting late," Sarah replies as she looks at both girls now facing her. "Turn around girls, and I will rinse your hair."

"Is our mom coming to see us tomorrow?" Calie asks as Sarah pours water on the back of Talia's head.

"I'm sure she will see you tomorrow. She was so excited to see you girls and play with you today."

"I can't wait to see her again tomorrow," Talia says.

"OK girls, time to dry off. Here are your towels and pajamas. Don't forget to brush your teeth after you get dressed and I will meet you in your room in a few minutes to brush your hair."

"Yes Aunty Sarah!" Talia shouts out being silly as Sarah leaves the bathroom. Calie laughs at Talia.

"Talia, you're goofy," Calie giggles.

"Hi girls," Joe says as Talia and Calie enter the bedroom. Sarah sits on one of the two beds in the spare bedroom as Joe sits on the other.

"Your dad is going to brush your hair so I will say goodnight." Aunty gives the girls a kiss on top of their heads and walks out.

"Jump up here girls," Joe says as he pats the bed in front of him. After jumping up onto the bed Joe carefully takes Calie's long curly blonde hair and brushes it from top to bottom. Calie gives her sister an elbow.

"What," Talia whispers.

"Ask him," Calie whispers back with a scowl on her face.

"No, you ask him."

"Girls, I'm right here. I can hear everything you are saying. Ask me what?" Joe stops brushing Calie's hair. Talia turns her head slightly towards Joe but not all the way that she can see him.

"Daddy, should we call her Kim or can we call her Mom?" Talia asks.

"I'm sure she would love it if you called her mom." Talia and Calie look at each other and smile.

"Daddy."

"Yes Calie," he answers with a grin as the brush stops halfway down her head. The curious girls turn around and face their daddy.

"Are we ever going to live with Mommy, or are we just going to live here?"

"That is a good question honey, but I don't have an answer for you. That will have to be Mommy's decision. There's so many things that your mom and I have to talk about before we do that."

"What do you need to talk about?" Calie asks.

"Things like where are we going to live, where will I work, and who is going to take care of you girls when we are working. Those types of things." Joe turns Talia around and starts to brush her hair slowly from top to bottom.

"How come Mommy didn't live with us in San Francisco?"

"Well Talia, it's because Mommy was mad at me for leaving her by herself for all those years while we were in San Francisco."

"Why did you leave her?" Calie asks.

"Boy oh boy, you guys are filled with lots of good questions tonight." Joe stops brushing Talia's hair and drops his hands down to the bed as he reflects on the past seven years. "Um, your mom was mad at me for acting bad and I was acting that way because it was a very sad time in our life... so... one day I left the house we were living in together and I moved away without telling her." Calie stares at Joe, and Talia turns to look at him too. Joe is looking down and talking slowly and low as if he is ashamed of himself for leaving Kim. Joe remains still for a moment then looks up at the girls.

"Are you sad Daddy?" Talia asks.

"I'm not, sweetie. I have my two favorite girls with me and that's all I need to make me happy. I just need to think about how I can fix this with Mommy."

Joe jumps off the bed, grabs Calie, lifts her in the air and drops her slowly on the other bed. "It's late and I think that you guys are going to be very busy tomorrow so it's time for bed." Talia gets under the covers and holds her arms out as if she is waiting for a hug. "Goodnight Calie, I love you," Joe says as he gives her a kiss on her forehead.

"Goodnight Daddy, love you too." Then he walks over to Talia who still has her arms stretched out for a hug. Joe bends over and engages Talia in a big squeeze hug.

"Goodnight baby, I love you."

"I love you too, Daddy." Joe starts to stand up but Talia doesn't let go. "Daddy."

"Yes," Joe replies softly as he looks into Talia's eyes.

"Don't be sad." Joe stares at Talia for a moment then smiles.

"OK, honey. Sleep well." Joe smiles as he flicks off the light switch on the way out the door.

Joe walks downstairs to the living room where Sarah and Marc are sitting close together on the couch.

"Hey Joey, sit down and have a beer with us. I'll grab you one," Sarah says then jumps up and walks into the kitchen as her brother plops down on the floor and leans back against the couch opposite Marc. She returns and hands Joe a mug of beer then sits back down on the couch next to Marc.

"Thanks. You don't know how much I need this right about now."

"I'm sure it's been an emotionally draining day," Marc replies as they both stare at Joe.

"How are you dealing with this?" Sarah asks as Joe looks straight ahead at his sister and brother in-law.

"I'm just not sure what the future holds. When Kim left this evening she said goodbye to the girls then got in her car and drove away, like I wasn't even there," he says as he shakes his head in disappointment.

"Joey, you knew this was going to be tough for her to deal with. I can't even begin to imagine what she's feeling right now."

"I have a bad feeling that Kim is going to want to take the girls home with her without me. That we are going to get into a battle over this and I'm scared out of my mind all of a sudden."

"I'm sure everything will be fine," Sarah says optimistically.

"You think so? What do you think?" Joe asks as he glares at Marc.

"I think I'll meet you both in the middle and say that there may be some bumps in the road along the way, but in the end, you and Kim both have the best intentions at heart for the girls." Joe nods his head slightly then takes a sip of beer.

"I assume that you and Kim will be talking about this in the next few days," Sarah says.

"I would assume so," Joe replies.

CHAPTER 32

The brilliant green numbers shine bright in Kim's eyes as she rolls towards her bedside table. Unable to sleep, she opens her eyes slowly to see the glow of the alarm clock shining 3:10 AM. With every toss and turn she grows more anxious to start her day. The excitement of seeing Talia and Calie again is overwhelming. She closes her eyes and tries to fall back asleep. After what seems like an eternity, her eyes open only to see the clock glowing 3:25 AM. As she pops up and rubs her eyes, she sits on the side of the bed for a few moments pondering her next move.

She turns her attention to the other side of her bed where Joe last slept seven years ago. Even though Kim is the only person that sleeps in the bed, she still stayed on her side all these years. Maybe, in some strange way she thought Joe would return home and want his side of the bed back. Now that the girls are back in her life, she can't seem to stop thinking about Joe.

When Kim decides to get out of bed, she walks to the stairway and stops before heading down to make coffee. With a smirk she turns and walks to Talia's bedroom door. Calie and Talia's bedroom doors have remained closed for the last seven years. Maybe it was just too hard for her to look inside the rooms everyday as she passed by them.

Kim opens the door slowly and peeks inside with a smile on her face. As she slowly closes the door she stops. Kim stands still taking in the moment then she slowly pushes the door open and leaves it. The smile doesn't fade away as she continues down the hall to Calie's bedroom. She slowly and quietly pushes the door all the way open.

It's 8:00 a.m. on Sunday and Sarah, Joe and the girls are eating breakfast at the table. The cordless phone rings as Sarah answers it.

"Hello," Sarah says before pausing for a moment. "Hi Kim. How are you?" Joe looks at Talia and Calie as they perk up and smile at the thought of their mother being on the other end of the phone. "Hold on one second." Sarah holds the phone out in Joe's direction. "She wants to talk with you." Joe gets up as he looks at the girls then takes the phone from his sister.

"Hi Kim," Joe says as he looks at the girls and smiles back at them. "Sure, that would be great. Let me ask them, hold on a second." Joe looks at the girls. "Mommy would like to come over in a few hours and pick us up. She wants to go to the park and get lunch then maybe some ice cream. What do you guys think?" Calie and Talia look at each other briefly then back at Joe.

"Yes!" both girls scream in unison.

"Did you hear that?" Joe asks Kim. "Great, see you then. Bye." Joe looks down at the phone and pushes the off button. Talia and Calie stare at Joe as he looks back at them. "Mom will be here to pick us up at eleven, which is about three hours from now." Joe sits back down at the table and smiles as he looks at Sarah.

Later that morning, Joe and Kim are walking in the short cut grass in the middle of the park while Talia and Calie play on the swing set. The town park is twenty acres with a walking track around the perimeter, a large swing set with climbing structures and a fountain in the middle. At this time of day in July, the park is filled with people having picnics, playing ball or just walking around the track. As they walk slowly towards the swings, Kim breaks the silence with conversation while they watch the girls.

"What made you want to come back home after so many years away?" Kim asks. With his eyes still fixed on the girls, he glances at Kim and smiles slightly.

"There was this park down the street from where we lived. It was called Freedom Park." Kim looks at Joe as they stop walking. "The girls loved that park. We would go to Freedom Park at least a couple times a month." He takes a moment and looks around the park. It was actually a park similar to this one. "A little more than a month ago while we were at the park, the girls all of a sudden stopped dead in their tracks. They were fixated on this family that was in the park, close to them." Kim looks inquisitively at Joe as he continues to watch the girls.

"Did you know them?"

"No. The girls didn't know them either, but there was, what I assumed, a mother, father and two daughters playing together." I knew right away what the girls were thinking as they were watching that family." Kim looks at the girls.

"A mother," Kim says with a smile.

"Not just a mother, but someone to hold them, love them and care for them. They needed someone to be proud of them when they do something good and someone to pick them up when they fall down. I was that person for the past six years, but they needed someone else in their life. They needed their mother. They needed their mother's hugs, kisses and laughter, as all kids do." Kim wipes a lone tear teetering on the edge of her eye. Joe looks at Kim with a frown.

"Kim," Joe says softly. "There wasn't a day that went by when I left and especially when the girls were born, that I didn't think about you. I wanted so badly to be with you and have you be a part of this amazing journey." Joe pauses for a moment. "I just didn't think you would embrace the idea." Kim wipes another tear from her face as she looks like she's about to break down. "As the years went by I watched the girls grow, I knew I had to bring them home. When the girls asked me why they didn't have a mother, it tore me apart. It was then that I made the decision to tell them about you and bring them home." Joe and Kim gaze into each other's eyes.

"Thank you for bringing them home." Kim steps towards Joe and puts her arms around him. Joe holds Kim for a moment and closes his eyes as he fights to hold back the gratifying emotions he is feeling. This is the first time he felt that Kim didn't hate him and he didn't want this feeling to end. "Thank you." Kim says again softly.

"Mommy, are you sad?" Talia says as Joe and Kim separate and look down to see both girls standing next to them. Kim crouches down to the girl's level.

"Mommy is good, sweetie. Hey why don't we go get that ice cream we talked about?" Kim looks at Calie and caresses her cheek. "OK, honey?"

"OK, Mommy," Calie answers. The family starts walking towards the ice cream stand next to the fountain in the center of the park.

"Girls, tell Mom what flavor of ice cream you like the best. Kim stops and looks at the girls.

"Mine is mint chocolate chip," Calie says enthusiastically.

"I love strawberry ice cream with rainbow sprinkles," Talia says. Kim turns and looks at Joe.

"Oh my God, that's the same..."

"I know. They both just chose that on their own one day. It's amazing, isn't it?" Joe says as they continue walking towards the fountain. Joe and Kim walk side by side as the girls lead them to the center of the park.

"Thanks for the ice cream, Mommy," Calie says with a smile as green ice cream drips down her chin.

"You're welcome, Calie."

"Thanks, Mom."

"You're welcome, Talia."

"Calie, let's go back over to the swings. I'll race you," Talia says as they start running toward the swings with their ice cream in their hands. Joe and Kim slowly walk together and follow the girls to the swing set.

"Maybe you and the girls should come home," Kim says as she continues walking and watching the girls. Joe stops abruptly and stares at Kim.

"Are you talking about all of us moving into your house?" Kim stops and turns towards Joe.

"Technically, it's your house too."

"Don't you think it's too soon for that? I mean we just got into town and until two days ago, you hated me. Now you want me to move back home?"

"Let's be clear about something Joe. I'm still very angry with you. Most likely, I will never get over the fact that you abandoned me when I needed you the most. If you feel this strongly that it's too soon, then the girls can come home and you can stay at Sarah's, but I'm sure you won't allow that to happen." Kim looks at the girls and starts walking towards the swings again with Joe right behind her. "So if it's a matter of all three of you or not having my girls with me, then I'll take all of you." Kim stops and turns her head back to Joe who is still walking slowly behind her. "Are you good with that?" Joe gives Kim a smirk and nods his head slightly.

"OK," Joe says somberly.

"Good." Kim turns towards the swing and watches the girls as Joe stands next to her.

"Wow," Kim says softly.

"What?"

"I just can't believe how much they look like Calie and Talia."

"Kim, they are Calie and Talia," Joe replies while standing next to Kim looking at the girls swinging. Kim and Joe look at each other and Kim gives Joe a little smile.

"Yeah they are. Hey girls, let's get going," Kim shouts to Calie and Talia and waves to them. "Do you want to bring them over to see the house now?" Kim asks.

"I think that would be great. The girls will be excited to see their bedrooms. I'm actually a little nervous myself," Joe replies. Kim looks at Joe and giggles slightly.

"Shit," Kim says as the girls get closer.

"What's the matter?"

"I haven't touched the girl's bedrooms besides cleaning them. All of the pictures of them and us together are in their rooms."

"Oh. Good thinking. That would have been bad. Why don't you drop us off at Sarah's house and you can take care of their bedrooms. I will bring the girls over around five o'clock and we can get pizza for dinner. It's been seven years since I've had East Street Pizza."

"That sounds good," Kim replies.

Joe and Kim walk towards her car in the adjacent parking lot. Joe holds Calie's hand while Kim walks and holds Talia's.

"Girls, I had lots of fun with you at the park. Thanks for coming with me." Kim opens the car door as the girls climb in the backseat and into their car seats. After strapping the girls in, Joe and Kim get into the front seats.

"Where are we going?" Calie asks.

"Mommy is going to bring us back to Sarah's house for a little while."

"No, I don't want to go to Auntie's house. I want to stay with Mommy," Talia says as she starts whimpering.

"Me too, Daddy." Kim looks at Joe with a frown then smiles.

"Girls, it's just for a little while. Then what do you think about Daddy bringing you to my house? I have a surprise for you there."

"OK," Talia says as she calms down and stops pouting.

"We were thinking that we would show you Mom's house," Joe says as Calie and Talia look at each other as they are sit in the back seat, quietly nodding their heads.

"We want to see Mom's house," Talia says loudly.

CHAPTER 33

"Do you really think this is a good idea? I mean think about this. You've been home for two days, Joe," Sarah says as Joe stands in the kitchen looking out the window at Calie and Talia chasing a butterfly in the backyard. He chuckles to himself as he is watching the girls and listening to Sarah.

"You should have seen how happy the girls were today at the park. We were a family again and not only did the girls have fun together, but I loved being with Kim again too." Joe looks down at Sarah sitting at the kitchen table. "Maybe we are moving fast, but it just feels right. For the first time in over seven years, everything feels good to me." Joe nods his head and looks out the window again. "It just feels good."

"I'm not saying you shouldn't be together," Sarah says now standing next to him looking out the window at the girls. "I just thought you would have taken it slower." Joe turns and smiles at Sarah as she looks up at him.

"You sound like Mom." Joe laughs to himself. "I miss her. I can imagine how happy Mom would be right now playing in the backyard with the girls seven years after we buried them." Joe stares intently at the girls as he remembers his mother's smile and the joy she brought to everyone. Even though Joe was young when his mother died, he thinks about her constantly and pictures her in his life and spending time with her granddaughters.

"I miss her too Joe, but if she was still alive today, I'm not sure she would be happy about this."

"I think your wrong, Sis. I think if she were here today, she would appreciate and embrace the moment, and the idea of having her granddaughters back. Think about her in the backyard right now, playing with the girls. It brings a smile to my face." Sarah giggles at the thought.

"Joe, I just don't want you or the girls to get hurt by moving in so fast. That's all." Joe puts his arm around Sarah and pulls her close to him.

"I know. Thanks. Thanks for everything."

"Maybe I'm being a little selfish too. There's a piece of me that thinks if you leave I won't see the girls that much," Sarah says as she looks out the window again.

"I have a feeling you're going to be spending lots of time with your nieces," Joe says while watching the girls run towards the back door. The back door swings open with a bang and the girls charge in excited and out of breath.

"Daddy! Auntie Sarah! Did you see the butterfly?" Calie shouts as she tries to catch her breath. Both Joe and his sister crouch down.

"Yeah, did you see it? We almost caught it," Talia adds as Sarah puts both her hands in the air for a high-five from Talia and Calie.

"Give me five girls. Next time you'll get it." The girls slap Sarah's hands.

"We did see it. That was awesome. We were watching you from here." The girls are all smiles as they continue to gasp for air. "Girls we need to get going soon if we're going to get to Mom's house," Joe says.

"I hope you guys have fun at your mom's and I want to hear all about it. OK?" Sarah kneels down and gives both girls a hug at the same time as the girls hug her back. Sarah stands up and takes the girl's hands. "Come on, I will walk you guys out to the car."

The driver's side window rolls down and Joe turns his attention to his sister standing next to his door. "I hope it goes well Joe. Shoot me a text later and let me know how everything is going."

"I will. Everything will be fine. Trust me." Joe smiles at her as he starts driving forward. Sarah waves to the girls in the back seat as they go by.

<hr />

"Daddy, how much farther is it to Mom's house?" Calie asks.

"It's right down the…" Joe stops as he stares out his window at the side of the road and slows the car down.

"Daddy! What are you looking at? Why are we slowing down?" Talia asks.

Joe pulls to the side of the road, out of traffic and stops the car. The window goes down as Joe stares at the side of the road. He was caught completely off guard by where he was. Joe's now at the very spot that Kim, Calie and Talia crashed before the Valentine's Day Dance.

"Daddy," Talia shouts as she tries to get his attention.

"Sorry, sweetie. I was just looking at something on the side of the road." Joe turns his head around and looks at the girls.

"Daddy, why are you crying?" Calie asks while pointing to Joe's cheek.

Joe wipes a tear from his cheek just as it drips out of his eye. "Daddy remembers something very sad that happened here a long time ago, but I'm good. Let's get to Mommy's house, OK?"

"Yeah!" Calie shouts as she throws her arms in the air to celebrate.

"I can't wait to see Mommy," Talia said.

Joe checks the rear view mirror for traffic then pulls out into the road slowly after one more quick glance at the gully where Kim's car came to rest on its hood. Joe sees his wife's car upside down and the blood inside on the seats and roof. "BANG" Joe get's startled as he hears and feels Kim's car getting hit seven years ago. Joe turns his attention back on the road and continues on his way to Kim's house that is just minutes away.

"Here we are girls." Joe pulls into Kim's driveway for the second time in the past three days and stops the car near the garage. Kim walks onto the porch then down the stairs. Calie and Talia both unbuckle their booster seats and open the doors.

"Mommy!" Talia yells as she runs towards Kim with Calie following right behind her.

"There's my girls," Kim says as she runs to meet her daughters with open arms and scoops them up in a big hug. Kim spins around once while holding the girls and laughs with excitement. "I am so glad my girls are home with me again."

"What do you mean again, Mommy?" Talia asks with a look of confusion.

"Mom was talking about when you girls were here a few days ago for the first time. Isn't that right, Kim?" Joe looks at Kim nodding his head, with his eyes wide open trying to get her to agree.

"That's right because you were just here a couple of days ago," Kim giggles. "Let's go inside," Kim says as she slowly sets the girls down on the grass then starts walking with them towards the front porch. Joe stands behind Kim and the girls, watching from behind and alone, as if he isn't wanted at the house. Other than Kim replying to him about not confusing the girls, she hasn't really acknowledged Joe's presence.

Talia turns and looks at Joe by himself then stops walking. She runs to Joe and takes his hand as Kim turns to watch Talia. Kim and Joe make eye contact with each other then she continues to the house. The tension and anger is still present just masked. Joe looks down at Talia.

"Come on Daddy. We are going to Mommy's house together." Talia says looking up at her Daddy with nothing but love in her eyes.

"Thanks sweetie."

CHAPTER 34

"Girls, did you have enough to eat?" Joe asks. "There's salad and breadsticks left over."

"I'm stuffed," Calie says as she rubs her belly. Kim sits between Calie and Talia at the kitchen table where they have eaten dinner as a family so many times before. Kim reaches over to Calie and softly pokes her stomach.

"Look at that big belly," Kim says as Calie breaks out in laughter.

"I can't eat anymore either," Talia says as Kim reaches over and pokes her belly too. Talia laughs then tries to poke Kim's stomach as Calie joins in and Kim breaks out in uncontrolled laughter.

"OK goofballs. I'll clean up the table. Why don't you guys go hang out in the living room." Kim looks at the girls with an excited grin.

"I have a great idea. Why don't we go play some board games? I have a whole trunk filled with games," Kim says as Talia and Calie perk up at the table.

"Yeah," Talia says with excitement.

"Let's go," Calie shouts.

The girls bound from their seats and push them under the table. Joe begins cleaning up and moves everything over to the sink area as Kim collects the cups and puts them in the sink next to Joe.

"Do you remember where everything goes?" Kim remarks with a sarcastic tone while never looking at Joe. She turns and walks towards the living room. "After all, it has been seven years." She continues on into the living room without looking back.

"I'm good, thanks," Joe barks back as he opens numerous cabinet doors looking for the garbage can. He glances back to make sure Kim doesn't see him opening the cabinets.

Calie and Talia light up with excitement as Kim opens the large brown wooden toy trunk in the corner of the living room. The trunk hasn't been opened since Calie and Talia died. Kim smiles when she sees the toys in the box she remembers playing with seven years ago. As Joe enters the living room and sits down next to the girls on the floor, he can see the excitement in their eyes as they look into the toy box. Joe and Kim share a smile with each other. The toy box, like a time capsule, has Joe and Kim thinking about the past and remembering Friday game night in the Walker house.

"This is incredible. I loved playing these games," Joe says with a smile.

"Can we take some out, Mom?" Talia asks. Calie next to Talia, is grinning from ear to ear and giggles at the thought of Kim removing the games from the trunk.

"We can take them all out. How about that?" Joe reaches in the trunk and pulls out a stack of board games as Kim reaches in and takes out some toy cars, a pink castle and some small dolls. Kim and Joe share another smile as Kim inconspicuously wipes a tear from her cheek. Joe scoots over slightly and gently rubs Kim's back in a comforting way. Over the next two hours, the family plays with every board game and toy in the trunk.

"Girls, Mommy and Daddy want to talk to you about something." The girls stop playing with the castle and dolls for a minute. "Come here Talia. You sit here." Joe picks up Talia and sits her next to him. "And Calie, you sit next to Mommy." Kim pulls Calie close to her and hugs her. Joe looks at Kim briefly, then takes a deep breath and lets it out. "How would you two feel about all of us living here with Mommy?" Calie smiles at Kim and stands up and hugs her.

"Daddy, are you serious?" Calie shouts with joy.

"Yes, I am."

"Thank you Daddy," Talia says as she hugs Joe then jumps onto Kim and hugs her tight. With laughter and happiness throughout the house like old times, Kim wipes the tears that are flowing down her face.

"Mommy, why are you crying?" Talia asks as she wipes a wet line, from where a tear traveled, off Kim's face. Kim grabs Talia and hugs her again.

"Oh sweetie, Mommy isn't sad. I haven't been this happy in a long time. I'm so happy that you're going to stay with me and never leave me."

"We're never going to leave you Mommy. Right, Calie?"

"No way. I'm going to stay here forever," Calie says. Joe gets emotional so he stands up and walks into the kitchen to get a bottle of water out of the refrigerator.

"OK now we have a special surprise for you. Mom, are you ready to show them?" Joe says as he looks at Kim with a smile after he walks back into the room.

"Another surprise for us?" Calie asks while clapping her hands and smiling.

"Talia we have lots of surprises at Mommy's house," Joe says.

"I love surprises," Talia replies as she jumps up in anticipation.

"Girls, are you ready to see your surprise?" Kim stands up and reaches out for the girl's hands. Calie and Talia each take a hand as Joe leads the way.

"Follow me girls," Joe says as the family makes their way to the center hall of the large colonial house, then upstairs. At the top of the stairs, the family stops in front of the first bedroom door. "Come right up to this door, Talia." Joe stands behind Talia in front of the closed bedroom door with his hands on her shoulders. "This is your bedroom sweetie." Joe reaches for the handle and opens the door. The door swings open to a large bright yellow bedroom with plush cream carpet and a large bed against the left wall. The pink comforter on the bed accents the white and orange curtains on the two large windows straight ahead. In the corner of the room stands a doll house with some dolls next to it.

"Wow!" Talia has a huge smile on her face and her eyes are wide open as she looks up at her father. "Daddy, this is my room?"

"It's your room, honey. Everything in it is yours." Talia walks in slowly as she is in awe of her room. She looks all around the room turning in a circle to take it all in. Kim and Calie are right behind Joe as they all walk into Talia's room. Joe looks around in amazement. This is the first time he's seen Talia's room since he left seven years ago.

"Talia, look at the animals on your bed." Calie points to the stuffed animals all over her sister's bed. Talia giggles as she walks over to her bed and slowly picks up a small black kitten stuffed animal resting against the pillow.

"He's so cute," Talia says. She holds the kitten close to her and snuggles up to it. "I like this one the best." She runs over to Joe and Kim and grabs both of their legs. "Thank you, thank you, thank you! I love my room." She lets go and turns to Calie. "Calie, let's go see your bedroom."

   "Come with me, Calie," Kim says as she reaches out for her hand. When Calie takes her hand, Kim leads her into the hallway and down to the next closed door. Kim crouches down next to Calie and gives her a kiss on her forehead. "Are you ready?" Calie nods slightly with anticipation and a big smile as she looks at her mom then looks at Joe and Talia behind her. "Go ahead, open the door," Kim says softly. With a twist of the black handle, she pushes the door open.

The door opens to a large bright sky blue room with pink curtains. Her bed is covered with a blue comforter and big pink pillows. Calie enters her bedroom and looks around in bewilderment, her smile never faltering. She turns and smiles at her mom and dad then she and Talia walk over to Calie's bed to look at the stuffed animals set up neatly. Out of the five stuffed animals on her bed, the one that catches Calie's attention is the small brown puppy in front of all the others.

Joe walks up behind Kim who is watching Calie in disbelief. He now comprehends what his wife is looking at. When Joe sees Calie pick up the brown puppy, he moves to Kim's side. Stunned by what she's witnessing, she turns to see that Joe is astonished by the sight too.

   "This one is my favorite," Calie says as she holds the puppy close to her face.

Kim walks up behind Calie and Talia and puts her arm around both girls. Joe stands in the doorway watching Kim and the girls. "Do you like your bedrooms?" Kim asks.

"I love my room, Mommy," Calie says.

"Me too," Talia answers.

"Good. I'm so glad to hear that. Just so you know, your closets and dressers are filled with clothes." Calie and Talia look at Kim with a smile, as they giggle at each other. "You can go through those and see what you have for clothes if you would like to."

"Girls, if you pull clothes out, please make sure we put them back and clean up when you're done," Joe adds.

"OK, we will," Talia answers.

CHAPTER 35

"The house looks good. You've done a great job keeping it up." There's an awkward silence in the living room as Kim looks at Joe. Calie and Talia are playing in their bedrooms while Joe and Kim are talking. Joe is sitting on one end of the couch and Kim is sitting at the other as he looks around the living room and remembers all the years of family gatherings and birthday parties they shared together.

"I took some of the money from the settlement and used it to do some repairs and updating. The house needed a new roof shortly after you left. Seemed like everything started falling apart at the same time, but that's life I guess."

"Kim, I know you have questions and things you want to say, so let's just start. I am just as uncomfortable as you are about everything going on right now." Her rage festers internally at Joe's remarks.

"I don't think you are anywhere close as uncomfortable as I am right now." Kim sits up slightly takes a deep breath and looks deeper at Joe as he stares back at her. "My world ended over seven years ago when my daughters died and my husband walked out on me to find himself." Her voice staying low so the kids don't hear their conversation. Kim's clear and incensed tone stings Joe's ears. Maybe this was a bad idea. Joe thinks to himself. "With no contact for seven years, not even a fucking hello or I'm OK, my husband shows up at my door with my dead daughters. I don't think your uncomfortableness is anywhere close to mine you selfish...." Kim stops herself and takes a deep breath. "I told myself I wasn't going to let my emotions get the best of me and ruin the day I had with my girls." Joe looks down slightly then back at Kim as to concede to her. Kim's eyes well up then tears flow from both eyes as she wipes her face with her bare hands then stares back at Joe.

"Your right, I'm sorry. I didn't mean to minimize your pain and suffering over mine. Obviously you suffered much more than I did and I will forever be sorry for leaving you, but if I had stayed, Calie and Talia wouldn't be upstairs right now." He moves his body slightly closer to Kim and turns his whole body towards her. Kim's head is down, as she stares at the couch. A calming comes over her, as she recognizes that Joe is right. Happiness has consumed her since her girls came home. With another deep breath, she looks at Joe, ready to talk calmly.

"I find myself afraid to go to sleep at night because I fear when I wake up this will all have been just a dream. I can't decipher right now what is real and what is my imagination. I tell myself that this has to be a dream." Joe continues to listen intently to everything Kim is saying. He wants to comfort her and hold her, but he knows she will reject him. "It has to be a dream."

"I know what you're feeling Kim, I do. I had the same reaction the first couple of days after the girls were born. I can assure you, this is real and it's wonderful. You have your daughters back."

"Where have you been? How did you do this? How are my daughters upstairs playing in their rooms again?" She glares deeply at Joe as her facial anxiety softens. "I just don't understand. I have so many questions."

"OK, do you want me to start from the beginning?"

"I don't even know if I want to hear it," she says glaring at him. "Sarah filled me in a little about what you did. It's just so crazy to think about."

"Well, why don't we do this? Since it's your first night with the girls at home, how about you put the girls to bed? Spend some one-on-one time with them. Read them a story or just talk with them. I'm going to run back over to Sarah's house and pick up some stuff for me and the girls. I will be back in about an hour or so. What do you think?" Joe gives Kim a smile as he stands up. "When the girls go to sleep, we can talk and I will tell you as little or as much as you want to hear."

"OK," Kim says as she stands up and walks towards the stairs. Joe turns and grabs his keys off of the side table in the living room and starts for the front door. "Joe," Kim says as Joe stops and looks up the stairs. "I want to know. I want to know everything," she says as she gives Joe a half-hearted smile. Joe gives Kim a bigger smile back. "Just so there are no surprises later on down the road." Joe turns the door knob and walks out onto the front porch.

The doll house in the middle of the room is filled with furniture for the various figurines that Calie and Talia are playing with. Kim stands in the doorway to Talia's room as the girls are lying on their bellies in front of the doll house. As the girls play and talk back and forth, Kim listens and watches. She closes her eyes momentarily just to take in the sounds of her daughters talking and playing as she remembers all the days the girls played together, filling the large house with laughter. She opens her eyes and steps into the bedroom. As she sits down behind the girls and puts her arms around them, they smile at Kim.

"Hi. What are you playing?" Kim asks with delight.

"Dolls. Do you want to play with us?" Calie responds while continuing to play.

"I would love to play, but it's getting late and we need to start getting ready for bed."

"OK. Where's Daddy?" Talia asks.

"Dad went to Auntie Sarah's house to pick up some things. He should be back soon. There are some pajamas in your dressers and by the time we clean up your rooms and get ready for bed, Dad should be home."

"Hi guys," Joe says as he walks through the front door of Sarah's house. Sarah and Marc are sitting in the living room watching a movie as Sarah hits the pause button on the remote.

"Hey Joey. Is everything OK?" Sarah asks. Joe sits down on the chair next to the couch and looks at Sarah and Marc.

"There's some tension in the air. We'll just leave it at that."

"I'm sure there is," Marc replies. "So what's your plan for tonight?"

"The plan is that we are spending the night at Kim's house. We are supposed to talk after the girls go to bed. I think I will have a better idea of where we stand after tonight." Sarah smiles at Joe.

"Joey, when you guys are alone tonight talking about what happened and why you left and where you went, just remember where Kim ended up. She will be angry, sad and happy all at the same time so be patient and understanding with her." Joe nods his head while listening to Sarah.

"I will. I just need to pick up a few things for the girls then I'll get out of here and give you your home back." Joe stands and walks upstairs.

"It's not going to be good," Marc says softly as he reaches for the remote and turns the volume on. Sarah looks at Marc with a scowl. A few minutes later, Joe comes down the stairs with a duffle bag in both hands. He puts the bags down next to the front door and walks over to Sarah. She wraps her arms around the little brother she took care of after she graduated high school and started college.

"Thanks for letting us stay here. I really do appreciate it," Joe says as he holds his sister tight.

"You're welcome Joe. You and the girls are always welcome here. You know that, right?" Sarah asks after Joe releases his hug and stares deeply into her eyes.

"I know Sis, thanks again." Joe looks at Marc and extends his right hand out to him. Marc stands up and shakes his hand. "Thank you Marc."

"Anytime Joe. Don't be a stranger now that you're back in town. I kind of liked having another guy around." Joe nods his head and smiles as he turns and walks out the door.

The girls are in bed on the first night back in Kim and Joe's house. Kim is lying next to Calie in her bed, gazing into the eyes of her daughter. "I'm so happy you're my mommy," Calie says as she reaches her arms around Kim and pulls her in tight. Kim gives Calie a kiss on her forehead as she nestles her head into Kim's chest.

"Oh Calie, I'm glad you're my little girl. I love you sweetie. Sleep well," Kim says as she slowly slips out from under the covers and gives her another kiss on her forehead.

"Love you too," Calie whispers as she cuddles up to her brown puppy. Kim looks at her one more time before she walks out the door and down the hall.

"Hi baby," Kim whispers as she enters Talia's bedroom and sees Talia's face sticking out of the covers. Talia was waiting for her mom to walk through the door.

"Hi Mommy," Talia whispers back. Kim sits next to Talia on her bed and smiles.

"Can I snuggle with you for a few minutes?" Kim asks. Talia nods slightly then squirms toward the opposite side of the bed to give her mom some room as Kim curls up next to her. "How do you like you room?" Kim asks before giving Talia a kiss on the top of her head.

"I love it and I love all my toys and all my clothes."

"Good, I'm glad honey," Kim replies as she pulls Talia close.

"Mommy?"

"Yes."

"Have you always been our mommy?" Kim looks down as Talia props her head up and looks at her. Kim takes a moment and smiles.

"Yes, I've always been your mommy. It's a long and weird story that we will tell you both about someday, but for right now, I'm just glad the two of you are home with me." Kim continues to smile at Talia as she returns the smile back at her mom. "Goodnight Talia. I love you."

"Goodnight Mommy. I love you." After rolling off the bed, Kim stands up then walks towards the door. "Mommy, I'm glad I'm with you too." Kim stops and smiles at Talia, then closes the door halfway. She stands against the hallway wall with a tear in her eye and a smile on her face.

CHAPTER 36

"Where do you want me to start?" Joe asks with a calm easy voice.

"If you are back in my life, I assume we will have plenty of time to talk about the damage that our relationship has suffered because you left." Joe nods slowly. "I really have to know, but I'm not sure I want to know it all." Kim pulls a tissue from the box sitting on the coffee table and holds it in preparation of tears flowing down her face. "OK, I'm ready," she says as she stares at Joe.

"After I left, I found myself in many different cities across the country. I was just roaming. I didn't have a purpose or a plan and most of the trip is a blur." Kim listens intently. Two months after leaving, I was drunk in a hotel in a small town outside of Tacoma, Washington. On some news program was an interview with a scientist from San Francisco that claimed he could clone a human." Kim closes her eyes briefly and tilts her head back in a clear sign of disapproval.

"You found this doctor in San Francisco?"

"I sought him out and ultimately found him in San Francisco." Kim suddenly sits up and points her finger at Joe.

"It was you," Kim said.

"It was me what?"

"It must have been a little more than a year after you left. I received a phone call at about five in the morning and my caller ID showed up as San Francisco, but the person hung up. That was you." Joe gives a slight smile. "Somehow I knew that was you."

"It was one day after Talia and Calie were born." Joe pauses for a few moments and gathers himself. "I wanted so badly to share it with you." Joe's voice cracks and he rubs his eyes as they begin to water. Kim pulls another tissue from the box and hands it to Joe. "Thanks."

"Go on," Kim says.

"So I was able to persuade Dr. Marxx into cloning Calie and Talia."

"How did you do that?"

"He was going through a tough financial time. His wife left him and took everything he had, and his company was cutting off his funding for the project he was working on. If Dr. Marxx had no funding to continue the research, it would have destroyed any advances he made in perfecting the DNA sequence from egg to embryo. So I made him an offer he couldn't refuse."

"I don't understand what all that means. How do you clone a person?"

"Simply put, an egg is inserted with the DNA of the person being cloned and the DNA and egg are fused together with a faint shock of electricity. This process is the most delicate part of the cloning process, and also the time when the cloning process fails the most."

"Oh, I'm starting to get it now."

"Well Dr. Marxx was working on this stage of the cloning process with grant money from his company and he was starting to make significant progress as to why and how so many eggs reject the DNA and die. His company cut him off, reduced his budget and relocated staff to other areas of the company."

"Why would they do that if he was so close?"

"That's the million dollar question. Dr. Marxx theory was that the company didn't think he would actually be able to perfect the cloning sequence. Once they found out that Dr. Marxx was close to completing the sequence, the company panicked and took the remaining grant money and funneled it to other parts of the company. Gene Tech receives millions of dollars a year from the federal government in contracts and grants. Because the US Government had no real cloning legislation in place, Gene Tech thought the government would shut them down once it found out the cloning process was a success."

"So, how could he have done this without someone knowing?" Kim asks.

"Dr. Marxx ran the science lab and sometimes he was the only person working on this project. The company couldn't have more than a few people working on this assignment. They needed to keep this project a secret."

"So this scientist was able to complete the cloning sequence?"

"Yes and after he cloned Hope the ape and knew it was a success, he cloned his brother's daughter, Meghan." Joe's nodding his head at Kim who looks at Joe with skepticism. "It's true. I met Meghan shortly after I persuaded Dr. Marxx to clone the girls."

"This is unbelievable."

"Dr. Marxx had a network of women, mostly college girls that wanted to make money and help parents that couldn't have children. They all signed up to be surrogates in this program. We picked two women and Dr. Marxx inseminated them with the fused eggs. They carried the girls to birth, were paid for their service and then they walked away." Kim stares at Joe, motionless then stands up and walks around the room.

"Calie and Talia are the very same girls, biologically as our first daughters?"

"Besides a little different personality and the girls being the same age, they're identical. I've seen little nuances here and there that are slightly different from our first daughters, but nothing extraordinary." Kim turns and looks at Joe.

"How safe is this? Is there any scientific data to show the cloning process is safe?" Kim asks as she continues to pace back and forth. Joe stands up and walks over to Kim.

"It's safe Kim. Dr. Marxx assured me the process was safe. The girls are healthy and happy." Joe says to her as Kim stares into his eyes. Joe pulls her close and puts his arms around her as she hugs him too. "You have your beautiful daughters back. We can continue with life where we left off, if you want to. We can see our girls go to the prom and graduate high school and college. I'll be able to walk them down the aisle at their wedding and someday Kim, someday we will get to hold our grandchildren." Kim breaks down crying in Joe's arms. "Our family is getting a second chance.

"Thank you Joe."

CHAPTER 37

"Just go in and say hi," Joe whispers to himself. Two weeks after getting back into town, Joe finds himself in downtown Jacksonville after taking a drive. He pulls to the side of the road and coincidentally parks across the street from Target Security. The big fifteen foot tall windows of the storefront cover the façade of the old block long building with multiple businesses inside. With his heart racing a mile a minute and beating through his chest like a drum, Joe considers visiting his former partner and lifelong friend.

He knows the interaction may be uncomfortable but at some point, they will run into each other on the street. Joe takes a deep breath before exiting his car and jogging across the street to avoid the traffic. As he stands in front of the door to his old business and grabs the door handle, he has second thoughts. Will his old friend still be a friend? After all, Joe hasn't talked with Bill since he left town.

After a few more moments of building his courage up, he opens the door and steps inside. As the door opens a loud beep saturates the room to alert Bill that someone has entered the business. Joe has a smile on his face as he looks around at the interior of the office. For nearly fifteen years of his life, after resigning from the police department to follow his dream, this was his home away from home. This is what he loved to do. More than the job, he loved meeting new people and learning about their story. He walks over to the wall near the reception desk and looks at a picture. The wall is covered with framed photographs from years past, but the photo that Joe is glued to is special. It's a photograph of Bill and Joe in their high school football uniforms, standing next to each other after a football game. The picture has been hanging on the wall since the business was opened.

"I will be right with you," Bill says from his office. He can't see that the man standing in his lobby is his former partner. "Hi sir, how can I help you today?" Bill says as he walks into the lobby from his office. Joe still has his back to Bill.

"I remember this day like it was yesterday," Joe says pointing to the photo. Bill's eyes grow big. "That was the game you threw the bomb to me in the end zone to win it all and I dropped the ball."

"Joe?" Bill says with a crack in his voice and a smile on his face.

"You ran down to the end zone to comfort me, then helped me up. You always were a good friend," Joe says before turning around to see his old pal.

"Holy shit!" Bill walks over to Joe and both open their arms and hug each other.

"Hi pal. It's good to see you," Joe says as they break their hold on each other.

"Holy shit dude. When did you get back?"

"I got home two weeks ago. I'm sorry I didn't stop by sooner. It's been a crazy few weeks."

"Yeah, I imagine it has. Come on in and have a seat." Bill leads Joe into his office.

"So, how's business?" Joe asks as he sits down in the black leather chair in front of Bill's desk.

"Joe, business is insane. I'm so busy that I have to turn people away. There's not enough time in the day."

"That's good, right?"

"Yeah, I guess so," Bill replies as he shrugs his shoulders. Bill stares at Joe for a moment. "Have you seen Kim since you've been home?"

"I have and we have worked everything out and we are living back home." Bill closes his eyes, shakes his head then opens his eyes quickly and looks at Joe.

"Sorry. Did you say your back home?" Bill questions.

"I know Bill. That's why it's been a crazy few weeks."

"Don't take this the wrong way buddy. You know I love you like a brother, but you took off for seven years and abruptly come home with no notice and you move right back into your house? That is the craziest thing I've heard in a long time. And did you say we are living back home?" Joe nods slightly. "Who's we?"

"That's a great question, but unfortunately I don't have the time it will take to answer it." Joe stands up and starts walking back out to the lobby. "How about we get together for a few beers tonight and I will fill you in on everything?"

"Sounds good, but what's your hurry? You just got here." I know, but I was driving around town and I thought I would go out and try to find a job. I need to get back to living a normal life again."

"I have the perfect job for you." Bill says as Joe looks at the door to his old office.

"No. I don't think that's a good idea. I didn't come here to get my job back. I came here to see my friend and tell him I'm back in town." Joe slaps Bill's shoulder as he smiles and turns towards the front door.

"Come on Joe! It's a great idea and you know it. I need some help here and you love this kind of work." Joe shakes his head "No" as he continues to walk towards the door. "Just so we are both clear about something. You still own half of the business." Joe stops walking after opening the door. He stands motionless looking outside with the door ajar. The hot Florida air hits Joe's face as the cool air conditioned room chills him from behind. Joe turns to look at Bill, as Bill smiles at him. Joe pushes the door slowly until it closes.

CHAPTER 38

"What the hell!" The woman shouts with terror in her voice, as she stands motionless in the middle of the aisle staring at Kim, Joe and the girls. The sound of panic grips the shoppers in the store as they jockey for position to find out what the commotion is about. Its four months after Joe and the girls came home to Jacksonville and they're shopping in the local grocery store.

"Lisa," Kim says as she walks toward the shocked woman. Kim and the woman lock eyes on each other as Kim gives her a hug. The woman, Lisa Babcock, was one of Kim's closest friends prior to the accident, but they slowly drifted apart when Joe left. Lisa spent time at the house playing with the girls as they were infants and was close to the girls up until the accident. As she stares at the girls, Talia and Calie cower behind Joe for protection and glare at Lisa.

"Daddy, what's wrong with that lady?" Calie asks.

"Nothing honey," Joe explains. She hasn't seen Mommy in a long time."

"Why is she staring at us?" Talia asks. A store employee arrives on the scene to assess the situation as Kim holds Lisa's shoulders, doing her best to comfort her.

"Lisa, it's OK. I can explain everything to you," Kim said. "Lisa," Kim said sternly to get Lisa's attention as she looks at Kim again.

"How are..," Lisa pauses for a moment as Kim turns and looks at Joe and the girls. "What's going on?" A tear rolls down her left cheek as she wipes it away.

"Girls, stay here for a second," Joe says as he walks over to Lisa and Kim.

"Hi Lisa," Joe said softly as he gives her hug.

"Hi Joe, I didn't know you were back in town," Lisa said as her voice and body tremble in shock as she tries to hold back her emotions.

"I've been home for about four months now. Lisa, we want you to meet two special little girls." Joe looks back at Calie and Talia. "Girls, can you come here please?" When the girls walk over to Joe and Kim, they grab a hold of Joe as he crouches down. "It's OK girls." Joe stands up as Calie and Talia still hold Joe's hand but have loosened slightly.

"Lisa, we would like you to meet our daughters. This is Calie and Talia." Lisa looks at Joe, then at Kim. Kim smiles and nods her head slightly.

"Hi," Lisa says as her eyes tear up and overflow her eyes.

"Hi," Calie says apprehensively.

"Hello," Talia responds. Lisa looks at Kim.

"Is that Calie and Talia?"

"Yes," Kim says with a giggle and a smile.

"How?" Lisa asks flabbergasted by the sight of Calie and Talia. Her mouth still open slightly and eyes locked in a daze on the girls.

"Why don't you and Kurt come over for dinner tonight and we will explain everything then. How about six o'clock?"

"Oh, ah, OK. We will see you then," Lisa says as she walks away but continues staring at the girls.

"It was good to see you again Lisa," Joe says as he waves to Lisa and Lisa gives him a lethargic wave back.

The doorbell rings promptly at 6 p.m. Calie and Talia run towards the door as Joe and Kim follow.

"I'll get it," Calie yells.

"No, I will," Talia yells as Calie opens the door. Lisa and her husband, Kurt Babcock, are standing outside the door.

"Hello girls," Lisa says with uncertainty in her voice as she's once again shocked at the sight of the girls. Kurt looks at the girls with a silent stare.

"Come in guys," Kim says as she approaches the front door. Joe extends his hand to Kurt. Kurt reaches out and shakes his hand and Joe gives him a slight tug to welcome him into the house and to distract his attention. Upon entering the foyer, Kurt's attention is shifted from Joe back to the girls.

"Hey Joe, how've you been? It's good to see you again."

"I'm good! How about you Kurt?"

"I'm doing well thanks." Kurt leans in close to Joe. "I don't believe what I am seeing," Kurt says quietly so only Joe can hear him. "I saw the girls. I went to the funeral. How's this possible?"

"Come in, have a drink and we will tell you all about it," Joe said.

Joe, Kim, Lisa and Kurt are sitting in the living room after finishing dinner as Calie and Talia play upstairs. Joe and Kim sit close together on the couch while Lisa and Kurt snuggle together on the loveseat.

"So I went through this really bad time after the girls died, and I decided that I needed to get away from here for a while," Joe explains. "While I was away, I saw a story on TV about human cloning and that a doctor in San Francisco had cloned an ape. I sought this doctor out and talked him into cloning Talia and Calie."

Fifteen minutes later, Joe finishes telling Kurt and Lisa the story about Talia and Calie.

"Is this legal in the United States?" Kurt asks.

"The United States has some of the simplest laws on record regarding cloning of human beings. What the lawmakers didn't realize is how close scientists were to actually cloning a human," Joe explains. Joe looks at Kurt's almost empty beer glass. "Kurt, do you want another beer?"

"No I'm good for now, thanks."

"Officials in San Francisco don't know about Talia, Calie or Meghan. They knew about Hope the ape, but I think once the fanfare was over, everyone forgot about her. I would ask you guys not to broadcast this among your friends. Lets just keep this between us."

"Of course Joe. I can't even imagine what your reaction was when you saw the girls for the first time," Lisa says as she looks at Kim.

"I was shocked to say the least," Kim says as she laughs softly then looks at Joe and smiles. "It's an amazing feeling to have my family back home with me." Calie and Talia come running down the stairs and jump into Kim's lap as she begins tickling them. Calie, Talia and Kim are all giggling as Kurt, Lisa and Joe look on with smiles.

CHAPTER 39

"Talia, do you want to play hide and seek?"

"Sure," Talia responds.

"OK, your it! You count to 30 and I will hide first," Calie says. It's a Saturday afternoon, six months after Joe and the girls returned home. The girls are in the family room playing hide and seek while their parents clean up from lunch.

"Ready, set, go. 1, 2, 3, 4, 5....," Talia counts out loud as Calie races upstairs to the second floor. Calie runs down the hall and stops. She turns to open the attic door and walks quietly up the creaky stairs to find a hiding spot.

"....29, 30. Ready or not here I come." Talia starts looking for Calie and makes her way up to the second floor of the large colonial house. "Calie, where are you?" Talia asks as she finds the attic door ajar. She creeps up the stairs slowly to surprise Calie and finds her sitting on the floor in front of some boxes. "Calie?" Talia says unsure of what her sister is doing. She walks over to Calie and stands behind her. Talia hasn't acknowledged her sister yet and sits motionless on the floor. "Calie?" Calie looks up at

Talia with a blank stare while holding some photographs. "What are you doing?"

"I found this box when I was trying to hide. Have you ever seen these pictures?" Calie asks while staring at a picture. Talia sits on the floor next to her sister and Calie hands her the photo. The photograph is a picture of Joe, Kim, Talia and Calie at Disney World with one of the characters behind them.

"Is that us?" Talia asks. In the picture Talia is noticeably younger and shorter than Calie but it's clearly Calie and Talia in the picture. Calie looks to Talia with confusion. "Look at how little I am."

"Talia, we've never been to Disney World."

"I know. Look there's a bunch of pictures in this box. Talia reaches into the box and pulls out a white envelope with pictures inside. "Look at this one," Talia says. Leaning against Calie, her sister holds the photo so they can both see it. The picture of Joe, Talia and Calie in a boat sitting next to Sarah and Marc shows Talia and Calie holding fish they caught.

"I don't remember fishing with Auntie Sarah and Uncle Marc," Calie said to Talia. Calie drops the picture and reaches into the box and pulls out more. There are hundreds of photographs in this box and the girls look through all of them. They look at each other in amazement as to what they are seeing.

"Who are these girls?" Talia says.

"I don't know, but they look like us," Calie responds. "Look at this." Calie finds a newspaper article with a picture of a car flipped over on its roof. Calie starts reading the article out loud as best as a seven-year-old can.

2 LOCAL GIRLS DIE IN HEAD ON CRASH, MOTHER SERIOUSLY INJURED

"On Friday, February 12, 2009 an accident on Holmes Road between a car and a box truck claimed the lives of two little girls and seriously injured their mother. The two girls, Calie and Talia Walker, were in their car seats when the box truck veered into their lane and clipped the rear end of their car. They were transported to the hospital where they were pronounced dead shortly after. Kim Walker was rushed to the hospital with serious injuries and is in critical condition."

The girls hear a creek in the floor and turn to see Joe staring at them. Standing on the stairs looking down at the girls, Joe sighs as he shakes his head in regret.

"Daddy what are these pictures? We don't remember these, and why does this story say that we died? We didn't die. We are right here," Calie says while tears form in her eyes as she looks up at her father.

Joe walks over to them and kneels down on the floor. He grabs the girls and hugs them tight.

"You are both here with me right now." Joe gives them both a kiss on the side of their heads. "I'm so sorry you found this box. Calie begins sobbing uncontrollably.

"What happened?" Kim turns the corner to the attic and meets Joe and the girls as he carries them down the stairs. "Baby, why are you crying?" Kim asks Calie while caressing the side of her head.

"We found a box with pictures of girls that look like us and the newspaper said we died," Calie blurts out sobbing. Glaring right through Joe, Kim takes Calie from him and holds her tight. Calie's agonizing cry brings Kim to tears as she walks down the attic stairs as Joe follows with Talia.

"You weren't supposed to see that stuff. That box should've been out of sight!" Kim says angrily as she sneers at Joe again.

Later that evening, Calie, Talia and Kim are sitting on the floor in Calie's room playing with dolls. An eerie silence fills the room as Calie and Talia play with their dolls in a slow methodical dance. They are lost in deep thought, not truly present in their play but trying to grasp the reality of their earlier discovery.

"Mommy," Calie says softly.

"Yes sweetie?"

"Who were those girls in the pictures we found in the attic?" Kim stops playing and sits stationary for a second.

Calie and Talia stop the animation with their toys and look to their mom. Kim raises her head and her eyes meet Calie's as she looks back at her with sadness.

"It's a very long story honey. You're father and I have to talk about this and then we will all sit down and talk about it together. OK?" Calie nods in disappointment as Kim rubs her back then goes back to playing with the dolls in the same disinterested manner as before.

The day's events have created a somber mood throughout the house. The girls are in their parent's bed snuggling with Kim and Joe.

"Daddy needs to tell you girls about those pictures." Calie and Talia both look at Joe simultaneously. "So tomorrow after dinner we will talk all about it and you will understand then what those pictures were about. OK?" Calie nods her head then rests her head on Joe's chest.

"OK." Talia says sleepily.

CHAPTER 40

The whole family is sitting on the living room floor in a circle. Joe opens the box of photographs the girls found in the attic as he looks apprehensively at Kim. She gives him a quick nod, expressing her approval to proceed. To say the least, she doesn't condone this activity, but feels that they have no choice but to tell the girls the truth. A picture emerges from the box in Joe's grasp as he shows the girls the photo of the whole family together. Talia is two years old and Calie is a newborn. Kim is lying in a hospital bed after giving birth to Talia. Joe explains this to the girls.

"But Daddy, when we were little, Mommy wasn't with us. It was just me, you and Talia," Calie says.

"I know sweetie. What I am about to tell you both is going to be very difficult to understand, but it's time you knew the truth." The girls look at Joe attentively. "Mommy and Daddy had two little girls a long time ago and their names were Calie and Talia." Calie and Talia look at each other in disbelief. "They died in a car crash when Talia was five and Calie was seven."

"That was us in the newspaper?" Talia asks with an indecisive tone.

"Well not exactly," Joe says with a nervous chuckle. "After they died in the crash, Daddy took their blood and had someone make you from the blood. Therefore, you look like them and sound like them, but you have different personalities." Calie stands up and walks around the room, lost in thought.

"We aren't your first daughters?" Calie says confused.

"No honey. You two were born about a year after our first daughters died."

"Why wasn't Mommy with us all that time? I don't understand this Daddy."

Kim has tears collecting in her eyes at the sight of her daughter in distress as Joe looks to her with a panicked stare. Kim's starting to think that this was a bad idea. Calie begins to get upset as Talia looks through the pictures, trying to make sense of what her father just told her.

"Come here baby," Kim says to Calie as she wraps her arms tightly around her mother and begins to cry.

"I don't understand. How can we be the same girls that died?" Kim holds her daughter close while trying to reassure her that everything is OK.

"Let's not talk about it anymore tonight," Kim whispers. "You and your sister are our girls now and you're Daddy and I love you more than anything in this world. That's all that matters."

"This was a bad idea," Kim hisses to Joe as she lifts Calie up and walks into the kitchen. "Get rid of those pictures Joe." Joe picks the pictures up off the floor as Talia still sifts through them. He gets all the pictures in the box and puts the top on it. Talia, who is staring back at him, hands the box to Joe.

"I don't care who they are Daddy."

"No?" Joe asks.

"As long as I'm here with you, that's the only thing that matters." Talia stands up and hugs Joe tight. "I love you, Daddy."

"Thanks sweetie. Daddy loves you too."

CHAPTER 41

It's about fourteen months after Joe returned home with Calie and Talia and the girls are almost eight years old. Joe and Kim have slowly mended their differences and she has forgiven Joe for leaving her. Their relationship has evolved rapidly and they have started to rekindle their emotional bond with each other. The family is hanging out on a Saturday morning in Joe and Kim's bed. Joe tickles Talia as she screams for mercy.

"You want some more tickles?" Joe tickles Talia more and more.

"OK, OK!" Talia yells as she laughs hysterically. "Stop Daddy, I'm going to pee my pants!" Kim joins in and starts tickling Calie.

"Do you want some too?" Kim says to Calie. Calie laughs now as the whole family rolls around and messes up the bed.

"OK, everyone stop for a second." Everyone sits frozen on the bed as if they are mannequins in a store display. "Who wants pancakes for breakfast?" Kim says softly. Joe, Calie and Talia all raise their hands as high as they can and now are competing with each other to see who can put their hands up the highest.

"Me, me, me!" they all yell as Joe leaps out of bed and heads toward the bathroom.

"I will go make coffee for us, you guys hang out in bed for a few." Joe exits the bathroom after brushing his teeth and blows the girls a kiss as he runs down the stairs. Kim's lying in the middle of the bed between Calie and Talia and has her arms under the girl's necks, holding them close.

"Mommy loves you girls very much. Don't ever forget that. You guys are the best thing that has ever happened to me." Calie and Talia both look up at Kim.

"Mommy, do you ever think about your other daughters? You know the other Calie and Talia," Talia asks as she looks away from her mom. Kim looks to the ceiling as she ponders the question while Calie looks up at her.

"I think about them occasionally. They were a very special part of my life before you were born." She looks down at Talia, but Talia is still looking away. "Hey," Kim says as she shakes the girls slightly trying to get them to look at her. When they finally do look at their mom, she gives them a big smile. "Now I think about how much I love you two more than about what I had years ago." Kim smiles at the girls. "I am right here with you two and you are my life now, no one else." Calie and Talia smile and look away as Kim pulls them in close once again. "Let's go make some pancakes."

The doorbell sounds as the family is enjoying breakfast at the table and talking about their plans for the day. Everyone stops eating as they are all mystified that someone's at the door at this time of the morning.

"Who could that be on a Saturday morning?" Joe asks curiously. "I'll get the door girls, you enjoy these yummy pancakes." The door opens and Joe looks in disbelief at the man standing at the door. "Steve," Joe says stunned as he freezes in place.

"Hi Joe, it's good to see you."

"It's good to see you too," Joe replies. Joe stands motionless looking at Dr. Marxx.

"Can I come in Joe?" Dr. Marxx inquires.

"Of course, I'm sorry Steve, come in." Joe reaches out and shakes Dr. Marxx's hand.

"Thanks," Dr. Marxx says.

"Come in! We were just having breakfast. Are you hungry?"

"No thanks, I'm all set."

"How about a cup of coffee?" Joe asks.

"Sure that would be great. Thank you." Joe escorts Dr. Marxx down the hall into the kitchen.

"Girls, look who's here." As Calie and Talia see Dr. Marxx they jump out of their seats and run over to him.

"Uncle Steve," Calie yells.

"Hi Uncle Steve," Talia says as Dr. Marxx gets down on one knee. Both girls give him a big hug and Dr. Marxx hangs on and closes his eyes for a few moments. Joe and Kim lock eyes with each other with a straight faced look.

"It's so good to see both of you. I've missed you both so much."

"Uncle Steve, why are you here?" Talia asks.

"Well, I came to Jacksonville for a science conference and I wanted to stop in and see all of you to see how much you've grown. And wow, have you really grown." Joe walks over and interrupts.

"Steve, this is my wife Kim." Kim walks over to Dr. Marxx and gives him a hug.

"Joe has told me so many wonderful things about you. It's nice to put a face with the stories," Dr. Marxx compliments.

"I'm so happy to finally meet you," Kim says with a smile. "Thank you so much for everything you did for our family, you are an amazing person," Kim whispers low enough that the girls can't hear her. Dr. Marxx, with his back to Joe, has a sad look on his face as he closes his eyes.

"Thank you very much that's very kind of you to say," Dr. Marxx replies as they break their hug and he looks at

Joe. "I can't believe how big the girls have gotten in such a short time. How is everything going?" Dr. Marxx asks inquisitively.

"Everything is great with us." Joe puts his arm around Kim's shoulder and pulls her close. "How about with you? How's the research going?" Joe asks.

"The research has been halted for the time being. We have more funding in place, but the heads of the company want to re-evaluate some recent discoveries," Dr. Marxx replies as Joe has a look of concern. "Can we talk in private for a few minutes Joe?"

"Ah…, sure Steve," Joe says with a cracked voice.

"I will clean up. Why don't you guys go out back and talk," Kim says. Joe and Dr. Marxx walk out the back slider as Kim watches and stands motionless with an uneasy look about her. Kim senses that something's wrong. "Why would Dr. Marxx visit after all this time if everything was OK," Kim says to herself silently. Kim looks at the girls who are back at the table finishing their breakfast. Kim's eyes tear again as she wipes them dry.

"How have the girls been doing? Any health issues or problems?" Dr. Marxx asks.

"No. They are as healthy as can be. They haven't even had a cold since I brought them home."

"That's good, I'm happy to hear that," Dr. Marxx replies as he turns his back and looks toward the house. As he looks through the patio doors at the girls sitting at the table, he smiles then catches a glimpse of Kim as they make eye contact.

"Steve," Joe says softly. Dr. Marxx is still looking at Kim. "Steve. What's going on?" Joe demands.

"I'm glad to hear that everything is going so good for you and Kim, and that the girls are doing well." Dr. Marxx turns and looks at Joe. "I have to go now Joe, I will be at the Sunrise Hotel in Jacksonville for the rest of the week, and then I'm going back to San Francisco. Dr. Marxx extends his right hand out to shake Joe's hand. "Take care of yourself, Joe. It was good to see you again." Joe extends his hand out and locks onto Dr. Marxx.

"Is everything OK, Steve?" Worry has suddenly occupied Joe's face as he refuses to release Dr. Marxx's handshake.

"Everything is good Joe. Tell the girls I said goodbye." Dr. Marxx replies as Joe lets go of his hand. The doctor walks away toward the side of the house as Joe stands completely still watching the man who travelled thousands of miles just to say hi. Joe doesn't buy the idea that he's in town for work. Dr. Marxx came to Florida for a reason. Joe turns and looks at the kitchen window and sees Kim staring at him frozen with the same concerned look on her face. Joe looks at the girls sitting at the table coloring, completely oblivious to the anxiety their parents have at this moment.

The back door closes and Kim walks over to Joe as he makes his way to the front of the house. Joe and Kim stare at Dr. Marxx as he walks to his car. He opens the driver's side door and stops before getting in then raises his hand slightly in a dispassionate wave to say goodbye. They stand motionless next to each other near the driveway and don't acknowledge Dr. Marxx's wave. As he gets into his car and pulls out of the driveway, Kim looks at Joe terrified at the thought of something being wrong with the girls.

"What's going on Joe?" she asks.

"I don't know, babe! But I'm going downtown tomorrow to find out." Kim hugs Joe tightly, as Joe rubs her back slowly while looking towards the road.

Its bedtime on the same day Dr. Marxx surprised the Walkers with a visit. Joe's lying on Calie's bed while she reads a children's book to him as he stares at the rotating ceiling fan.

"Daddy." Calie looks at Joe lying next to her.

"Yes princess," Joe replies. "I'm sorry sweetie, I was lost in thought."

"What were you thinking about?"

"I was thinking about how much I love my big girl." Joe says with a big smile as he gives her a kiss on her forehead. "I was also thinking that it's time for my big girl to go to bed." Joe takes the book out of Calie's hands and folds the page over so she doesn't lose her place. Calie pulls the covers up to her chin.

"Goodnight Daddy!" Joe turns the light off on her bedside table then looks down at her.

"I love you very much princess," Joe tells Calie as he stares into her eyes and smiles.

"I love you too, Daddy." As Joe was about to stand up, Calie grabs his arm to stop him. "It was nice to see Uncle Steve today. Did he come all the way here just to see us?" Joe looks at Calie intently and pauses for a minute then looks away briefly.

"I'm sure he did honey. He probably missed you girls so much, that he had to stop by and see you." Goodnight sweetie."

CHAPTER 42

"Kim," Joe whispers. Kim opens her eyes slowly from her deep morning sleep to see Joe looking down at her. "Hi babe."

"Hi," Kim whispers back. "What time is it?"

"It's about seven. I'm leaving shortly and I'm not sure what time I'll be back. I'll call you later."

"What are you going to say to him?"

"I don't know. He came all this way for a reason. He had something to say but for whatever reason, he didn't say it."

"Well drive carefully."

"OK, I will. I love you."

"Love you too, Joe."

"Hi Mommy," Calie whispered into Kim's ear as she stands on the side of the bed.

"Hi baby," Kim whispers back while opening her eyes slightly and shifting her body towards the middle of the bed as Calie climbs in and snuggles up to her mom.

"Mommy, where's Daddy?"

"Daddy had to drive to Jacksonville this morning to see Dr. Marxx. He left early this morning." As the sun was peeking through the shades, Kim looked at her clock on the nightstand. The alarm clock shines 8:05 AM. "Daddy should be at the hotel by now." Talia walks into the bedroom and climbs into bed with Kim on the opposite side of Calie. She pulls the girls close to her like she used to do with the girls before the crash.

"Did you say Daddy is in Jacksonville?" Talia asks.

"Yes, honey."

"Why is he going to Jacksonville?"

"Daddy just has some things to take care of today." Calie pokes her head up from the other side of Kim and looks at Talia.

"He's going to see Uncle Steve," Calie says.

Its 8 a.m. and Joe pulls into the large parking lot of the Sunrise Hotel. After turning the car off he sits for a moment, taking a big breath and letting it out. Joe is questioning himself about coming to see Dr. Marxx. He's running scenarios through his head why Dr. Marxx traveled all this way to see the girls. One more deep breath goes in then he lets it out, closing his eyes as he exhales. The large automatic sliding glass doors open to the expansive bright lobby as Joe walks over to the reception desk.

"Hi, can I help you?" the female receptionist asks.

"Hi, I'm looking for Steve Marxx's room please." The receptionist types the name into the desk computer.

"Here we go. It's room 207 sir. If you go into the elevator to your right, second floor and room 207 should be a few doors down on your left."

"Thank you." Joe takes a few steps towards the elevator then stops and turns around. The receptionist looks at Joe.

"Sir?"

"Is there a science conference here at the hotel this week?"

"No sir, there's not much going on this week."

"Thanks." Joe stops for a moment and shakes his head slightly.

"Sir, are you OK?"

"Thanks." Joe turns and continues to the elevator. As the silver door opens, Joe pushes number two on the panel. Joe's breathing becomes heavier and his heart rate starts to accelerate. "What the hell is wrong with me? Maybe he really did just come to see the girls," Joe says to himself. The elevator chimes and the door opens up to floor number two. Joe steps out of the elevator and turns left. Three doors down on the left, Joe stops in front of door number 207. He takes a deep breath and knocks on the door.

CHAPTER 43

The door to room 207 opens. "Joe," Dr. Marxx says surprised.

"Hi Steve. I'm sorry to bother you, but I had to come see you." Dr. Marxx looks down and sighs. "Can I come in for a few minutes?" Dr. Marxx looks at Joe and pauses for a moment. Joe is staring at Dr. Marxx. "Please, Steve." Dr. Marxx nods his head as Joe walks in. "Steve, what's going on? You show up at my door two years after I left San Francisco. I can't help, but think there is something wrong," Joe says in obvious distress.

"I figured you would have come sooner or later. Sit down Joe." Joe sits down in a chair at the small table in the middle of the room and Dr. Marxx sits down in the chair opposite Joe.

"Doc, you're really starting to scare me right now. Please tell me what's going on." Joe demands in a firm nervous voice.

"Joe, Meghan died two weeks ago in San Francisco." Joe stares at Dr. Marxx without saying a word. Joe's face turns pale as his heart and mind are in sudden distress. Joe stands up and takes a few steps backward. Joe's breathing begins to increase as he continues to stare at Dr. Marxx. "Joe, I'm sor..."

"How did she die?" Joe asks as he interrupts Dr. Marxx.

"Joe, it's complicated..."

"How did she die?" Joe slams his hands down on the table, startling Dr. Marxx as he leans back in the chair. Dr. Marxx stands up and looks at Joe. Joe's eyes fill with tears as the shock and reality of what Steve told him sets in.

"Meghan died of heart and lung failure while she was performing in a play at school." Joe sits down on the corner of the hotel room bed. Tears stream down his face as he looks at Dr. Marxx for some sign that this isn't really happening. "The autopsy results revealed that Meghan's internal organs were simultaneously deteriorating and shutting down." Joe buries his face in his hands.

"Oh God no," Joe cries as he looks up at Dr. Marxx. His face is flush and his eyes are wide open as he does his best to stay focused on the moment but then buries his face in his sweating hands again.

"Joe the medical examiner told me that all of Meghan's internal organs were showing signs of internal corrosion. The doctor said it was something they had never seen before. Joe sits up and pulls his hands away from his face and takes another deep breath to try and slow his heart rate. Tears continue their escape from Joe's bloodshot eyes, rolling down his cheeks as he tries to keep up with wiping them away. As he stands up and tries to regain his composure, denial sets in.

"That must have been a fluke thing with Meghan. That doesn't mean it will happen to my girls." Joe looks at Dr. Marxx. "Right?"

"Joe. Hope, the gorilla I cloned before Meghan, died six months after you left San Francisco. She was almost eight years old. Meghan was almost nine years old when she died."

"Things will be different with Calie and Talia. It has to be! The girls can get transplants. I can save them." Joe looks at Dr. Marxx while nodding his head. "We can save them, Steve."

"Joe the cloning process is flawed. At some point their internal organs will start to break down too. You can't transplant every organ in their body." Dr. Marxx stands up in front of Joe and grabs his upper arms and squeezes them. He pulls Joe closer to him. "I'm sorry Joe, I really am." Joe leans forward and breaks down crying on Dr. Marxx's right shoulder as his tears soak Dr. Marxx shirt. Dr. Marxx wraps his arms around Joe and rubs his back slightly. Joe pulls away and looks at Dr. Marxx.

"Thank you for giving me the time I had with Talia and Calie. Take care of yourself Steve." Joe walks toward the door and opens it.

"Joe." He turns towards Dr. Marxx. "Spend every minute you can with the girls."

"I will. Goodbye Steve!" Joe walks out the door as Dr. Marxx stands dejected.

One hour later Joe pulls into his driveway and stops the car near the garage. He looks at the house then down at the steering wheel and sits motionless. Kim steps out onto the porch and stares at Joe sitting in the car as Joe looks up at her and stares back. Knowing in her heart that something is very wrong, she shakes her head and begins crying while Joe still sits motionless and stoic in the car.

CHAPTER 44

"Aaah!" Calie screams with a blood curdling echo through the entire house. It's the middle of the night, three months after Dr. Marxx's visit and the house is filled with darkness. Joe and Kim jump out of bed from a dead sleep and start running for the hallway.

"Calie!" Joe yells as he flicks Calie's light on. Sitting up in bed crying, Calie stares at her hands.

"Calie? Oh my God," Kim says as she runs to Calie's bed side. The front of Calie's pajamas is stained red with blood along with her face and hands. Comforting her crying daughter, Kim cries with her as Joe checks to see what injuries she has. Her hand touches the pillow covered in dry blood as Kim realizes Calie's been bleeding for many hours during the night.

"I don't see anything wrong with her," Joe says while holding Calie's arms and checking her head.

"Calie what happened?" Kim asks hysterically while wiping the blood from Calie's face.

"I don't know, I was coughing and I felt something wet on my pillow." The horrified frown on Joe's face sends

Kim into an emotional tailspin as she begins to sob uncontrollably.

"I'm getting dressed and bringing Calie to the hospital," Joe says as he runs into the hallway then his bedroom.

"Mommy, my belly hurts," Calie says while holding her stomach and curling over in pain. Calie's mother holds her from the side as Calie begins to cry hysterically from the pain. "Aaah, Mommy!" Looking for comfort from her mother, Calie panics again at the sight of her blood all over her bed as Kim continues to hold her.

"Joe!" Kim yells. As Joe runs back into Calie's room, he sees her curled over in pain as she spits blood into her own hand. Joe, now in full panic mode after seeing Calie spit blood, runs back into his bedroom and begins dialing 911.

"Calie are you OK?" a soft voice asks. Talia stands in the doorway watching silently as her sister sobs and curls over in gut wrenching pain. Kim looks at Talia and gives her a little smile.

"Calie's fine honey. She just has a belly ache. Why don't you go back to bed sweetie?" Joe comes up from behind Talia and picks her up, giving her a comforting hug. Calie grimaces in agony again, breaking from the few moments of relative calm before whaling violently from the sharp pain.

"Come on. Let's get you back to bed," Joe says as he starts walking down the hall towards Talia's bedroom after glancing in at Calie and Kim.

"Daddy what's wrong with Calie? Is she sick?" Talia asks as Joe pulls the covers back over her and tucks her in.

"I don't know what's wrong with Calie. We are going to the hospital with her and Auntie Sarah is coming over to stay with you until we get back." He gazes into Talia eyes for a few moments and gives her a smile. "OK?" Talia nods her head in approval. "I love you sweetie."

"Love you too, Daddy."

"Goodnight." Joe kisses Talia on her forehead as Talia closes her eyes then rolls over away from Joe.

The white and red ambulance in the driveway shocks Sarah as she sprints from her car and meets up with Joe as he watches the EMT care for Calie. Running from the house and over to Joe and Sarah, Kim gives her sister in-law a quick hug before climbing into the back of the ambulance.

"What's going on with Calie?" Sarah asks flustered.

"We don't know. It looks like she was spitting up blood during the night before we found her. Talia's in her bed but probably awake. Thanks for coming over so quickly. We will call you when we know more," Joe says to Sarah quickly while walking toward his car. The ambulance siren wails as it pulls onto the main road from the Walker's driveway while Joe follows in his car.

The door creaks as Sarah peers in at Talia in her bed. Talia rolls over, wide awake and looks at Sarah. She smiles at her niece as she shuffles excitedly to the side of the bed and kneels down. "Hi Talia."

"Hi Auntie," Talia says as she sits up and gives Sarah a big hug and holds her tight. "Is Calie sick?" Talia asks while still locked in the hug with Sarah.

"She will be fine, I promise." Talia pulls away from Sarah and smiles at her as she lowers her head back onto the pillow. "Try to get some sleep. I'll be downstairs if you need anything," Sarah says caressing Talia's cheek softly with the back of her hand. Sarah closes Talia's door a little then makes her way downstairs.

"Daddy, I'm scared!" Calie screams as she turns to see her father behind the stretcher, then reaches for his hand. Joe takes her hand and runs up alongside the stretcher as Calie's wheeled to a vacant room in the emergency department. Kim and Joe sit down on the bed next to Calie and hold her as the intake nurse enters the room with her computer.

"Hi my name is Kristen. I just need the patients name, age and address please."

"Calie Walker, seven years old and she lives at 24 Williams Street," Joe replies.

"Are you Calie's father?"

"I am," Joe says staring at the nurse. The nurse has a puzzled look about her as she sees something on her monitor that's confusing.

"I'm sorry I can't find a seven year old Calie Walker in our system? Are you Joe and Kim Walker?"

"Yes, we are," Joe says as he holds Calie's hand.

"My system says you have a fourteen year old Calie Walker, but the system also says she's...." The intake nurse stops abruptly. "Clearly something is wrong here." Kim's eyes are closed as she shakes her head in disgust. "The doctor will be right in to see you folks. I hope you feel better Calie," the nurse says with a smile as she walks out of the room and slides the curtain closed. Joe softly takes Kim's hand to comfort her but she quickly pulls it away from his grasp. She wipes the tears flowing from her eyes off her cheeks with her hands and looks at him with repulsion.

<hr />

It is 10 hours after Calie was brought to the hospital in an ambulance. The front door opens and Joe carries Calie in with Kim following behind them. Sarah and Talia meet them in the foyer as Joe brings Calie upstairs to bed. The medication given to Calie at the hospital knocked her out as she sleeps in Joe's arms for the ride upstairs to her bed.

"Mommy is Calie better?" Kim kneels down on the floor in front of Talia and gives her a hug.

"She's very tired right now baby, but she will be fine." Kim gives Talia a reassuring smile and Talia smiles back. "What have you and Auntie Sarah been doing?"

"Auntie Sarah made pancakes this morning and we played outside and then played some games." Kim looks up and smiles at Sarah then looks at Talia again. "Auntie Sarah is the best, isn't she?"

"Yeah," Talia says with a smile looking up at Sarah.

"Talia, can you go play in your room for a few minutes so your mom and I can talk?" Sarah asks Talia with smile.

"OK." Talia turns and walks up the stairs to her bedroom as Sarah steps towards Kim and hugs her. Emotionally drained, Kim breaks down crying in Sarah's arms. Sarah gives her a few moments in her arms then takes a step back from Kim.

"What did the doctor say?"

"They did test after test and took blood and we have to meet the doctor tomorrow afternoon at one to talk about Calie's diagnosis. They gave us some medicine to ease her internal pain and help her sleep but that's it." Kim looks at Sarah, her terrified demeanor sends chills up Sarah's spine as she has a flashback of Kim from eight years ago. "Sarah, I'm really scared." They both look towards the stairs as Joe somberly walks down and joins them.

"Calie is sleeping comfortably, for the time being," Joe says as he reaches around Kim and pulls her close. "She will be OK, I just know it." Kim glares through Joe, hardly persuaded by his optimism.

"I need to get home, but I will be here tomorrow at noon to watch Talia for you," Sarah says as Kim gives her a smile.

"Thanks Sarah," Kim replies as she gives Sarah a prolonged and loving hug.

"Yes, thank you Sis," Joe adds while rubbing Sarah's back as she hugs Kim. As she walks out of the house and closes the door behind her, Joe and Kim hold each other in a long painful embrace. Kim breaks down and cries like she's done many times since early this morning.

CHAPTER 45

The waiting room at Dr. Wilson's office is quiet with only the sound of the occasional ringing of the office phone. Kim looks around the room as her leg erratically bounces up and down while Joe sits calmly. Joe grabs her leg and looks at her.

"Honey, try to relax."

"I can't Joe. Something doesn't feel right."

"Everything will be fine. Be positive," Joe says as he gives Kim a kiss on the forehead. A tall older man wearing a brown suit with a grey mustache and short grey hair walks out to the waiting room.

"Hi, I'm Tim Wilson," the man says as he extends his right hand out to Joe. Joe reaches out and shakes his hand.

"Hi, I'm Joe Walker and this is my wife Kim."

"Hi, Dr. Wilson. It's nice to meet you," Kim replies, then looks down after making eye contact. Her uncomfortable body language shows as Dr. Wilson gives her a slight smile.

"Follow me. We will go into my office where we can talk." Joe and Kim follow Dr. Wilson down a hallway to an open door. "Have a seat please," Dr. Wilson says while pointing towards two black leather chairs in front of his desk. Dr. Wilson sits at his desk and opens two large red folders. "I have reviewed your daughter's case extensively and I can't find any scientific or medical reason for what I'm about to tell you." Kim's eyes begin to fill with tears. Calie has RCD, which stands for Rapid Cell Disintegration. There's no scientific or medical explanation for this, but Calie's internal organs are shutting down rapidly."

Joe looks down and starts crying softly to himself as Kim's face is indifferent to the news. Tears have stopped flowing from Kim's eyes as Joe stands up and turns away from the doctor. Standing motionless facing the wall, Joe's head lowers.

"How long Doc?" Joe says as Kim turns to look at Joe still facing away from her and the doctor.

"Four days, maximum, or it could be as little as three hours. I'm sorry." Kim begins crying hysterically in her hands.

"No! This can't be happening! How can this be happening to us?" Joe walks over to Kim and kneels down in front of her. As he wraps his arms around her, she pushes him away and stands up. "No! No! You did this to me! You did this to Calie! This is your fault!" Kim loses it in front of Joe and the doctor. "I hate you for what you have done!" Kim says as she walks out of the doctor's office and slams the door behind her. Joe stands motionless with tears running down his face as he looks down at his trembling hands. The magnitude of the news setting in as his breathing intensifies rapidly while standing in the doctor's office. His eyes open wide and fixated on his hands. He's losing control of his mind and body. He closes his eyes and takes a deep breath as he tries to gather himself. The heads up by Dr. Marxx three months ago did nothing to lessen the impact of the news now.

"I'm sorry you had to see that Doc."

"It's OK Mr. Walker. You don't have to apologize for something like that. This is a stressful event to go through and it's expected that there will be strong dynamic and dramatic feelings." Joe nods slightly as he wipes the tears from his face. "I'm writing a prescription for pain medicine for Calie. She will need it during the course of the day and it will help her to sleep. She's going to need this medication in the next few days."

"Thanks Doc, I appreciate you being upfront with us," Joe says.

"Please don't thank me Mr. Walker, just spend what remaining time you have with your daughter. I'm really sorry." Joe again nods slightly as he walks out the door.

Later that evening Joe and Calie are together in Calie's bed. Calie is sedated but still wakes up every few minutes.

"Daddy, it hurts," Calie cries softly.

"I know baby. I promise the pain will go away soon," Joe says quietly as he kisses Calie's head softly and holds her head on his chest. A tear slowly finds its way down Joe's cheek as he looks up towards the ceiling. His chin quivers as he tries to hold back his intense anguish. He closes his eyes and embraces the moment with Calie. Kim and Talia are hanging out in Kim's room, reading before bed.

"Talia, Calie is very sick right now and she needs to hear how much we love her. Do you want to go in with me and say goodnight to her?" Talia nods her head.

"Can I tell her anything?"

"Anything that you think may make her feel better."

"OK, let's go," Talia says as she takes Kim's hand and leads her out of bed.

"Is she sleeping?" Kim asks softly as Talia stands next to Calie. Joe nods as Kim bends over and kisses Calie's cheek. "I love you Calie. Mommy will always love you." Calie doesn't respond to her mother's voice.

"Goodnight Calie." Talia gives Calie a kiss on her cheek. "I love you Sissy. You are the best sister ever." Joe waves Talia over to his side of the bed.

"Joe turns his head towards Talia face and gives her a kiss on her cheek. "I love you baby. Goodnight." Talia and Kim walk back out to the hallway.

"Daddy." Calie whispers lightly with what little energy she has.

"Yes sweetie."

"Do you love me as much as you loved the other Calie?" Joe silently weeps as he tries to keep it in so Calie doesn't hear him cry.

"Sweetie, Daddy loves you so much. You are the best daughter I could have ever dreamed of having."

"I love you too, Daddy." Calie whispers. "Daddy, I'm sorry I got sick." Joe's sobbing becomes more aggressive and uncontrollable. "Don't cry Daddy.., I will always be with you," she says barely audible as she tries to hug Joe tightly. Her weakened muscles only provide her enough power for a few seconds of a hug before she loosens her grip. Tears stream down the sides of Joe's face while he silently screams in agony as heartbreak rips through his body.

During the middle of the night, Joe wakes to find Calie in the same position with her head resting on his chest like a pillow. Joe slowly takes her hand in his and holds it gently. Calie's hand is cold. "Nooo." Joe's face crunches and his cheeks rise while he cries as quietly as he can and pulls Calie's lifeless body close to him. He holds her tight as he cries uncontrollably. I love you Calie. Don't ever forget how much Daddy loves you." Joe continues to sob and hold Calie close to him.

"Kim," Joe says softly. Kim wakes and looks up to see Joe crying while standing over her.

"No, Calie," Kim says as she starts crying and rolls out of bed, then runs into Calie's bedroom. Joe stands motionless in his own bedroom as Kim's agonizing cry pierces through the second floor of the house.

CHAPTER 46

Joe sits on the ground in front of Calie and Talia's grave stones. Their stones are in the same location as their sisters before them, only to the right of the birch tree. It's been three months since Calie died. Talia developed the same devastating ailment that took her sister's life and was buried two days ago. Kim blamed Joe for the deaths of Calie and Talia and left Joe after Talia's funeral. Even Joe's sister was angry with him for what had transpired as word spread around town of Joe's story.

"I'm sorry girls. I brought you into this world for my own selfish reasons because I couldn't live without you. Now, I don't have you. I thought I knew what I was doing. I had all the answers." Joe shakes his head, disappointed in himself. "I was wrong and for that, I'm sorry. I hope wherever you are, you're not angry with me. I miss you so much already and I'm lost without you." Joe sits slumped over and wipes the tears from his face. After a few moments he looks up at the stones. "I love you both and I will never forget you."

He stands himself up and kisses his hand then touches both grave stones as he walks away. As Joe walks to the left side of the birch tree, he looks at his first daughter's grave stones then blows a kiss to them and continues walking towards the dirt road. He reaches into his coat pocket and pulls a bottle of vodka out as he starts drinking from it while walking to his car. A short time later, Joe pulls into his driveway. Staggering from the car, he meanders his way into the house through the front door and grabs another bottle of vodka from the refrigerator.

Joe sits down in the living room with a picture of the girls on the coffee table. He just drinks and stares at the photo for the next hour. The empty bottle falls from Joe's hand to the floor as he passes out in the chair. He opens his eyes and looks to the floor at the empty bottle. When he attempts to reach for the bottle, he falls out of the chair and lands face down on the floor.

 Joe groans in pain as he rolls on his side. He begins shedding tears as liquid flows down his cheeks onto the hard wood floor. "Ahhhh." Joe looks at the walls covered in pictures of the girls and the family. He rolls back over on his stomach and closes his eyes. While lying motionless on the floor, Joe cries out loud as the empty house fill with his agonizing cries. That dark place has found Joe again and the demons he escaped from eight years ago are coming for him.

As he opens his right eye slightly, he sees something under the couch. With both eyes open wide now, Joe slowly reaches his hand under the couch as he can barely touch the colored paper. He stretches with everything he has and grabs the paper and slowly pulls it towards him. Joe pushes himself up with all his might and sits with his back against the chair he fell out of. After wiping his face and rubbing his eyes, he pulls the paper up to see it clearly. Joe's face awakens and his eyes open wider as he gazes at the pamphlet he took from the Jacksonville Blood Bank waiting room. Now shaking wildly as anxiety courses through his body, he mumbles something to himself while fixated on the brochure.

"Calie? Talia?" Joe says before a smile fills his face.

THE END

Acknowledgements

Five years has elapsed since I first starting writing this book and it has been a satisfying, but time-consuming experience that I will remember forever. I have appreciated all the kind words and encouragement from family, friends, and co-workers throughout this long and challenging process. I would be doing a great injustice to my family if I didn't mention the tremendous support of my wife, Lisa, and my daughters, Kasey and Sydney, while working on this project. None of this would have been possible without their support. So many ideas and thoughts were bounced off Lisa, who's incredibly creative in her own right, while writing this book. A big thank you to my editor, Emily Loux. You are awesome at what you do and I look forward to working together for many more years to come.

This book is dedicated to my Mother, Miriam, and my Father, Patrick. You are both missed.

Finally, if you bought this book, I want to thank you from the bottom of my heart for the support. I hope you enjoyed this read and keep an eye out for my next book, *My Father's Prison*.

Gary Herland

Made in the USA
Middletown, DE
07 May 2017